AND TYLER NO MORE

A NOVEL

STAN HAYNES

This is a work of fiction. All of the characters and events portrayed in this novel are either products of the author's imagination or are used fictitiously.

AND TYLER NO MORE
A NOVEL

Copyright 2021 by Stan Haynes

SMH Publishing

Cover design by Jennifer Quinlan of Historical Editorial

ISBN: 978-1-7377669-0-2 (print)
ISBN: 978-1-7377669-1-9 (e-book)

Printed in the United States of America

To Mike and Paula

CHAPTER 1

*J**une, 1852*— The page delivered the envelope to the young congressman from Ohio as he sat at his desk on the floor of the House of Representatives. The congressman was barely awake, his senses fading from a dreary debate on a bill to fund the War Department. It had already dragged on from morning into mid-afternoon, far longer than necessary, in his opinion, and still more of his colleagues were eagerly waiting their turns to speak. How they love to hear themselves talk, he thought, and such a waste of time. There would be no votes taken today. He gazed at the barely legible words scrawled on the envelope, "Hon. Montgomery Tolliver," thinking that he recognized the feeble handwriting, especially the "H," slanted and with a large loop. He quickly opened it and the brief note inside confirmed his suspicion. It was from his old boss, requesting a meeting at the National Hotel, today, if possible. He had not visited the gentleman for almost two months. As weak and sick as his host had been at that time, he thought it may have been their last visit, not wanting to impose again, unless invited. Perhaps the end was now near. He needed to go.

Monty, as everyone called him, left the House chamber, walked down the steps of the Capitol, and hailed a cabriolet. His eyes squinted from the brightness of the sun on the pleasant early June day. The oppressive swampiness for which Washington summers were known had not yet settled in. The ride to the National Hotel, located on Pennsylvania Avenue at Sixth Street, less than halfway to the White House, took only a few minutes. He entered the lobby, familiar to him from having stayed at the National for a couple of weeks at the beginning of his first term, until he found lodging in a nearby boardinghouse. Since then, he had been there for several dinner meetings, never developing a taste for the terrapin that was considered the specialty of the house. The handsome Ohioan, tall and square-faced, with chestnut hair and cornflower blue eyes, was known and liked by the staff, who took pride in recognizing every member of Congress who walked through their doors.

As he walked through the lobby toward the front desk, he overheard a group of men discussing the upcoming 1852 presidential election, which had just reached a crucial phase. Like most people in the nation's capital, Monty lived and breathed politics.

"Nominating Pierce was an ingenious move by the Democrats. Lightning will strike again in November, as it did with Polk in '44," Monty heard one of the men seated on a stiff high back chair say, smugly, as he watched him bring his fat fingers to his mouth for a puff on his cigar.

"Will never happen. Polk had Jackson's support. Old Hickory's dead and there's no one of stature this time among the Democrats to sell Pierce to the voters," said another man on the adjacent sofa. "The Whigs meet next week and my money is on General Scott getting the nomination and winning the election."

Monty had been hearing similar conversations everywhere he had been over the past few days. The previous week, he and most of the country had been shocked that the Democratic Party, at its convention in nearby Baltimore, had nominated as its standard-bearer, on the forty-ninth ballot, Franklin Pierce of New Hampshire. A former one-term senator, out of office for a decade and virtually unknown outside of New England (even Monty had barely heard of him), Pierce was the second dark horse candidate to have been nominated by the Democrats in the past eight years. In 1844, they had won the presidency with the similarly unknown James Polk.

"I'll take that bet. You're both wrong!," he heard another man on the sofa state with confidence. "President Fillmore will be nominated by the Whigs and win it all. He's done a good job and deserves a term of his own."

Millard Fillmore, the sitting president, Monty thought to himself, America's second accidental Whig president in a decade. At least Fillmore was truly a Whig, unlike the first one, John Tyler, who had betrayed the party and, in Monty's opinion, the country. The mere thought of Tyler brought back dark memories, which he tried to quickly erase from his mind.

He approached the front desk and told the clerk whom he was there to see.

"Good afternoon congressman. Yes, I passed his note to the messenger this morning. He's expecting you. Go right up, you know the way."

Room 32 was a suite, one of the nicest in the hotel, with a large parlor room adjacent to the bedroom. He knocked on the door. After a few seconds, it was opened by a free Black servant, James Marshall, whom he had met during his last visit. Marshall, well-liked and a good companion, had been the old man's valet for a year. His services had become more needed as his boss's health had deteriorated. The room was dimly lit, its dark curtains drawn. Monty could not help sensing gloom as he walked in.

"Good afternoon. He sent for me," he told James. The servant recognized Monty, went to the door of the bedroom and announced the guest to the old man, who stirred in his bed, suddenly energized. He motioned for James to show the guest in and to leave the two alone.

"Monty! Thank you for coming so soon, I hope that my note did not alarm you."

The man stretched out on the bed, propped up by pillows and surrounded by newspapers, looked better than expected. There he was, Monty's hero and mentor, America's greatest living statesman, Senator Henry Clay of Kentucky.

The mere sight of the man still gave him chills. On the ride from the Capitol, Monty had reflected on Clay's career. He had been at the forefront of every major issue in Washington City for the past forty years. As the youngest speaker of the House of Representatives in history, he made innovations to that office that forever increased its power and influence. He had been a peace negotiator in Ghent and helped draft the treaty that ended the War of 1812. Clay had successfully led through Congress the Compromise of 1820, easing sectional concerns over slavery for almost a generation. He had devised his American System, with tariffs and infrastructure improvements, to build the economy of the growing nation, and had served as secretary of state under the second President Adams. He moved to the Senate and, in 1833, crafted a way to diffuse the Nullification Crisis. Clay became a leader of the National Republican Party and, later, a founder and leader of the Whig Party. Now in the twilight of his career, he had recently worked tirelessly to pass the Compromise of 1850 through Congress, again, as in 1820, keeping the nation together as divisions over slavery between the North and the South had threatened to tear it apart. Over a career of working out and solving political issues, Clay had earned his nickname, The Great Compromiser. There had been setbacks too, multiple losses in presidential elections, never achieving his dream of becoming president of the United States. As he had once famously said, "I had rather be right than be president." He had come so close. A shift of twenty-five hundred votes in New York in 1844 and history would have been different.

Fresh out of college in 1838 and a newcomer to Washington City, Monty had gone to work for the senator, and became what was in effect his chief of staff. After Clay initially left the Senate in 1842, Monty had stayed on in the capital for a few years, left to go back to Ohio, and now had returned to begin his own political career. Like Clay, he was a Whig, and proudly so. In 1849, Clay had returned to the Senate and had again become one of the nation's most influential men. Monty always admired Clay's love of country, his style and wit, and those intangible qualities that caused people to look at him and think, this is a leader.

Monty glanced at the newspapers strewn across the senator's bed. "I see you've been reading about the Democratic convention. Interesting outcome."

"Frank Pierce. God help us," scoffed Clay. "What a stretch, even for the Democrats. Too fond of the bottle, from what I knew of him in his Senate days. A backbencher among backbenchers. Rarely spoke on the floor. Now, they think he can be president?

Five days in a hot convention hall, and an itching to get back home, leads men to make strange decisions."

"Seems like they would have been smarter to nominate Senator Cass again. A known entity."

"Agreed. Of course, the joke may be on us. There may be a method to their madness. Remember, they beat me with that rascal Polk."

"At least he had been the speaker, and a governor. People had heard of him outside of Tennessee. And you *almost* beat him."

"You humor an old man, Monty. A shameful loss it was."

The two exchanged pleasantries about family and mutual friends. Monty learned that the senator's son, Thomas, had arrived in May from Kentucky to help attend to him, to answer correspondence, and to report back to the rest of the family. Clay, Monty readily saw, was a shadow of his former self. Known as a great orator, the best of his generation, his voice was weak and raspy from the frequent coughing caused by the consumption that had sapped the strength from his once vigorous body. For six months now, since December, he had been holed up in this hotel, too weak to attend sessions of the Senate, save one brief time, and most assuredly unable to survive a trip home to Lexington and his beloved Ashland estate. His face was gaunt, his hair disheveled, but his blue eyes were still piercing. Monty could not help but recall the senator in his prime. More than six feet tall, he always stood ramrod straight, and his presence had dominated any room he entered.

The banter over, Clay became serious as he stared at his young friend. "Monty, I am a dying man and do not know how many more days I have. Before I leave this earth, I need to know the truth. Tell me about your plot to assassinate President Tyler back in 1844."

Monty could feel the blood drain from his face as he heard the words. How did the old man know? Exactly *what* did he know? Dare he tell him the truth?

CHAPTER 2

June, 1852— Monty caught his breath after the unexpected inquiry from the senator, tried not to look concerned, and asked, as innocently as possible, "What do you mean?" Clay coughed several times, brought a handkerchief to his mouth, and coughed some more. Monty could see specks of blood as Clay pulled it to his side, crumpling it into his frail hand. Such a terrible way to go, he thought. This good man deserved better.

"We've known each other too long, young man, and I can tell by the look on your face that you know exactly what I mean." His tone began to show some irritation. "I know that you were involved in some plot to kill President Tyler. I hope it was not some misguided attempt to benefit me politically. I deserve the truth."

"You *hated* Tyler. We all did. You should have been elected in 1840 and should have been the president then, not him. Of all people, not Tyler."

The old man smirked and let out a small laugh, his prior annoyance seemingly gone. "Well, if it had not been for those damn fools running my campaign at the convention in Harrisburg, I would have been."

Monty nodded in agreement. "You don't have to tell me, I was there."

"That's right. I'd forgotten that I sent you to the convention to observe things for me."

"You did. December of 1939. I'd only been working for you for just over a year then. Remember it like it was yesterday. That damn rule change. I tried to stop it, but no one wanted to listen to a kid."

"Caused me to lose the nomination to ol' Granny Harrison. What an embarrassment."

* * *

The contest for the nomination for president of the relatively new Whig Party in 1840 was a three-man race between Henry Clay, the party's primary founder, and two military men, William Henry Harrison and Winfield Scott. Going into the convention, Clay, whose base of support was in the South, had more delegates than each of his two opponents, but was short of the majority that was needed. It was the first time that the party held a convention to select its nominees, an innovation that other parties had been using since the campaign of 1832.

William Henry Harrison, then sixty-six years old, had been a hero at the 1811 Battle of Tippecanoe, fought against Native Americans a generation earlier. "Old Tip," he was called. In the ensuing years, he'd had an undistinguished career—a brief stint in Congress, minister to Columbia for a year, and some administrative positions. An Ohio resident for several years, Harrison had been born into a prominent Virginia family, his father having been a signer of the Declaration of Independence and a governor of the Old Dominion. In 1840, Harrison was supported for president by several states in the West and a few in the North.

The other contender was Winfield Scott, still an active general in the United States Army and, like Harrison, also a hero on the battlefield, long ago, during the War of 1812. The political boss of New York's Whig Party had lined up the majority of the Empire State's delegation behind Scott. As the largest state, New York had the most delegate votes at the convention and this made Scott a formidable contender for the nomination.

On the convention's second day, leaders of the Harrison and Scott campaigns conspired and offered a change to the proposed nominating rules that was damaging to Clay. Under it, a committee of three delegates from each state would poll the rest of that state's delegates, and would keep polling them until a majority favored one candidate. Then, *all* of that state's delegate votes would be cast for the candidate supported by the majority. It silenced the votes of the minority of delegates in each state. Clay would lose at least fifteen votes under the amendment. Clay's floor leaders at the convention were slow to realize the impact of the rule change and did not strenuously oppose it. Once it was passed, they tried to get it reversed, but were unsuccessful.

The next day, on the first ballot, Clay led with 103 votes of the 128 needed to win. Harrison was second with 91, and Scott third with 57. The votes of the fifteen or so delegates who supported Clay in three large states were cast for his opponents, under the rule adopted the previous day. Had they been cast for Clay, he would have been within reach of the votes needed for victory, and positioned for a win on the second ballot. Instead, he slipped to 95 votes on the second ballot, and Harrison won the nomination on the third.

* * *

As Monty sat in an uncomfortable wooden chair by Clay's bed in the senator's room at the National Hotel, they reminisced about the Harrisburg convention.

"I went over the figures in my head when the rule change was first proposed and realized how many votes you would lose. Went up to Mr. Johnson," said Monty, "and told him it would doom your chances and that he had to oppose it. He caucused with those around him. Said you would still win and that it was not worth antagonizing the Pennsylvania delegation, where the proposal had come from. A few minutes later, someone handed him a piece of paper with some numbers on it, and his face went pale as a ghost. By then, it was too late."

"Basic arithmetic. Gotta count every vote. You saw it right away. Why couldn't they?" said Clay. "I was none too happy. That was my best chance at the presidency."

"I never had the nerve to ask you back then. When you first heard the news of your loss back here in Washington City, did you really say 'My friends are not worth the powder and shot it would take to kill them?'"

"I surely did. One of my better lines in the heat of the moment, if I say so myself." Clay added, "It was a joke. Well, *mostly* a joke. Anyone could have beaten Van Buren that year." Clay's words were not spoken in anger, but in a matter-of-fact way. He had long ago gotten over that defeat. There had been successes, and more defeats, since then. Such was politics.

"And then they compounded their sins," added Monty, "by putting Tyler on the ticket with Harrison."

"So they did. I would never have given it my blessing," said Clay. "John Tyler was a Whig in name only. A states' righter and still a Democrat at heart. Not one of my backers. They didn't give it more than a minute's thought." He paused and let out a few coughs. "Our so-called party leaders didn't care a tinker's curse who was in the second spot. They got a military man, Harrison, in the top one. Someone who would attract votes. Never mind that his battles were fought more than thirty years before and that his career since then had been . . . how can I say this politely . . . rather *mundane*. They were already planning a campaign that was all about imagery, not issues. Log cabins and hard cider. Tippecanoe and Tyler Too. How many times did we have to hear that idiotic slogan?"

"You can say that again," responded Monty. "If Tyler's name had not started with a T, maybe the country would have been spared all of the trouble he caused. What did someone later write about putting him on the ticket, 'There was rhyme but no reason to it?'"

Clay laughed, precipitating another coughing spell. Monty could see that the old man had tired, so he stood up to take his leave. "Come back tomorrow?" asked the senator, adding, "It is good to reminisce, but don't think for a moment that I didn't notice that you avoided talking to me today about the subject I asked you here to discuss. Assassination plot. I am dying, but I'm not senile."

So much for trying to distract him, Monty thought. "We have floor votes scheduled most of the day tomorrow. How about Monday, same time?"

"Not like I'm going anywhere. God willing, I will see you then."

* * *

As he walked out of the hotel, Monty pulled out his pocket watch. Not quite six. Too late to go back to Congress. The House would be adjourned by now. He decided to walk to his boardinghouse. Only about a mile. As he strolled along a half-empty Pennsylvania Avenue, he began to think of the best way he could explain how he had gotten involved in a plot to assassinate the president of the United States.

It had all begun in the winter of 1841, he recalled, in the middle of the fourth-month long transition in administrations from Van Buren to Harrison. After beating Clay for the Whig nomination, Harrison had gone on to win the election. The Democrats, after a twelve-year hold on the White House, were headed out of power and, for the first time in their brief history, the Whigs were about to take charge, not only of the presidency, but also with majorities in both houses of Congress. Despite his loss of the nomination, Clay had campaigned hard for Harrison and Tyler and was ready to reap his reward. Enacting into law the Whig Party's agenda was at hand. A new national bank, tariffs to protect industry from foreign competition, and the building of roads and canals. It would just be a matter of time. So it was thought. During this time of hope and anticipation, Monty made friendships that, when unexpected political events occurred, led to fateful decisions.

CHAPTER 3

July, 1841— "You see the look in their eyes as well as I do," John Tyler, III said, with a tone of disgust in his voice. "They treat him like he doesn't belong here. Senators, congressmen, the cabinet. Even the servants."

The comment was made to his older brother, Robert, about their father. They faced each other, sitting at the two small desks shoved together in their cramped office on the second floor of the President's House.

Only twenty-two, John was handsome, strikingly so, with a long face, dark eyes, and black curly hair, which he wore long. His nose was narrow and straight, having avoided the aquiline nasal feature that characterized most of the men in his family. He and Robert both worked as secretaries for their father, the tenth man to serve as president of the United States.

"They need to get over it," John continued. "He *is* the president, as surely as Harrison was."

"It's only been three months,' responded Robert. "Give them time. A president has never died in office before."

A typical Robert response, John thought. Robert, always an optimist. John had noticed that the tension between the two of them had grown over the past few months. Close proximity, he decided, would do that, especially among siblings. He had always resented how Robert, the firstborn son and three years his senior, had an engaging manner and an air of confidence. "You need to be more polished, like Robert," he remembered his mother telling him when they had been in their teen years. John had a darker, brooding personality, and a stubbornness about him. The best in men was not something that he looked for, nor cared to find. He took more after his father, he thought. A trait of which he was proud.

* * *

President John Tyler was a Virginia aristocrat to his core. Raised on a plantation between Richmond and Williamsburg, worked by the family's forty or so enslaved people, he had followed in his father's footsteps, attended the College of William and Mary, and became a lawyer. Public service was expected of men of his class. Beginning in his early twenties, Tyler served in a succession of political offices of increasing prestige, from the Virginia legislature, to Congress, to governor of Virginia, and then to the United States Senate. In each, he was known as an ardent defender of states' rights and of slavery.

Tyler had aligned himself with the Democratic Party of President Andrew Jackson, but broke with Jackson in the early 1830s during the Nullification Crisis, when Jackson had threatened federal military action against South Carolina to force compliance with tariff collections. When it came to federal power versus state power, Tyler's inclination was to stand with the states, and he was not a man open to changing his mind. Obstinate, he had been called in his Senate days. He left the Democratic Party and moved to the new Whig Party. It was an awkward fit. The Whigs welcomed all who opposed Jackson, but their economic policies were based on the American System, an agenda devised by their founder, Senator Henry Clay, which called for a national bank, high tariffs, and the funding of roads and canals, all of which Tyler opposed. A federal government that had the power to do such things, Tyler and his fellow slave-holding southerners believed, was also a federal government that could interfere with the slavery system that was the bedrock of the southern economy. That was not going to happen, not if he had his way. To Tyler, the South's "peculiar institution" not only needed to survive, it needed to expand.

More than three years after leaving the Senate in 1836, Tyler attended the presidential nominating convention of his new party, the Whigs, in Harrisburg in late 1839. When Kentuckian Henry Clay lost the presidential nomination to William Henry Harrison of Ohio, the convention, hoping to appease southerners who had supported Clay, put him on the ticket as vice president with the aged Harrison. The Whigs soundly beat the Democrats in the 1840 general election, turning the incumbent Democratic president, Martin Van Buren, out of office, and taking both branches of Congress.

After briefly presiding over the Senate in his constitutional role as vice president on Inauguration Day, March 4, 1841, Tyler returned to his home in Williamsburg. No official tasks had been given to him by Harrison, typical of the relationship between presidents and vice presidents of the era. There, he planned to spend most of the next four years in relative seclusion.

Tyler's stay in Williamsburg lasted only a month. On the morning of April 5, at dawn, in a nightshirt and cap, he answered a loud knock on his door. The young man standing before him was exhausted, having ridden by horseback all night at breakneck speed. Tyler's presence was needed in Washington City immediately, the almost breathless messenger relayed. President Harrison was dead, likely from pneumonia.

In the nation's capital, a debate soon raged. Harrison was the first president to have died in office. Was Tyler now the president, or merely the *acting* president? The Constitution was not clear, stating that upon the president's death, the "powers and duties" of the office "shall devolve on the Vice President." It did not state that the vice president *became* the president. In Tyler's view, he was the president, not a mere caretaker. He took the oath of office shortly after his arrival in the city and, within days, issued a lengthy statement that was, in effect, an inaugural address.

Opponents believed that he had assumed power that was not rightfully his and referred to him as "His Accidency." Not only was he not really the president, in their opinion, he was in over his head. A former president, John Quincy Adams, who viewed Tyler as only the acting president, wrote in his diary of the low opinion he had of the man, and of his political philosophy: "Tyler is a political sectarian, of the slave-driving, Virginian, Jeffersonian school, principled against all improvement, with all the interests and passions and vices of slavery rooted in his moral and political constitution—with talents not above mediocrity, and a spirit incapable of expansion." Fate, wrote Adams, had placed "in the Executive Chair a man never thought of it by any body."

Within a few months, Tyler, the accidental president, was at odds with the political establishment in Washington City, both the Whigs and the Democrats.

* * *

"Give them *more* time? There you go again, Mr. Sunshine," said John, as he reached into a drawer on his side of the two desks, pulled out a silver flask, and took a swig.

"John! What are you doing? Its only ten in the morning," scolded Robert.

"Mind your own business. I can handle it."

"Apparently Mattie doesn't think so."

If looks could kill, John's icy stare at the comment would have. An unfair jab, he thought. He was sure that, in time, his wife, Mattie, would realize that she needed him and she would come around. Yes, she had decided to stay behind with their young son and live with her family in Virginia, rather than join him in Washington City. And she was not responding to his letters. But that had nothing to do with the alcohol, he kept telling himself.

John decided to ignore Robert's remark and shift the conversation away from him and back to the political atmosphere in the city. "You're too nice, Robert. Too passive. Don't be naive. Politics is war. We have to fight back. I've talked with father and he agrees. It's been long enough. The slights, the condescending remarks. They will never come around. He's done with it and is ready to put the bastards in their place."

CHAPTER 4

January, 1841— Most of the large crowd in the Hall of the House of Representatives was already seated when Monty entered the room. Snow flurries in the late afternoon of the raw January day, combined with the poor heating of the large room, led most to keep their coats on. "Dammit, I'm later than I should be," he muttered to himself, as he walked up the aisle to see if there were any seats left near the front. He spotted one in the third row and took it, between two men who appeared to be slightly younger than he. Both were clean shaven, had short hair, and sat erect. Possibly military, he speculated.

Turning first to his right, he held out his right hand. "Monty Tolliver, pleased to meet you."

"Ben Geddis, same here," came the response from the red-haired chap, along with a smile and a firm handshake.

Moving to the left, Monty repeated the greeting. "Sam Shipley," said the black-haired recipient of his second handshake.

Ben—red, Sam—black, he told himself, as he committed their names and hair color to memory. If there was one thing he had learned in his brief career in the political world, remembering names and faces was a key requirement of his job. Ben, he noted, had a long triangular face, highlighted by forest green eyes. Light freckles dotted his face and hands. Sam, with hazel brown eyes, had black hair and a youthful-looking round face that Monty was sure had rarely seen a razor.

"Where are you fellas from?" he asked, knowing that no one was actually *from* Washington City.

"Rhode Island," said red.

"Pennsylvania," said black.

"Ohio here" offered Monty, without anyone asking.

Monty looked up at the ceiling and walls of the familiar semi-circular room, which always gave him a sense of awe when he entered. Redesigned by architect Benjamin Latrobe after the first chamber of the larger house of Congress was burned by the British during the War of 1812, it gave the impression of an ancient Grecian amphitheater, with dark green marble columns lining the flat wall behind the rostrum, and also along the rounded wall. Crimson swags hung between the columns, and the room was capped by a half-dome ornate ceiling. The desks of the members of Congress had been removed for this meeting, and rows of chairs added, to increase the seating capacity. Monty pulled out of his coat pocket a pencil and several sheets of folded foolscap. He was not here for enjoyment. He was working. His boss would be speaking soon, without prepared remarks, and would be expecting on his desk tomorrow a concise summary of his words of wisdom to distribute to the press.

"Notes? You take this pretty seriously?" asked Ben, raising his barely visible reddish eyebrows.

"Have to, it's my job," Monty answered.

At that moment, five men entered the room from a doorway on the left. The clicking of their heels on the marble floor resonated around the room. They took seats in front of the rostrum, to polite applause from the crowd. One then walked to the lectern.

"Welcome to the twenty-fourth annual meeting of the American Colonization Society," he bellowed. "I call this meeting to order."

After an opening prayer and a financial report, the featured speaker of the evening and the president of the organization, Senator Henry Clay, was introduced. Monty leaned forward, pencil in hand and paper on his knee.

"Gentlemen of the Colonization Society," Clay began, "I hope that 1841 has begun well for you. I have just ended an arduous journey of hundreds of miles from the great state of Kentucky, made in midwinter's frost, and have come here with no formal nor highly polished address to deliver. Yet, I feel obliged to say some words to you tonight, as I was one of those who met some twenty-five years ago to form this Society and you have honored me these past few years by naming me as your president. Our goal was then, and still is, to establish a colony on the shores of Africa, where free persons of color may go, of their own voluntary desire, without coercion, to establish better lives for themselves and for their children. We have sought this based on the incontestable fact that the white and black races, due to prejudice, cannot, on equal terms, live harmoniously together in the same community. Our benevolent purpose is that the black race may enjoy, without molestation, all of the benefits of a free and democratic society." He expounded further on the organization's history and outlined its efforts, with limited success, over the past quarter century.

"Yet," continued the senator, "we are attacked on all sides. Those who support the institution of slavery assail us as seeking its demise, and for encouraging runaways and revolts. Conversely, the abolitionists attack us for condoning and encouraging the perpetuation of slavery. Why do they all criticize us? We do not interfere with either of them. Our purpose concerns only free persons of color, not slaves. The abolitionists seek to emancipate at one blow the entire colored race. Well, if they can do that, so be it. If they succeed, the work of colonization of those souls will commence only when the work of abolition has ended."

A good line, thought Monty, scribbling out a note. Better include it in the summary.

Clay moved on. "We are also attacked for having transported, to date, only a few thousand souls to Africa, and it is said that the mortality rate from disease of those who have emigrated there is prohibitive and, due to this, our cause should be ended. Let me remind you that most great enterprises of men have had small beginnings, and setbacks. Jamestown and Plymouth both languished for years after their founding, barely surviving, and their rates of death from disease were higher than among those who have gone to Africa under our supervision. And, lo, look what has become of those slow-growing seeds planted in the soil of Virginia and Massachusetts—the United States of America. Imagine what a successful colony in Africa of men of color, most baptized as Christians, who have knowledge of democratic institutions as we have here, can do to transform that dark continent. A land that has lain so long in barbarism, and in the worship of unknown and forbidden gods, can be brought into the everlasting light of Democracy and Christianity."

After comments congratulating the officers of the Society and their hard work over the past year, the man who was considered the greatest orator of his generation then closed in for his conclusion. "Let all men look on our Society as it is, and judge our purpose with fairness and impartiality. Go on, then gentlemen, go on in our noble cause. Our African republic will come to be and will change the world. Continue to give our goals of freedom, civilization, and social happiness to free persons of color your best energies and most fervent prayers, until our great object has been fully accomplished. Invoking on this great and good cause the blessings of Almighty God, without whom nothing is strong, nothing is holy, and whose smiles, I believe, have hitherto been extended to our efforts, I bid you a cordial farewell."

When Clay finished, there was a loud round of applause and, shortly thereafter, the meeting was adjourned.

"The man can turn a phrase," said Ben, as he turned toward Monty.

"I know. He's my boss. I never get tired of hearing him speak and seeing the effect he has on an audience," responded Monty, as he slipped his notes into his coat pocket. "Gents, the evening is young," he said to his two newfound acquaintances on either side, "How about a drink?" Both nodded and the threesome headed out of the House chamber and down the steep marble steps.

"I know just the place," said Ben, as he led the way to a tavern on B Street.

A round of ale was ordered. Sam started off the conversation with an interesting proposal: "Each one of us tells his life story in one hundred words or less. Monty, you're first."

After a feigned grimace and a deep breath, Monty started, "Well, here goes. Born and raised in Dayton, Ohio. Oldest of four kids. My father owns a foundry. Went to college at Miami College in Oxford, near home, and graduated in '38. Was interested in being a lawyer and came here to read law in the office of an attorney who is the brother of one of my professors. Got bored with that after a few weeks. In politics, I've always been an admirer of Henry Clay. On a whim, about three years ago, I walked into his office here and asked for a job. The senator hired me as a clerk and I am now his chief aide. I'm excited about the new administration. Some great things are about to happen. How am I doing on the world count?"

"Real close," grinned Sam.

"No wife, no sweetheart. Oh, twenty-six years old. Done," finished Monty.

"Good job, I feel like I've known you forever," joked Sam. "Ben, you're next."

"Hard act to follow," started Ben. "I do *not* work for one of the most important men in America, but I do carry the name of one. A dead one. Named after Benjamin Franklin. I'm from Newport, Rhode Island. Grew up on the water. Twenty-three years old. My father was an officer in the Navy, left that, and started a sail cloth factory that he runs now. One younger brother. I did a year of college at Brown, near home. Found out that I was not much of a college boy. Got an officer's commission as a lieutenant and joined the Navy, like my old man. Assigned here to the Navy Department about a year ago. We've been working on plans to build new and better ships. We hear that Harrison will push for this when he comes in as president in a few weeks. I hope to someday be a captain of one of those ships.

My politics—abolitionist. Lady friend at home? Had one, but no more. And I love beer!," Ben ended, as he took a big swig from his pewter tankard.

"Sam, your turn. Go," said Ben.

Sam chuckled, "Do I have to? I really didn't think you guys would do it."

"Yes!," came the reply, loudly and in unison.

"I'm a farm boy from near Harrisburg, Pennsylvania. We grow mostly wheat and raise cattle. Five siblings, two sis's and three brothers. I'm younger than you guys, only twenty. I tried college too, at Franklin in Lancaster, and also found it was not for me. My uncle is a captain in the Army and I was able to get a commission as a second lieutenant and am posted here in Washington City at the War Department. I've been working with a group developing new artillery and hope to get transferred soon to a fort's artillery unit. Lady friend? I have to confess I haven't had one yet. Politics? Also an abolitionist. Heard about this meeting from a friend at work and came to see what the colonization society was about. Can't say that I was impressed. Is that enough?"

"Not quite. Do you love beer?," asked Ben.

"Almost as much as my mother!"

"Ben," Monty said, "I love that quote from your namesake, that 'beer is proof that God loves us and wants us to be happy.'"

"I like that one too, although I've heard that he may have actually said it about wine."

"Say it isn't so! If he wasn't talking about beer, he *should* have been," replied Monty. "A wise man, ol' Benjamin."

The three raised their tankards in unison and each took another sip of the amber brew.

They talked about the colonization movement. Monty defended it. Sam dismissed it as ineffectual. "Don't get me wrong, I think Senator Clay is a good man," said Sam, "but colonization is not about ridding this country of slavery. It doesn't even pretend to do that. He admitted as much tonight. My parents do more to oppose slavery than this highfalutin American Colonization Society. Our farm is not far from the Susquehanna River, near the Maryland line, a big crossing point for slaves seeking freedom. They have hidden a few escaped slaves for a couple of days and helped them move further north. What are they calling it, the Underground Railroad?"

"I have to agree," Ben chimed in. "Maybe if Clay had beaten Jackson back in '32, he would have taken on the slave interests and gotten something done. Gradual emancipation. Anything. But he lost and slavery is now a bigger mess and more divisive than ever. The slavers have way too much power in this country."

"That's for sure," said Sam.

"Almost makes me ashamed to be an American," Ben continued, "Just look around the streets of Washington City at the way these people are treated. No freedom. We've all seen some of them being led around in chains. And if you go outside of the city into Virginia and Maryland, it's much worse there. Folks in the North won't stand for it much longer, I'm telling you."

Monty found himself on the defensive, responding as best he could. "The majority of the colored people here in the city are free, and most of the ones who are slaves are hired out by their owners to hotels and restaurants as service workers. It's not like they're working in the fields and are beaten. Gradual emancipation, followed by colonization, which Senator Clay has advocated for years, is the answer."

Ben pounced. "Well, they are still slaves. *Owned* by someone. And if they are not worked to death and beaten here, they surely are in the South, and more so the farther down you go. Gradual emancipation and then colonization? How can you tell someone, 'Don't worry, you spend your life in bondage and maybe we'll let your children or grandchildren be free, and then we'll ship them off to Africa?' That's the solution I heard tonight."

"Don't you care about our country?," asked Monty. "Our Union? Sometimes you don't like how some family members act or what they do, but they are still family. Southern slaveowners are still our countrymen. We all live under our Constitution, and it permits slavery."

"Some things are more important than country," replied Ben. "I feel like all of us from north of Mason and Dixon's Line are tainted, have blood on our hands, because we condone this evil within our borders."

Sam spoke up, trying to be the peacemaker. "Probably wasn't a good idea to talk so much politics at our first meeting, gentlemen. We are not going to solve the slavery issue tonight and I, for one, have to go to work tomorrow morning. How about we meet here again Saturday night?'

"Sounds good, I can do that," said Ben.

"Agreed. Maybe we can discuss our opinions on religion then," responded Monty, with a wink.

The three laughed.

CHAPTER 5

ugust, 1841— John watched as the six members of the cabinet shuffled out of the room, the smoke from their cigars hanging in the hot air. It had been a contentious meeting. Voices had been raised. A lack of proper respect, he felt, for the office and for the man who held it. The look of disgust on his father's face matched his own.

"You heard it, son. To a man, they are telling me to sign it," said President Tyler.

A good thing Robert had not sat in on the meeting, John thought. His older brother would, he was sure, urge going along, or at least a compromise. Sign it? To hell with that, John had determined, with certainty. Now was the perfect time to get his father to commit. "You don't have to listen to them. They are Harrison's men, not yours. They don't have your best interests at heart."

"They *are* right. Harrison would have signed it."

"He's dead. God rest his soul." John put his notes from the meeting aside, got up from his seat, and began to pound his right index finger repeatedly on the president's desk. "If you sign this bill, you will hand over the leadership of the Whig Party to Senator Clay and you will have no hope of getting the nomination in '44. It's Clay's bill. He wrote it. He will be the hero, not you. A veto is your best path to taking over the party. Chart your own course. And if that fails, you will be positioned for the Democrats to take you back in and nominate you."

"My old Democratic friends would surely love me to veto it. I have always been on record as opposing a national bank."

"Old Hickory certainly used opposition to it to his advantage. Got him a second term. You can do it too."

"The Whig press will crucify me if I veto the party's blessed bank bill."

"Let them. Not like you have ever had many supporters there."

* * *

Political divisions over a national bank had been around since the first term of George Washington. The primary purpose of such a bank was to establish a national system of credit for borrowing money by the federal government, and by business and industry, thereby promoting economic development. But was it within the power granted to the federal government under the Constitution? There was the rub. Explicitly, no; implicitly, probably so. Opinions were passionate on both sides. The First Bank of the United States, the brainchild of Secretary of the Treasury Alexander Hamilton, was established in 1791, but Congress did not renew its twenty-year charter when it expired in 1811. The economic benefit of a national bank was evident when, five years later, President James Madison, a states' rights

Virginian who had opposed the First Bank, signed into law in 1816 a bill creating the Second Bank of the United States. The support of Madison, known as the father of the Constitution, seemed to have settled for many the constitutionality of a national bank, if not its propriety on its merits.

But controversy over a national bank did not die. When the Second Bank's charter came up for renewal in the early 1830s, President Andrew Jackson, the leader of the Democratic Party, who was running for a second term in 1832, whipped up opposition to it, portraying the bank's renewal as a battle between the nation's working men and farmers, and the political and business elite. The opposing party strongly supported the bank. Jackson rode opposition to rechartering the Second Bank to another four years as president.

Almost a decade later, the tables were turned. The Whigs had won the 1840 election, tossed the Democrats out of office, were calling for a new national bank, and had successfully steered a bill creating one through Congress.

* * *

President Tyler rubbed his forehead and looked at the abandoned chairs around the empty table before him. "I wish I had my own men in those cabinet seats."

"Another reason to veto the bank bill," responded John. "Give them a reason to resign. Will save you from having to fire them."

John watched his father's head begin to gently nod. "Interesting thought," commented the president. "Your mother always said you were our most cunning child."

"Doubt she meant it as a compliment."

"Surely not. But that's her opinion. Not mine. I have only been here a short time, but I am coming to the belief that being cunning is necessary for survival in this damn office. It may be time to shake things up."

"Do it."

"I have a lot to think about, my boy, a lot to think about."

CHAPTER 6

August, 1841— Ben looked over the drawings and plans one more time, rolled them up, and knocked on the half-opened door of his boss's office. "I have the information here for your appearance on Thursday afternoon before the committee," he said to John Simms, the chief clerk to the secretary of the Navy. "Whenever you are ready."

"Let's go ahead and do it now, Lieutenant Geddis. I hate it when Secretary Badger asks me to fill in for him at the last minute. It's not the first time. Between you and me, not sure I believe that he is as ill as he alleges, but so be it. The president wants the funding for this ship in the Navy's congressional spending bill coming up for a vote next week and we can't delay it."

"We have everything you need. Should be routine."

"I don't know. Those old coots in the House hate any change. They love the traditional warships under sail. Getting them to agree to fund a steamship as an alternative is going to be a hard sell."

Ben unrolled the detailed diagrams for the USS *Princeton* across Simms' desk.

"She sure looks impressive, at least on paper," said Simms, as he glanced over the drawings and puffed on his pipe, giving gentle nods of approval. "Refresh my memory again on the background of this captain. Stockton?," he inquired. "Richard is his first name, correct?"

"It's Robert, sir. Captain Robert Stockton," Ben began. "Experienced. Served in the War of 1812 and in the Barbary Wars. Captured enemy ships, but sometimes by exceeding orders. A swashbuckler. At least that is his reputation. According to his file, higher-ups thought him to be stubborn and untrustworthy, but he got the job done. He's from a wealthy New Jersey family. He's naming the ship *Princeton* for the town there where he was born. I understand that he is a close personal friend of President Tyler."

"Yes, yes, I recall him now. So he is. A friendship built on political support. He used to be a big Democrat. Came to us here at the department a few years ago with basically these same plans, but Van Buren's folks were not interested. He then contributed substantially to the Whigs in the election last year and, *viola*, he's back, and now the Navy is supporting his ideas. Of course, none of that will pass my lips when I am before our esteemed members of Congress."

"It will be an amazing ship, sir," said Ben, "despite how we got to this point."

"Agreed, lieutenant. Tell me about this Swedish inventor, Eric-something. He's the brains behind all this, right?"

"Yes, sir. John Ericsson. Stockton met him in England a few years ago. A brilliant man, from all I have read and heard. The Brits weren't interested in his ideas, so Stockton told him he would promote them to our Navy. Ericsson has solved the two main problems that we have had with military use of steamships—the exposed paddlewheels with engines on deck, and limited range. The *Princeton* has a screw propeller system that he devised, with the engines housed within the hull and underneath the waterline, making them almost invulnerable to enemy attack. They connect directly to a shaft that goes to an underwater propeller. No need for a paddlewheel."

"Where is that on the diagram?"

"Here, sir, the enlarged area," said Ben, pointing to the right side of the desk. He continued. "The boilers are more efficient than any designed before, and they burn anthracite coal, meaning more range with less fuel. Our steamships will be able to do more than patrol the coastline. She can also run under sail and, when doing so, the smokestack on the deck collapses, reducing wind friction and increasing speed."

"That's ingenious. The old codgers should like that."

"Her wooden hull will be covered in a thin sheet of iron. Three masts. About a hundred and sixty feet in length. Not particularly large, which means greater maneuverability. She will have a crew of around one-hundred and fifty."

"What do you think, Geddis? Is this ship really a step forward?"

"A hundred steps, sir. Our Navy needs this."

"If she turns out to be as good as these plans indicate, we can build a fleet of them and, for once, finally get some respect on the seas."

CHAPTER 7

*A*ugust, 1841— Monty had a good seat in the third row of the packed Senate gallery. It was late afternoon on a hot August day in 1841, five months since John Tyler, the man still called "His Accidency" by much of the press, had been in office. The temperature outside made the indoors almost sweltering. Typical Washington City heat and humidity, he thought, having grown more accustomed to it over the past few summers. A crowd of hundreds more, maybe even a couple of thousand, waited in the Rotunda and outside along the steps on both the east and west sides of the Capitol. The event that they had come to see was expected soon.

* * *

Under the Constitution, the president has ten days to veto a bill passed by Congress. The signature item on the Whig Party's agenda, the reestablishment of a national bank, which they had run on in the 1840 election, and upon which President Harrison and the party's majorities in Congress had been elected, had been passed and put on the president's desk. But it was a different man sitting behind that desk than the one who had been elected. Harrison was dead and his vice president was now in charge. Years earlier, when a Democratic senator, John Tyler had opposed a national bank as, in his view, an unconstitutional expansion of the power of the federal government.

The Whigs in Congress knew that President Tyler, although now also a Whig, based on his prior statements and states' rights history, was a wild card. They had revised some portions of their bill, hoping to appease him and alleviate some of his known objections. But was it enough? Would he sign it, or veto it? Everyone in Washington City seemed to have an opinion, but no one knew for sure.

* * *

Monty pulled out his handkerchief and wiped the beads of sweat from his forehead. Nine days had passed since the bank bill had landed on Tyler's desk. It was rumored that today would be decision day. That had brought the crowds to the Capitol. He looked around the gallery. Mostly men, dressed in dark colors, as usual, but with an occasional colorful oasis from the bright dress of a lady. Every now and then, his eye caught a fluttering motion. Those who had brought handheld fans looked very pleased with themselves. The tension among the spectators was as thick as the air.

As the Senate debated a bill concerning the proceeds of the sale of federal lands, Monty saw several heads turn to the main door at the rear of the chamber. A young man, whom Monty recognized as the president's son, John, suddenly appeared, an envelope in hand. The sergeant at arms greeted young Tyler and escorted him up the main aisle to the secretary of the Senate. The eyes of everyone in the gallery fixed on the two men. This was it, they all knew. Many, including Monty, leaned forward, elbows planted on knees and faces buried in hands, as if their heads had suddenly doubled in weight and needed support.

As the secretary opened the envelope, all eyes shifted to him. "From the president of the United States," he bellowed, and then read the seven-paragraph message from Tyler. As it was being read, Monty focused on Senator Clay, who was sitting at his desk, motionless, a look of disgust on his face. "Unconstitutional," said the secretary, reading Tyler's words, "I regard the bill as asserting for congress the right to incorporate a United States bank with power and right to establish offices of discount and deposit in the several states of the union, with or without their consent, a principle to which I have always heretofore been opposed, and which can never obtain my sanction."

The deed was done. A Whig president had vetoed the major economic recovery bill of the Whig Party. People gasped. Monty then began to hear hissing, both to his right and to his left. Senator Benton of Missouri, one of the president's supporters, demanded that the sergeant at arms be ordered to clear the gallery. The president *pro tem* refused, but the Senate quickly adjourned, diffusing a potentially dangerous situation. The crowd poured out of the Capitol, most angry and disgusted.

* * *

The next evening, Monty knocked on the door of Ben's room at his boardinghouse. "Sorry, I got held up a bit," he said when his friend opened the door.

"Are you sure that Sam is going to like this?" asked Ben.

"It's his twenty-first birthday. What red-blooded American male would not?"

"What's that in your hand? Bringing a book?"

"A little something for you. Found it in a bookshop the other day. A little worn, but thought you would like it," said Monty, as he handed it to Ben.

"*Quotations of Benjamin Franklin*," said Ben, reading the title. "My father had a similar one. Thank you! I suppose I should learn to recite more of the wit and wisdom of the man I am named after than 'A penny saved is a penny earned.'"

"You're welcome. We should get going. There's probably something in there about the rudeness of being late."

* * *

They met Sam at their favorite tavern on Second Street. Monty and Ben extended birthday wishes, each putting an arm around Sam's shoulders. "It's just another day, nothing to celebrate," said Sam.

"You are such a Pennsylvania farm boy," said Monty. "You are twenty-one, my friend. We are in the nation's capital and we will be doing some celebrating tonight!" Ale and dinner were ordered. As usual, the conversation turned to politics.

"Can you believe that Tyler vetoed the bank bill?," asked an incredulous Ben. "Who does he think he is? He is elected vice president as a Whig, takes over when Harrison dies, and vetoes the most important legislative item of the Whig Party. And don't even get me started on whether he is really the president, or should be just an acting president, carrying out Harrison's policies."

"I have never seen Senator Clay so angry," said Monty. "We heard rumors all last week that Tyler was going to do it, but still held out hope that he would back down. I was in the Senate chamber and people were shocked when the veto message was read. When he got back to the office, he threw down his papers and slammed his hand on the desk. 'Damn that arrogant Virginian!,' he shouted, and added a few more choice words. He said it's all about the 1844 election, that Tyler is trying to take over the party and, if he fails at that, to cozy up to the Democrats. It's been two days now and he still hasn't calmed down."

"Can't Congress override the veto?," inquired Sam.

"That takes two-thirds of both the House and the Senate, and the votes are just not there," said Monty. "There's talk of kicking Tyler out of the Whig Party. Not that it would really accomplish anything. More symbolic than anything else."

The waitress arrived with dinner. "Meat and potatoes for all," she said, distributing the plates. Another round of ale was requested.

"She's gorgeous," said Sam. "It would be nice if we had three young ladies like her on our arms tonight."

"The evening is young, my boy," said Monty, winking to Ben.

"Seriously, what can be done with Tyler?," said Sam. "I know I'm young, but have our politics ever been this bungled? How can this be fixed?"

"Have to wait to the election in '44 to do anything," said Monty.

"Not necessarily," replied Ben. "There is a quicker remedy. Someone could kill him before then. That would solve a lot of problems. Not like he's the real president."

Monty and Sam chuckled.

"I'm not joking," added Ben, a serious look on his face. "Not that I would do it but, mark my words, there are people giving it serious consideration right now."

"You're probably right about that," said Monty. "But we're not some European monarchy. We can't go lopping off heads, like the Brits did with Charles I and the French with Louis whatever number he was. And God knows what the Spanish, Russians, and others have done. We are a republic and we elect our leader."

"That's just it, Tyler wasn't elected our leader. He was elected second fiddle, a spare wheel," retorted Ben, as the waitress came to clear away the empty plates.

"Enough talk about Tyler for tonight," said Monty. "We do have something more constructive that we need to accomplish this evening," looking at Sam.

"And what might that be?," asked Sam.

"Just be patient. You'll find out soon enough," said Monty. He and Ben paid the bill and they walked out of the tavern. Outside, Ben hailed a passing barouche. As they climbed in, Monty noted that there seemed to be more people out on the streets than usual. It was a Wednesday. Shouldn't be crowded, he thought. He heard some shouting in the distance.

* * *

"Number 349. This is it." Monty said to the driver.

"Yes, sir, I've stopped here many a time," responded the driver, as he brought the two black horses pulling the rig to a gentle stop. He deposited his three passengers in front of the handsome three-story brick house on Maryland Avenue, not far from the Capitol. Senator Clay had told Monty about the establishment and had recommended it. It was one place in Washington City where partisanship ended at the door. Men in power, Whigs and Democrats, came and went, and the authorities looked the other way. Or ventured through the door themselves. The employees here had enough inside information about what was really going on in the federal government, Monty was sure, to make the best newspapermen envious. After arriving in the city three years ago, he had visited more often than he would like to admit.

They went up the steps and Monty knocked on the door. A small horizontal slat slid opened, revealing an eyeball. The clicking sound of locks being undone soon followed.

"Is this place what I think it is?," asked Sam. "A whorehouse?"

"I think the owner and the clientele prefer the term upscale brothel," replied Monty. He walked over to the desk in the foyer and recognized the proprietor, Mary Ann Hall. "Good evening. My name is Monty Tolliver. I stopped by earlier. There are three of us."

"Yes, Mr. Tolliver. Good to see you again," replied Miss Hall, a slightly plump, fair-skinned and big-bosomed woman of around forty years of age. She wore a flowered dress, low-cut but tasteful, with her long red hair draped in front of her right shoulder. Long eyelashes fluttered above her mint green eyes. "As you requested, you will be with my sister, Liz. We have Matilda for the young man celebrating his birthday, and Sophia for your other friend. They will be down in a few minutes."

As he walked back over to his friends, Monty noticed that Sam seemed to be pleased with how the evening was progressing. "I told you that he would like his present from us," said Monty to Ben, and then whispered into his ear, "Just the place for a young man to lose his virginity."

They sat down on an embroidered sofa in the parlor, a plush rug underneath their feet. The room, dimly lit by an ornate chandelier, was full of elegant Victorian furnishings. Oil paintings, all landscapes, were on the walls. The one with fields of lavender caught Monty's eye. On a greenish marble tabletop, there was a silver bucket containing ice and a bottle of champagne, decorative coupe glasses, and a tray of assorted hors d'oeuvres.

"We ain't got nothing like this back home in Harrisburg," beamed an excited Sam.

The three ladies of the evening came into the parlor and greeted their customers, Liz, a redhead like her sister; Matilda, a tall blonde; and Sophia, a petite brunette. "Now, who is celebrating a birthday today?" asked Matilda. Sam smiled. They escorted the young men up the spiral staircase.

An hour or so later, Ben was the first to make his way back down the stairs to the parlor, followed by Monty shortly thereafter. They poured some champagne and sat on the sofa. "Good time?," asked Ben.

"Oh yes, Liz is always very good to me. How about you?"

"No complaints here. I guess our special guest is getting some extra attention."

A few minutes later, a grinning Sam came into the parlor, sat between Monty and Ben on the sofa, put his head back, and looked up at the ceiling. "You two are the best friends a guy could have. Thank you!"

"We thought it was an appropriate gift," said Monty. "Glad you enjoyed it."

Back outside, while waiting for a carriage to arrive, they noticed several people walking by, some actually running. It was approaching eleven o'clock.

"Strange," commented Ben. "Middle of the week. The streets should be empty by now."

"Indeed," replied Monty. He shouted "What's going on?" to a man approaching them, and who had just broken into a trot.

"Everyone is headed for the President's House, to let Tyler know how we feel about his veto of the bank bill," came the response from the half-breathless man, as he increased his speed.

"Well, shall we?," said Monty.

"Hell, yes! We've got to see this." replied Ben.

"I'm definitely in," said Sam. "Not like I was going to be getting much sleep tonight."

They hailed down an open buggy and the three piled in. "To the President's House," Monty told the driver. "Follow the crowd."

* * *

As the driver turned onto Pennsylvania Avenue, they noticed more people joining the throng from the side streets. As they got to Lafayette Square, a mass of humanity had filled the street and the pace of the buggy came to a crawl. Monty noticed that some were carrying lit torches. A few had bugles. "Down with the veto!" he heard someone shout. "Huzzah for Clay!" yelled another.

"This is as far as I can go, boys," said the driver. They hopped out, and Ben thanked the driver and paid him.

As they walked closer, they could see that the crowd had become a full-fledged angry mob, having broken through the gate on the north side of the President's House and rushed to the portico. Monty, Ben, and Sam held back near the gate, but were able to see everything unfold in front of them. Although it was now approaching midnight, the torches made it seem almost like daylight. The shouting now came from everywhere. "Resign, you fool!" "Hustle him out here, so we can get our hands on him!" "Down with the traitor!" They saw some stones being tossed. Monty thought he heard a window break. A few rifles were fired into the air.

"What's going on over there?," said Sam, pointing to a large tree near the portico. "Do they have ropes?"

"That's what it looks like to me," said Ben.

Shortly thereafter, they saw a large object being hoisted into the air, suspended from a rope that had been flung over one of the larger branches of the tree. As it got about ten feet off of the ground, several torches were raised, setting it afire.

Monty immediately recognized what was going on. "My God," he said to Ben and Sam, "The president of the United States is being burned in effigy next to his own front porch."

"I told you at dinner that there were people ready to kill him," replied Ben. "I just didn't think it was going to be tonight."

"You know, there are no police or security here at night," said Monty. "This could really get out of hand."

Just then, a light appeared in a window on the second floor, and then two more in rooms on the first floor. People inside were stirring.

Monty looked at his two friends, his face still in a state of shock. "Unbelievable," he said, "I feel like we're in Paris during the French Revolution. Kind of scary."

"Good for them," said Ben, approving of the scene they were witnessing. "About time Tyler learned that his actions have consequences."

"I'm glad we don't have guillotines here," replied Sam, jokingly. No one responded.

Just when it appeared as though the situation may turn more violent, Monty noticed the mob begin to quieten and to slowly disperse. Likely, he speculated, they were concerned about shots being fired from inside the mansion, or perhaps felt that they had grabbed the president's attention and had made their point.

The three friends turned and headed back toward Lafayette Square. Given the early morning hour, there were no carriages for hire out on the streets. Walking was the only way home. Fortunately, no one lived much more than a mile away. They bade each other a good morning.

"Thank you. A birthday to remember, for a lot of reasons!," said Sam, as he shook the hands of his two friends and they each headed off to their boardinghouses.

CHAPTER 8

September, 1841— Monty sat in a chair in front of Henry Clay's large desk in the senator's office on the west side of the Capitol. It was the largest and most ornate of the offices for members of the upper chamber of Congress, a perk of Clay's status as the leader of the party that controlled a majority of the seats in the Senate.

Through the windows behind the desk, he looked out on an open expanse of unkept land, stretching for a mile, toward the Potomac River and the President's House. Acres that were to have been, he recalled the senator telling him when he had first been hired, under architect Pierre L'Enfant's plans for the city, a grand avenue with public parks and ornate gardens, flanked by stately homes, embassies, monuments, and public buildings. Instead, livestock roamed and grazed. A smelly and little-used canal ran along the northern end of the property, near Pennsylvania Avenue, turning at the base of Capitol Hill and winding its way south to the Anacostia River. In Washington City, Monty thought, in architecture as in politics and government, what was hoped for, and what existed, were starkly different.

In the few weeks since Tyler's veto of the bank bill, the political turmoil between the president and the Whigs in Congress had significantly worsened. A second bank bill was passed, an attempt to address some of Tyler's concerns in his veto message. He vetoed that one also. Within days, the president's cabinet, save one member, Daniel Webster, had resigned in protest. The Whigs hastily called a caucus and formally tossed the president out of the party.

Monty and the senator both took sips from cups of black coffee that had turned cold. Clay, with pages of notes before him and pencil in hand, was working on a speech that he was going to deliver to the Senate in a couple of days. As he often did, he wanted to try out his remarks on Monty and get some feedback.

"What a month it's been," said Monty. "My head is still spinning. I really thought Tyler would have resigned after the cabinet did. It would have been the honorable thing to do."

"Webster saved him," responded Clay. "His staying on as secretary of state gave Tyler the cover that he needed. Daniel's decision was, I am sure, all about me. His statement that he needed to remain in office to handle so-called ongoing delicate foreign negotiations was just a cover. If he resigned, it would have strengthened my position in the party. Daniel wants to be president. Hell, we all do. But Tyler is using him, and our friend from Massachusetts is willing to let himself be used, because it suits his own interests."

"The party was right to have expelled Tyler after the resignations," said Monty.

"Indeed. The Democratic newspapers say that I orchestrated it. I wish that I had such power. Each of the cabinet secretaries made up his own mind."

"Tyler betrayed the party," said Monty. "It is hard to believe that it was only six months ago that Harrison came into office, with Whig majorities in both houses. The party's agenda should have been easily passed and become law by now. Instead, everything is in tatters."

"Interesting that you used the word betrayal. Tyler's actions were treason to the party. That is the theme of the speech I am going to give on the floor this week. No one likes a traitor, not the people he betrays, nor those he seeks to curry favor with. One group hates him, and the other will never truly accept him. I compare Tyler to Benedict Arnold." Clay put on his spectacles and held his notes closer to his eyes. "Where's the key part?" His eyes moved down the page. "Here it is." He read his words to Monty. "Our policy has been arrested by an Executive that we brought into power. Arnold escaped to England after his treason was detected. Tyler is on his way to the Democratic camp. They may give him lodgings in some outhouse, but they will never trust him. He will stand here, like Arnold in England, a monument to his perfidy and disgrace."

"I like it," said Monty. "Tyler deserves to be a president without a party. He's earned it."

* * *

The standoff between Tyler and the Whigs in Congress continued for the rest of 1841 and through the rest of Tyler's term of office. The president was determined that no friend nor ally of Henry Clay would have any power or influence in his administration. He filled the cabinet vacancies mainly with former Democrats turned Whigs, like himself, who shared his states' rights views. Southerners dominated.

In the midterm elections of 1842, the Democratic Party took advantage of the disunion and disarray among the Whigs, picking up almost fifty seats in the House of Representatives and gaining control of that body. With only a third of the seats in the Senate at stake, Democratic gains were fewer there, only one seat, and it remained under Whig control. The Senate became the Whigs' last bastion of power, but a sufficient one to oppose Tyler and block his agenda. There was stalemate in Washington.

Knowing that nothing would be accomplished for the remainder of Tyler's term in office, Henry Clay resigned from his seat in the Senate in early 1842 and returned to Kentucky, to rest, and to prepare for the upcoming 1844 election, in which he hoped to be the Whig Party's nominee for president. Nothing would please him more than Tyler being forced to turn the office over to him.

After much thought, Monty decided to stay in Washington. Despite his disappointment with the political situation, there was an allure to the place. It gave him a feeling of importance, of doing things that mattered. He had his friends, Ben and Sam. One day, he would go back to Ohio, but that could wait. He obtained a job in the clerk's office of the Senate, keeping him in the center of the political world.

CHAPTER 9

April, 1842— It was the first crisis of Monty's new job. The second session of the Twenty-Seventh Congress was about to experience a calamity. The United States Senate was running out of paper. It was April 1842 and there were still four months to go. There would be endless talking, taking care of "the people's business," as those in Washington City liked to say, before adjournment in August and, hence, the need for much more paper. Almost everything spoken, considered, or studied in the world's greatest deliberative body was printed on paper—drafts of bills, committee hearings, federal budgets, final bills, reports, floor debates, and much more—and kept for posterity.

Monty wondered if it was all really necessary, but this was part of his job as a deputy clerk for the Senate. Would anyone really want to read this in ten years, or fifty years? But who was he to question tradition?

The usual supplier, near Capitol Hill, was out of stock and paper would have to be purchased and picked up from a backup source in nearby Alexandria. The staff member that Monty would have given this rather low-level task was sick and had been out of work for several days, so he decided to do it himself. It was a nice spring day, a good opportunity to get out in the fresh air. The afternoon before, he had taken two hundred dollars out of the Senate's cash supply, taking care to document his withdrawal, making sure that he had a sufficient amount of money to purchase enough paper to last several weeks. He took the early morning coach for the ten-mile trip down the Washington and Alexandria Turnpike.

From Alexandria's coach station, he walked up Duke Street and found the paper supplier's shop. Not opening until noon, according to the note on the door. He had more than an hour to kill. As he walked back down the street, he noticed a disturbing sight. Through an open gate, in the center of a high stucco wall, he saw a large number of Black people, milling about, in an enclosed area. Two White men, with guns tucked in their waistbands, guarded each side of the gate. From where he stood, he could see the faces of some of those inside. Faces of despair. Men stared into the distance. Mothers held their children tightly. No chatter. All had a look of helplessness, of resignation to an impending and unknown fate.

Next door, at 1315 Duke Street, stood a narrow three-story office building. The sign above the main entrance, in large letters, read Kephart & Co. and, below that, in smaller script, Dealers in Slaves. A sandy-haired boy, maybe thirteen, was standing in front and giving out handbills, shouting "Slave Auction Today!" to all passersby. Curious, Monty took one. The main auction, he read, was to begin at two in the afternoon and featured an "abundant number" of "strong and able" field hands. Men, women, and children. "Ready for transport," it said. Before then, at noon, "a limited few slaves, ideal for local crops and domestic use" would be offered. "Terms: One-third cash, remainder in thirty days."

Monty knew a bit about the slave trade. International trading in enslaved people had been outlawed in 1808, but domestic buying and selling at auctions such as this was common throughout the South. Auctions were also legal in the District of Columbia, although they were less common and held in more discrete locations there. In his time in Washington, Monty had never witnessed one. In recent years, the growth of the cotton and sugar markets in Alabama, Mississippi, and Louisiana had led to a massive transfer of enslaved labor. Slaveholders from places like Virginia and Maryland, who had switched from tobacco to less labor-intensive crops like wheat, began selling off their excess enslaved persons to brokers, who transported them to the Deep South and resold them there to plantation owners, at a handsome profit. Being "sold down the river," Monty had read, was how the unfortunates involved in the transactions referred to it. Some families were sold together as a unit, but most were not. Young women of childbearing age were sold at a premium. The enslaved were fed well in the days before auctions, and given new clothes, to increase their market value. Knowing about the process, and seeing it in person for the first time on the streets of Alexandria, were entirely different things. Monty felt physically ill.

At that moment, he heard a clanking sound. A line of five Black people, men and women, came up from behind him, no more than a couple of feet away, their hands and bare feet bound in chains. As the last one, a woman, went by, her right foot appeared to give way and she started to fall to the ground. Instinctively, Monty reached out and helped her up.

Within a couple of seconds, he felt a hard blow to his chest, knocking him backward a few feet.

"Hands off the merchandise, mister!" snarled a young White man who had been walking a few feet behind, holding the end of the chains in one hand and having shoved Monty with the other.

"Just trying to help," said Monty. He noticed a coiled whip at the man's waist.

"We don't need your help, move on!" came the shouted reply.

For a moment, he thought of challenging the ruffian, of letting him know the shove was unacceptable. How dare you, he imagined himself saying, I am here on business for the United States Senate. He quickly thought better of it, deciding that the bastard would likely pull out his whip and retaliate on those in his charge. He felt almost as powerless as the poor souls in chains.

The enslaved woman looked back at Monty, a look of appreciation on her face, like she wanted to say thank you, but knowing that doing so would not be a wise choice. As the line moved on, toward the walled off area and the guarded gate he had seen earlier, Monty noticed that the woman was limping and that her right foot appeared to be swollen.

"Register now to place bids. Excellent selection today. There's still time. Fifteen more minutes!" the sandy-haired lad shouted as he passed out more handbills to all who went up and down the street. Monty overhead a group of men talking nearby.

"Those will go cheaply," said one, referring to the line of five that had just passed. "They are older or have some problem. The brokers won't want them for selling down south. Not strong enough or young enough."

"No profit in them," said another.

A third man chimed in, "I know. They'll likely be sold locally for household or garden work. Wish I had a need for one. Probably would get a good deal today."

"Same here," replied the first man. "I got my Henrietta here about two years ago. Think I overpaid."

Reaching into his pocket and feeling the two hundred dollars of the Senate's money, Monty made a snap decision. He walked over to the boy.

"Where do I register?"

The process was easy. Too easy, he thought. Show you had enough cash for the deposit, sign a note agreeing to pay the balance, and you could buy a human being. Few questions were asked. He was given a program for the auction. Each enslaved person was listed by a number, with their name, age, physical description, and a brief summary of their past work. He read through the list. "No. 12, Delores." It had to be her. "Approx. 45. Offered for sale alone. Tall and muscular. Scar on right arm. Slight limp. Good attitude. Experience with vegetables and tobacco."

Promptly at noon, the auctioneer, a thin balding man, mounted the wooden platform adjacent to the building. "Welcome!," he shouted, to the crowd of about twenty-five men that surrounded the platform. Monty stood at the back, near the middle of the group. "We will start with our offerings that we think will be of interest to local buyers." George, a dark-skinned man who, according to the program, was fifty-two, was brought up to the platform by the man who had shoved Monty earlier.

"Good with horses," Monty read from the program, "some blacksmith work."

"Who will offer me $700 for this man?," asked the auctioneer, starting the bidding.

"Can he shoe horses?," a man in the front asked.

The auctioneer motioned to George to respond. "Sure can, yessir."

"Tell him to take off his shirt," said another. George did so, revealing a muscular chest for a man of his age. Another man requested that he be instructed to squat. Again, compliance.

"I'll bid $700," said a man near the back.

"I have $700. Who will give me $800?"

The bidding went on, among four prospective buyers, and George was sold for $950 to the man who had made the initial bid. Monty took it all in. Two more auctions followed, both of men around George's age, and both sold for slightly lower prices.

"Next up," said the auctioneer, "Number 12, Delores." Monty moved closer to the front. The man with the whip grabbed the enslaved woman's arm and led her up to the platform, her limp noticeable as she walked up its three steps. "Experienced field worker, but easily trained for household work," began the auctioneer. "Who will offer me $400?"

"What's wrong with her foot?," someone asked.

The auctioneer looked at Delores. "Wagon wheel runned it over," she nervously said, "Don't bother me none."

"Can she sew?," asked another.

"Sure can, pretty good at it." she proudly responded, followed by silence from the crowd. There were no bids.

"How about $300?," said the auctioneer, dropping the price and hoping to get some bidding started.

"I'll go $300," said a man to Monty's left.

Monty took a deep breath. "Four-hundred!" he shouted.

"I have $400, who will go $450?"

A man to Monty's left near the front raised his arm. "Four-fifty," he said.

A few more rounds of bidding and the price for Delores was up to $600, offered by a new bidder. "Going, going . . ."

Before the auctioneer could finish, Monty shouted, "I'll go $650."

The auctioneer looked at the prior bidder, who shook his head. "Anyone else?" Silence.

"Sold, to the gentleman in the middle."

Monty went into the office where he had registered and completed the paperwork, handing over $200 from the Senate and $18 of his own money as the deposit, and signing a note for the rest. He was given a certificate of ownership. He was not a wealthy man. He thought he had enough money in his bank in Washington City to repay the $200 to the Senate easily enough, but would have to dip into an account he had in Ohio, money he had inherited from his grandfather, for the rest.

"I have to run an errand, be back in an hour or so," he told the clerk.

"She'll be here."

As he walked up Duke Street to the paper supplier, he began to have second thoughts. "What have I done?," he mumbled to himself.

* * *

Several hours later, it was late afternoon when the carriage pulled up to the large brick house at the base of Capitol Hill. The trip from Alexandria had taken longer than expected. Monty got out and went up front to the driver, slipped him a few bills, and thanked him again.

"I only did it as a personal favor to you." said the driver, counting the cash and finding the amount to be acceptable. "Don't like colored riding up here with me."

"Here's some more for delivering the four boxes of paper in the carriage, as we discussed, to the clerk's office in the Senate. Monty handed over some additional cash. They will be expecting you. Tell them that the supplier will be shipping the rest and it should arrive on Tuesday."

Monty reached out his arm and helped Delores down. "Trust me, you will be safe here. It will just be for a few days, and then you will be on your way." In Alexandria, he had briefly explained to her his intention, that he had purchased her not to be his slave, but to free her. That had caused her eyes to light up, a broad smile, and some tears of joy. But it had last only briefly. How could she not be suspicious? She had to be dazed and frightened, he thought, and unsure what had happened to her. Could she really believe the word 'trust,' coming from a White man?

When she realizes that he has brought her to a brothel, Monty speculated, she may question his sincerity. He could think of nowhere else to take her, certainly not to his small room in the boardinghouse. Liz would be able to help him out, he was sure. He needed a few days to figure out how to get manumission papers prepared and filed, and to make arrangements to get her headed north. Monty mulled over what it said about his life in Washington that, when he needed a favor, he was turning to a prostitute. He motioned for Delores to follow him.

Monty's knock on the door was soon followed by the usual opening of the slat, an eyeball, and to sound of locks being opened. They walked through the heavy wooden door, flanked by stained glass sidelights. The dim gaslights in the foyer made the crimson wallpaper look even darker than he had remembered. He was glad to see that Mary Ann, the proprietor and Liz's older sister, was sitting at the desk in the foyer. "Miss Hall, it is good to see you again. I am looking for Liz, is she available?"

"She's with a customer just now. Shouldn't be too much longer. Did you have an appointment?"

"I do not. This is actually more of a personal call. I was hoping that she could assist me with something."

"I will let her know that you are here. You are Mr. Tolliver, correct?"

"That's right."

"Have a seat in the parlor and make yourself comfortable. She will have to stay here," said Mary Ann, nodding toward to Delores.

About a half hour later, Liz appeared and gave Monty a peck on the cheek. He explained the situation, and nodded to Delores, who was sitting on a bench by the front door. Liz said she would have to check with Mary Ann, who had stepped away. She returned in a couple of minutes. It was all set. Delores could stay there for a few days, longer if necessary, but she would have to work as a housemaid and laundress. She could sleep on the floor in the room of the other maid. He walked over to Delores and explained the arrangements. Her face brightened again. Perhaps, he thought, he had earned her trust.

"Come with me, my dear. Sure looks like you found your knight in shining armor today," Monty heard Liz tell Delores as he was leaving.

It was now dusk. He decided to walk home and to get a quick dinner on the way. He had not planned for this day to turn out as it did. He was not a proud man, but he had a feeling of accomplishment. A mundane trip to buy paper had turned into something more. He had struck a blow, albeit a small one, against slavery.

* * *

The next day, Monty walked down the marble hallway in the Capitol from his office near the Senate chamber to the Library of Congress. "You will find him where he always is, down the hallway and to the left," said the librarian to Monty. His job with Senator Clay over the past few years had frequently brought him to the cluttered rooms of the Library of Congress, the senator sending him to research a topic or to find a quote for one of his speeches. Housed in the north wing of the Capitol, the Senate side, Monty had, on occasion, taken time on those visits to leaf through some of the books that had been owned by Thomas Jefferson. They were the nucleus of the library's collection when Congress purchased them from the founding father a generation ago, after the British had burned the Capitol, along with all of the original library's books, during the War of 1812. To hold in his hands the books that the author of the Declaration of Independence and former president had owned, and read, always gave him chills.

Monty found Theodore Weld seated at a table, deep in thought, his spectacles on the end of his nose, perusing one of the ten or so books piled up in front of him. One of the leading abolitionists in the country since the early 1830s, Weld had been a leader of the American Anti-Slavery Society and editor of its newspaper, *The Emancipator*. He had moved to Washington from his home in New Jersey in 1841 to assist abolitionist members of Congress, most notably former president John Quincy Adams, then a congressman from Massachusetts, in lobbying their colleagues and arguing their cause in Congress and in the press. Weld spent most of his days at this table in the library doing research for Adams' speeches. Adams had already been dubbed by the newspapers in the North as "Old Man Eloquent" for the quality of his passionate speeches against slavery on the floor of the House of Representatives, and much of the credit was due to Weld's research. If there was anyone who could help with Delores, Monty knew that Weld was the man.

"Excuse me, Mr. Weld, I am sorry to disturb you, but I am hoping that you can help me." Monty introduced himself as a former aide to Senator Clay.

"Help you with what?," said a clearly perturbed Weld. "And using Henry Clay's name does not impress me, young man. He is all talk, and no action, as far as I am concerned."

"How to go about manumitting a slave here in Washington City; the process of getting it done?" Monty ignored the dig a Clay.

"Who owns this slave?"

"I do, as of yesterday. I purchased her at an auction." Monty explained to Weld the events in Alexandria the previous day and his spontaneous decision.

"God bless you, Mr. Tolliver," said Weld, now looking kindly on the young man who had interrupted his research. "Every little bit helps. Sit down and wait here."

Monty watched as Weld disappeared down a nearby aisle and returned a couple of minutes later with a book in his hand, which he had opened and was reading as he sat back down.

"Tell me your given name, the slave's name, age, and her physical description, including any distinguishing marks or traits."

Monty complied, and watched as Weld pulled a couple of sheets of paper out of a folder and began scribbling.

"Does she have a last name?," inquired Weld.

"I asked, and she said she was not aware of one."

"Well, she has yours now."

"The process of manumission is relatively simple," Weld explained. "You free her by filing a document with the court, and then the court issues an order confirming it." After a few minutes, Weld handed Monty the first of two documents that he had written. It was entitled Deed of Manumission. As he read through it, the last sentence brought a slight smile to his face. "I further declare," it said, "said Delores Tolliver to be discharged, in perpetuity, from all manner or service or servitude to me, to my family, or to the executors of my estate."

"You file that with the court and have the clerk execute and seal this," instructed Weld, as he handed the second document to Monty. It was entitled Certificate of Freedom, and had a place for a judge's signature and for the seal of the Court.

"Once you have the document from the court," Weld continued, "take her to Mrs. Sprigg's boardinghouse on First Street. It's just across from the Capitol. The landlady there can put her in touch with one of her boarders, who has contacts with the Underground Railroad. She must always keep a copy of the certificate on her person, or she can be thrown into jail. My advice is to tell her to keep going to Canada. Even with valid freedom papers, there are unscrupulous bounty hunters in northern cities who entrap and capture free colored people and sell them back into slavery. God help us in this country for perpetuating this evil. A day of reckoning is coming."

"I cannot thank you enough, Mr. Weld. How much do I owe you?"

"Nothing. It would be a sin to accept money for helping to free someone from slavery. You have done a good thing. The best reward you could give me would be to join us in the fight for the abolition cause. We need all of the help we can get."

Monty stood and shook Weld's hand and thanked him again. He knew that most in Washington City, and throughout much of the north, viewed abolitionists as extremists, little better than the die-hard slaveholders in the South. Weld seemed reasonable and sensible, as did his two abolitionist friends, Ben and Sam. Maybe in the future, he considered, he could do something more than save one enslaved person, and help put an end to this dreadful institution.

* * *

Within a few days, the papers were filed with the District Court of the District of Columbia and Delores was officially a free woman. As Monty gave her the Certificate of Freedom and explained it to her, she thanked him profusely. In doing so, she called him master. He took joy in correcting her. That was a term that she would never need to call anyone again. Her face broke into a grin, a larger one, Monty thought, than the ones before. He explained to her that Liz would be taking her to a boardinghouse, the one that Weld had recommended, and that she would soon be getting on her way.

CHAPTER 10

January, 1843— "Gents, it looks like we are stuck with Tyler for a couple of more years," said Monty to Ben and Sam, as the waitress dropped off the first round of ale. The three had not been together for a few months, since the previous fall. Each had been busy at work and had gone to visit their families for Christmas. Monty to Ohio, Ben to Rhode Island, and Sam to Pennsylvania.

"I've been reading about it in the papers," said Ben. "He deserved impeachment. Continues to slap the Whigs in the face. I was hoping that we could start 1843 off with some better news. It would have been nice to see Congress kick him out of office. Talking about it is one thing. Actually doing it is another. As Ben Franklin said, 'Well done is better than well said.'"

"I see that you have been reading your book," said Monty.

"I have," a grinning Ben responded. "Pearls of wisdom in there on just about any topic."

* * *

Since August, Washington City and the nation had been focused on the latest battle between the president and the Whigs in Congress. As in the fall of 1841 with the bank bills, the most recent dispute was over Tyler's vetoes, this time over the tariff. Due to falling government revenues, the Whigs wanted to extend existing tariff rates, which were scheduled to go lower, and to increase them on a permanent basis. They also wanted to extend payments to the states from the proceeds of the sales of federal lands. A bill accomplishing these goals, on a temporary basis, was passed in June, and was then vetoed. Another bill to permanently deal with these issues was passed in August, and it was also vetoed by Tyler. The Whigs lacked the two-thirds votes in each chamber of Congress to override the vetoes. Tyler had again thwarted the party's agenda, and the will of the majority of the Congress.

After the second veto, a special committee in the House of Representatives, chaired by former president John Quincy Adams, recommended the impeachment of Tyler. A few months later, in January 1843, Congressman John Botts of Virginia brought articles of impeachment to the floor of the House, the first use of the Constitution's impeachment clause against a president in American history. The charges noted Tyler's unique role as a non-elected chief executive, referring to him as "John Tyler, Vice President, acting as President of the United States." There were nine alleged "high crimes and misdemeanors" that warranted his removal from office, of which use of the veto power in an "arbitrary, despotic and corrupt" manner to "gratify his personal and political resentments" was but one. Others included "wicked and corrupt abuse" of the power of appointment in keeping and removing federal officeholders, withholding information from

Congress, and "gross official misconduct and shameless, duplicity, equivocation and falsehood" in his dealings with the initial Whig cabinet that he inherited from Harrison, and in his relations with Congress. A vote by the full House on the articles of impeachment failed, by a vote of 83 for and 127 against, a disappointment to Tyler's most vocal opponents, since the Whigs held the majority of seats. The vote came after the 1842 midterm elections, during a lame duck session of Congress. The Democrats had won the majority of seats in the new Congress and, given that, many Whig congressmen voted against impeachment, believing that it was too drastic a tool to use against Tyler by a party that was about to lose its control of the House of Representatives. "His Accidency" would remain in office.

* * *

"What a mess Tyler has caused. He should have resigned back in '41," said Ben.

"One would have thought so, but he will never give up the office voluntarily, even though he got it by another man's death. Tyler does everything eyeing next year's election," said Monty. "He wants a term of his own. He's filled most of the cabinet seats with southerners and is openly courting the Democrats to nominate him."

"How is the federal government going to function without the revenue from tariffs?," asked Sam. "We need new roads, we need canals, need to grow our industry."

"Tyler doesn't care about that," replied Monty. "Our industry is in the North. His focus is on the South. On slave labor. The people he is putting in office are some of the most vocal proponents of slavery. Mark my words, protecting slavery is at the root of every move he makes."

"Hard to believe that Daniel Webster is still secretary of state," said Ben. "I used to like him, but my opinion has really changed."

"Webster is a sly one," replied Monty. "He desperately wants to be president, has for years, and he is playing all the angles. He wants to be viewed as a loyal soldier working for the good of the country, and he hopes to use that to expand his base of support in the Whig Party and to get nominated in '44."

"Does he have a chance?," asked Ben.

"Doubtful," replied Monty. "Most of the Whig leaders can't stand him for staying in Tyler's cabinet. Webster and Clay have always been rivals to lead the party and, even though Clay left the Senate last year, he's the favorite for the party's nomination next year, after being passed over in '40 for Harrison. That's what got us in this disaster we've been living for the past two years. Imagine how much better things would be now if Clay had been nominated and elected last time."

"Ready for some dinner, gentlemen?," asked the waitress.

"Yes, please," said Monty, as Ben and Sam nodded. After ordering their food, the conversation continued.

"If Congress won't boot him out of office, maybe someone will take matters into their own hands," said Ben.

"What do you mean? Assassination?" asked Monty.

"Damn right. Would be best thing for the country," replied Ben.

"The word on Capitol Hill," said Monty, "is that he gets a lot of death threats in the mail. That's one reason why he rarely leaves the President's House."

"He probably gets more threats than he knows about," said Sam. "Doesn't he return to the post office unopened all letters addressed to Acting President Tyler? Didn't I read that in the papers?"

"So he does," said Monty. "His ego is really amazing."

Their dinner plates arrived. Monty, Ben, and Sam turned to other topics while eating, having had enough talk about Tyler for one evening. But silently, as he ate, Monty kept thinking about the president. If he opened a newspaper next week, or next month, and saw a headline that Tyler had died, it would please him. Was he a bad person, he wondered, for having such thoughts? A death, he envisioned, by natural causes, or by an accident. Surely Ben was just joking about suggesting that someone should kill him.

CHAPTER 11

March, 1843— "Why are you encouraging him on this?," Robert Tyler asked. "He will lose any support that he still has in the North. Even Jackson wouldn't touch it."

"You're wrong," responded his brother John. "That was then. This is now. Annexation of Texas is the best path forward for him for '44. He's determined to get it done. It has to be presented in the right way. Of course, we can't *say* that it's about slavery. Think like a Yankee, Robert. Folks in the North want to expand our borders, to go all the way to the Pacific. They want California. And Oregon. They hate the Brits. And they want to make money."

"I'm listening," responded Robert.

"Congressman Gilmer's January letter in the *Madisonian* laid it all out in terms that they can accept. Expanding our country, to the northwest *and* to the southwest, is in all of our interests. Annexation of Texas will give the Yanks a new market to sell their goods and their crops. It will keep the Brits from gaining influence there. They want all that more than they hate slavery. And look what we southerners would get. We won't have to worry about Texas abolishing slavery and dealing with a free nation on our border. We *expand* slavery. Think of the Senate. This will give us control of it for a generation. We can block any attempt to interfere with slavery. To us, it means survival and more power; to them, it can be sold as promoting patriotism and pocketbooks."

* * *

In the spring of 1843, over a year before the next presidential nominating conventions would be held, Henry Clay looked like a shoo-in for the 1844 Whig nomination. The frontrunner among the Democrats was a former president, Martin Van Buren.

John Tyler seemed like a dead man walking. He remained unpopular in the country, especially in the North and the West. He was a president without a party. The Whigs disowned him for having wrecked their agenda, and the Democrats distrusted him and held him at arm's length, due to his prior desertion from their ranks. He was considered by most political observers to be a caretaker in office until the next election, an unelected president that fate had unkindly thrust on the country.

Against all odds, Tyler saw a way to winning a term of his own in 1844, either by persuading the Democrats to nominate him, or by forming his own third party. The path forward, he believed, was through the annexation of Texas. It became, he said, the "great object of my ambition."

Since 1836, when the Texians, as they were called, (mostly expatriated Americans who had moved to that province of

Mexico), had defeated the Mexican Army in a civil war, the Republic of Texas had been an independent nation. Almost from its birth as its own country, there was talk of Texas being annexed as a state into the United States. It was an issue that most politicians would not dare touch. In the waning days of his administration, Andrew Jackson, an ardent expansionist, had avoided the temptation. His successor, Martin Van Buren, likewise did nothing during his single term as president to bring Texas into the Union.

Texas was a political hot potato because of slavery. There were about 30,000 enslaved persons in Texas in the mid-1840s and that number was expected to dramatically increase with annexation, which would bring a flood of slaveholders into the new state. A tenuous balance between the North and the South over slavery had existed since the Compromise of 1820. Under it, Maine was admitted as a free state, Missouri as a slave state, and a line was drawn from Missouri's southern border extending westward, above which slavery would be prohibited. After the Compromise, there were twenty-four states, twelve free and twelve with slavery. The balance was maintained with the two new states admitted in the 1830s, Arkansas, a slave state, and Michigan, a free one. With annexation of the approximately 400,000 square miles of Texas, slave territory would dwarf the amount of free land in the United States. The South would control the Senate. It was an issue that had the potential to tear the country apart.

Tyler's strategy for annexation began in January 1843 when he had one of his closest advisers, Thomas Gilmer, a congressman from Virginia, publish a detailed letter touting the annexation of Texas as a benefit to the entire country. Gilmer's letter was one of the first moves in a game of political chess, setting up a strategy that would play out over the next year. The prospective 1844 nominees of both parties, Clay for the Whigs and Van Buren for the Democrats, were opposed to the annexation of Texas.

* * *

"I can hear ol' Quincy Adams and the other abolitionists now," responded Robert. "Don't listen, they will scream. Tyler is pulling the wool over your eyes. It's a slaveholders' plot by a desperate man trying to hold onto his office. And what about Secretary Webster? He's been on record against annexation for years and has resisted father's prodding to get talks started with the Texians."

"Things are about to change. I've heard from a good source that Webster plans to resign in the next month or two," said John. "Father can then get a secretary of state who is his own man, and who will push this. Webster was an asset back in '41, staying on when all of the others resigned, but he long ago outlived his usefulness."

"Even if Webster goes, you really think folks in the North are going to stand by and let us almost double the amount of slave territory in the country? With a threat of war from Mexico? Father should tread warily on this, in my opinion."

"The Mexicans are bluffing," John replied with confidence. "We can crush them. Our army is stronger. And that's why we're building the *Princeton*. Once she is launched, we will excel at sea, as well as on the land. They wouldn't dare to start anything."

CHAPTER 12

April, 1843— Monty tugged at his starched collar with his index finger. It was tighter on his neck than he was used to. He looked over at Ben, in the carriage and seated facing him, who was fidgeting with his sleeves. Fashion comes at a price, he decided. It was a bright Saturday morning in late April. All around, the city seemed to be in bloom. Shortly after the two-horse rig made the turn onto the street of Sam's boardinghouse, Monty saw Sam bolt from his rocking chair and start down the porch steps to the street.

"You clean up pretty well, soldier. I like the waistcoat," said Monty to Sam, as the carriage came to a stop. "Aren't we a trio of dandies today?" he added, as Sam climbed in.

Each of the men had purchased new silk waistcoats for the occasion. Monty's was an azure blue paisley print, Sam's had black and gold vertical stripes, and Ben's a green and yellow in a gingham pattern. Each wore a wide cravat, a dark tailcoat, and narrow fitting light-colored trousers. They placed their silk top hats beside them on the carriage seats.

"Having trouble walking today?," Sam asked Ben, eyeing the cane leaning against one of his knees.

"Please, Samuel," replied Ben, in an affected tone, "A *gentlemen* always carries a walking stick." Everyone grinned. "I, for one, have been looking forward to this day," continued Ben, as the driver loosened the reins and signaled the horses to start moving. "Worth having to dress up for it. I've never been to a horse race. Tell me again, Monty, about the schedule and our companions."

"The race track is near Meridian Hill, a couple of miles north of the President's House. A one-mile oval. It's called the National Race Course. Today is the final day of the spring meet. The Washington Jockey Club runs it. Been putting on the meets for years. Old Hickory was a racing enthusiast and entered some of his own horses when he was president. It's been a high society thing for some time. Everyone will be dressed to the nines. See and be seen, as they say."

"As a great man once said," commented Ben, "Eat to please thyself, but dress to please others."

Sam rolled his eyes and grinned. "Let me guess, another Franklin quote?"

"Most definitely! You may hear some more before the day is done."

"Oh, joy. I can't wait."

"And our lady friends for the day?," Ben asked Monty.

"Ah, yes. I suspected that you would be more interested in them than in the horses. Sarah is the daughter of Senator Morehead of Kentucky. I got to know him through Senator Clay. He asked me to escort Sarah to the ball held at the end of the races last fall. We went out a time or two after that. Attractive and pleasant, but not my type for anything serious. Between us, a bit shallow. I remembered she had said that she wanted to see the races the next time they were held. I also wanted to see them. I asked and she agreed to accompany me."

"And the other two?," asked Ben.

"Her good friend and the friend's little sister. Emily and Anna Bishop. Pretty sure those are their names. I've not met them. I'll be with Sarah, you will be with Emily, and the kid here will be with sister Anna."

When they arrived at the Georgetown home of Senator Morehead, the three exited the carriage and went to the door, emerged a couple of minutes later with the three young ladies, and escorted them down the steps from the porch and to the street. Like the men, the ladies had dressed fashionably for the day at the races. Sarah, in her mid-twenties, wore an off-white chintz dress, with a green and red floral pattern and a white collar. Her dark hair was pulled up under a wide-brimmed straw bonnet. Emily, a brunette of the same age as Sarah, had on a forest green dress with a floral design and a fabric green bonnet. Anna, who was in her late teens, wore a royal blue dress with an ikat pattern. She wore her blonde hair down, with slight curls, topped with a straw bonnet with blue ribbons. Sarah and Emily carried closed parasols. As they took their seats in the carriage, the ladies adjusted their dresses and petticoats to make room for all. It was no easy accomplishment. On the half-hour ride to the race track, all chatted pleasantly and got to know one another.

The driver waited in the line of carriages as they approached the main entrance to the track, and discharged his passengers at the appropriate place. Monty purchased their tickets and they then walked across the dirt track to the infield, where all were gathering for the festivities. The three couples found an attractive spot and stood in a circle.

"It seems that all of Washington City has turned out," said an excited Sarah.

"Something Whigs and Democrats can agree upon, I guess—a love of fast horses," observed Sam.

"Or at least the racing of them. Everyone here loves winners. What are elections but horse races in another setting, and the winners get to come here to Washington City," observed Monty.

"Probably so. Whenever Tyler is running today, I'll be betting against him, just out of principle," joked Ben.

"I didn't see his name on the race cards," replied Monty.

"Very funny," replied Ben.

"How you men love to talk politics," said Sarah. "Seems to me like today is more about a love of good fashion, than of politics and racing. Just look at all of the gentlemen, yourselves included, as well as the ladies."

"You have a good point there," said Sam.

"From the number of walking sticks being used by you gentlemen, one would think that we humans were intended to be three-legged creatures," said Sarah.

"I have never seen so many," added Emily. "Should the weather turn cold, we shall definitely have enough fuel to start a bonfire."

"At least we're comfortable when walking," said Ben. "I wouldn't want to attempt it in those hooped dresses. You all look like lovely hand-painted teacups, placed upside down in the cupboard, and almost as fragile."

"Another piece of evidence supporting my belief," responded Sarah, "that all fashion is designed by men. You get walking sticks and waistcoats, and we get corsets, crinoline, and hoops."

"But the finished product with you is so much more attractive," replied Ben. "Would you ladies like to take a stroll to the other side of the track, to see the outfits being worn over there?"

"Most definitely," replied Sarah. The two Bishop sisters quickly agreed, as did Sam.

Monty looked at the printed schedule of races he held in his hand and pulled out his pocket watch. "The next race is supposed to start in five minutes. I told myself this morning that I was going to actually watch one today. You all go ahead. I think I'll go over and find a spot along the rail and see if I can catch the horses going by."

"As you wish, Mr. Tolliver. I think I can wait a while for that," said Ben. "Ladies and Mr. Shipley, shall we?" he added, as he pointed his walking stick toward the other side of the infield. Then, following up to Monty, "Meet you back here in half an hour."

Monty went to the railing and squeezed into an open spot on the front row. After a few minutes, he heard a thundering noise to his right and watched as the field of about ten horses raced by, leaving a cloud of dust behind them. It was over in a matter of seconds, although the sound lingered in his ears much longer.

"I never realized they ran so fast," he commented, as he turned his head to the red-haired lady standing next to him at the rail. Looking closer, he realized that he recognized her. "Miss Hall?," he asked.

Why, yes, I am," Mary Ann Hall replied, as her mind quickly raced to place the man's face with his name. She rarely forgot a customer's name, especially a repeat one like Monty. "Mr. Tolliver, it is good to see you. I hope you are enjoying the races and this beautiful day."

"I am. This is my first time here. Have you attended before?"

"Oh, yes. This is one of my busiest events of the year."

"Of course, I should have known that," replied Monty, somewhat embarrassed, realizing that the National Course races would be a prime day on the calendar of one of the city's foremost madams.

"Mostly, they visit us, but sometimes it works out better for us to come to them," replied Mary Ann. She remembered Monty's relationship with one of her customers from years ago, and asked, "How is Senator Clay?"

"As you may know, he left the Senate nearly a year ago. I've not set eyes on him since then, but I understand that he is well."

"And how is Miss Liz?," said Monty, inquiring about Mary Ann's sister.

"She is well and is here today."

"I have not forgotten her help, and yours, with that personal matter last year. Again, my eternal gratitude for your help then."

Mary Ann had to think for a moment, and then recalled the enslaved woman that Monty had purchased, and then freed, and who had stayed at her brothel for a few days. "You are quite welcome."

"Please give Miss Liz my regards."

"Certainly. We hope to see you stop in again soon."

"Perhaps you will. A pleasure to see you. I must now rejoin my friends, Miss Hall, and I suspect that you have business to attend to." Monty tipped his top hat and excused himself. He was glad, he thought to himself as he walked away, that Sarah and her friends had not been privy to that exchange.

On his way back to meet his friends, Monty got in a line to purchase lemonade for he and Sarah. He heard his name called from behind and turned around and saw John Tyler, III, the son of the president. Monty had met John a few times in the spring and summer of 1841 when Senator Clay and the president were at loggerheads over the bank bills and other Whig legislation. Their encounters then had been terse, reflective of the animosity between their bosses. According to the Washington City rumor mill, the younger Tyler had a problem with alcohol, leading to streaks of violence that, it was said, had ruined his marriage after only a few months and had caused his wife to refuse to accompany him to the nation's capital.

"John, good to see you again. It's been a couple of years."

"Yes, it has been. I was not aware that you were still in Washington City, with Senator Clay having left the Senate last year."

"Yes, still here. I am now working in the clerk's office of the Senate."

"How are things at the President's House?"

"Good," replied John. "We're just waiting to see what your scheming Whig friends are going to do next. First expulsion of my father from the party, and then that impeachment debacle a few months ago."

Monty noticed that John slurred some of his words and was a bit unsteady on his feet. It appeared that he'd already had a few drinks of alcohol, though it was early in the afternoon. "I would not know," he replied. "Not much into politics any more, just pushing paper in the clerk's office."

"Oh, I'm sure your old boss Senator Clay has some more cards up his sleeve. I hear he's definitely running in '44."

"Could be. I only know what I read in the papers."

"My father had some cards to play also."

"I am sure that he does, John," replied Monty, getting annoyed. He had hoped to avoid getting into any political discussions today, especially with a half-drunk man.

"Big cards. Your Whig friends will see soon enough."

Having reached the front of the line, Monty ordered two lemonades and paid for them. He took as sip from one. Refreshing, unlike his conversation with young Tyler. The son is as obnoxious as the father, he decided. Time to end this encounter. "My thirsty date awaits," he said, slightly raising his hands and holding the two beverages. "Take care, John."

Monty rejoined his friends and heard about the interesting outfits and people they had seen while walking around. The Bishop sisters then saw some of their friends and they were introduced to all and joined the group. After a while, all went over to the rail to see a race up close. Over the course of the day, Sam's wagers on races netted a few dollars. Monty and Ben were not so lucky, but had not lost much. The three men agreed that it had been worth it for the entertainment. After the last race ended in the late afternoon, the crowd began to depart. As they waited in line for a carriage, Monty suggested having dinner and recommended a restaurant that he liked in Georgetown, which was not far from Sarah's home. All agreed and felt that it would be a good ending to a most pleasant day.

CHAPTER 13

July, 1843— "Damn Yankees!" John heard the president snort, as he slammed the palm of his right hand onto the opened newspaper spread across his desk. They were sitting in the small room on the southeast corner of the second floor of the President's House. His father preferred its coziness to the larger adjacent room overlooking the south lawn, which Andrew Jackson had used as his office. The sympathetic son cocked his head back and sat more erect in his chair, almost dropping the sheets of paper that sat on his lap for his notes. This weekly meeting between the president and his top cabinet officer had started off with a bang. Literally. He had rarely seen his father so angry and, he thought, with good reason.

"We always knew, sir," said the third man in the room, newly-appointed Secretary of State Abel Upshur, "that there were risks in accepting the invitation for the dedication of the Bunker Hill Monument in Boston, and in making stops in northern cities. The trip wasn't all bad. You were well-received in Baltimore." Upshur, a stern-looking man with deep set eyes, a round face, and long gray sideburns, was a longtime friend and colleague of the president from Virginia. After two years in the cabinet as secretary of the navy, Tyler had just transferred him to the state department to fill the vacancy created by Webster's resignation. The move had been made for a reason. It would soon be election year and the two men saw eye to eye, especially on the political issue that concerned them the most—slavery, protecting it and expanding it.

"But after we crossed Mason and Dixon's Line, it was a different story," commented young Tyler, who had been along on the trip and had seen it all. "Those damn Whigs and abolitionists."

"The city council in Philadelphia boycotting the welcoming ceremony. The crowds there, and in New York and Boston, standing like mutes as we passed by," said a disgusted president. "It was embarrassing. Listen to this from a Boston paper," he added, picking up the newspaper in front of him. "'Tyler's procession through the streets was surrounded by a population as silent and demure as if a funeral pageant were passing.' Folks only showed up out of respect for the office, it says, not for the man. I didn't hear one damn cheer. Anywhere."

"Disrespectful, it was," responded John.

"The people will be backing me soon," said the president, again slamming his right hand on his desk. "In the North, as well as in the South."

"You mean annexing Texas?," asked Upshur, already knowing the answer.

"Absolutely. Abel, we are going to get this done. I want you to make annexation your top priority. I tried to get Secretary Webster to start negotiations for the past two years, but he always fought me on it. Upset the slavery balance, he kept saying. The hell with that."

"Thank God he finally resigned," young John chimed in, "or you would have had to fire him."

"Likely so. Daniel wasn't bad, for a Massachusetts man. But it was past time for him to go," replied the president. "Annexation will be a popular issue. I can feel it in my bones. No one in the South will oppose it and folks in the North care more about expanding our borders and making money than they do about slavery. Jefferson got Louisiana and was worshiped for it. And I'm going to get Texas."

"Understood, Mr. President," replied Upshur. "I agree completely. But we still need a few months to make sure that we have in place what we need to meet any foreign threats to annexation."

"I know what you are saying. It will take a while to get troops along the border. At sea, I am aware we need some time. That was the highlight of the trip. Stopping at the Philadelphia Naval Yard and seeing first-hand the progress on the construction of the *Princeton*. She will give us the naval firepower we need."

"That was some reception that Captain Stockton had for you at his estate in New Jersey," said Upshur.

"That was the best part of the trip for me," commented John. "Being met at Princeton by those twenty-six beautiful girls, one for each state, holding that long train of flowers. And then all of us being transferred to those grand coaches and traveling in style to the captain's mansion. I can't remember when I last ate and drank so much, or so well."

"The whole trip should have been like that, sir," said Upshur. "You *are* the president."

"Mark my words, gentlemen. Texas is going to be the key to winning the election next year," replied the president, his face beaming with a look of confidence. "A term of my own. Clay and those Whig bastards will be eating their words. *Accidental* President. There will be no more of that after next November."

CHAPTER 14

*D*ecember, 1843— "Sir, you asked me to remind you about preparation for your meeting next week with the secretary about the cannons on the *Princeton*," Ben said to his boss, Mr. Simms.

"Yes, yes. Thank you, lieutenant. Has their installation been completed?"

"Almost. In the final stages now. There were some delays due to problems with the test firings of both of them. Some cracks developed at the base. As you know, Ericsson is overseeing the one called the Oregon and Captain Stockton is overseeing the other one, the Peacemaker. Ericsson devised a method of dealing with the problem and I understand it has been taken care of, on both of them. They should be mounted to the deck any day now."

"Cracks? That doesn't sound good."

"Apparently, it is something that was not unexpected with these new wrought iron cannons. Fixable, as I understand it."

* * *

The *Princeton's* screw propeller system, and her engines and boilers, were not her only innovative features. She was a warship, with twelve standard cannons, called carronades, forty-two pounders, six on each side, for bombarding the enemy at close range. Each had a seven-inch bore and were nine feet in length. But what made the ship unique was that the plans also included two much larger ordnance for the deck, which could fire cannonballs weighing over two-hundred pounds downrange for almost five miles. No naval ship in history had ever been equipped with such firepower.

Both of the large cannons on the *Princeton* were made of wrought iron, an innovative design for such weapons. Prior to the 1840s, the standard method of forging cannons was by using cast iron, which involved heating iron into a molten state, pouring it into a mold, and then boring out the center. Wrought iron involved heating iron bars into a malleable state and then using heavy hammers to beat them into the desired shape. The two cannons made for the *Princeton* consisted of numerous iron bars, hammered and forged into one massive unit. The center was then bored. Wrought iron was lighter than cast iron, allowing for a bigger cannon that could fire a larger ball and at a greater range, gave the weapon a better trajectory, and incurred less erosion of the barrel. Some in the Navy disfavored wrought iron for cannons, believing that hammered metal bars had less strength than cast iron, retaining weak points between each of the bars.

One of the cannons on the *Princeton* became known as the Oregon, the name an intended threat to Great Britain, due to the tense standoff then existing over the boundary between the Oregon territory and Canada. American expansionists wanted the northern border of Oregon to be at the latitude of fifty-four degrees and forty minutes north. Their slogan was "Fifty-four Forty or Fight!" The Oregon cannon, Captain Stockton had declared, "will be the fight in Fifty-Four Forty or Fight." Forged in Liverpool, England, under the supervision of the Swedish inventor, John Ericsson, who had designed most of the innovations that Stockton had incorporated into the ship, the Oregon was made of wrought iron and had a twelve-inch bore. When being tested, small cracks formed near its base, which Ericsson remedied by having metal rings heated and placed on the weapon in the area of the cracks, which shrank when cooled. Additional testing went smoothly.

Stockton wanted another large cannon for the deck of the *Princeton*, also made of wrought iron and with a twelve-inch bore. He had it forged in New York, under his own supervision. The competitive Stockton wanted his cannon to be bigger than Ericsson's, so it was larger than the Oregon, both thicker at its base and longer. It weighed 27,000 pounds and was fifteen feet in length. Stockton named this gun the Peacemaker, the name also a threat to foreign powers, the implication being that peace came through military strength. As with the Oregon, small cracks developed near its base during testing. Stockton, aware that the Oregon had developed the same problem and that Ericsson had fashioned some remedy by putting metal rings over the cracks, also had metal straps affixed, by welding, to the base of his weapon.

Both cannons were mounted onto the deck of the *Princeton*. Stockton had his put on the bow of the ship, giving it a more prominent position than the Oregon, which was affixed to the stern. By the placement, he made it clear that the Peacemaker, his cannon, was going to be the ship's principal weapon.

* * *

"Stockton is sure getting a lot of headlines in the New York papers about the *Princeton* since the ship was launched in September," said Simms. "Did you read about the race with the British paddle-wheeler? Do we have anything from him on that yet?"

"Yes, sir. We just got in the captain's official report on it. The *Great Western* is said by the Brits to be the fastest ship afloat. Stockton challenged her to a race. According to him, the *Princeton* not only sped past her, but circled her twice, before coasting to a sizable victory. Hundreds watched from the tip of Manhattan."

"Jolly good. It's time we sent the Brits a message. We should still be on schedule for Stockton to bring the ship here to Washington City in mid to late February. We will show her off to Congress and, hopefully, get funding for a fleet of them."

"It will be exciting, sir!"

"And lieutenant, I have some news for you. I have spoken with the secretary and, on my recommendation, he has agreed to assign you to the officer crew of the *Princeton* when she arrives here. Stockton has approved it. I know that you have been itching for a field assignment for some time. Why not start with the best ship we have?"

Ben's eyes brightened and his face broke into a broad smile. "Thank you, sir! Thank you for the opportunity. I will not disappoint you."

CHAPTER 15

December, 1843— "The next item on the agenda is the USS *Princeton*," John announced to the president and the secretary of state at their weekly meeting.

"Much progress. If anything, we are ahead of schedule." Secretary of State Upshur directed his comment to President Tyler, who looked pleased with the news.

"This ship is a key part of our plans for the coming year," replied the president.

"She will be ready to play her role, sir."

* * *

With much fanfare, the *Princeton* had been launched from Philadelphia in September 1843. Captain Stockton, always ready and willing to promote himself, made sure of that. He had kept the press advised of progress during the ship's construction and, during the week of the launching, held lavish parties aboard her, which he personally funded. Headlines across the country touted

America's newest and most innovative warship. Great Britain was being put on notice, it was said, that its dominance of the world's seas was being challenged. From Philadelphia, Stockton took the ship to New York, where the newspapers wildly praised Stockton and the new propeller-driven steam warship.

Not everyone celebrated the *Princeton*. In the 1840s, every political issue had a northern and a southern view, with slavery being the underlying point of contention. The need for a better naval fleet was no exception. Were new and better warships a way to project strength and defend America, or would they be used as tools to protect and expand slavery, by war or the threat of war? Some believed that one of the reasons that the Tyler Administration wanted a stronger Navy was to annex the Republic of Texas into the United States, and to use naval power to threaten or attack Mexico, or the British, if they tried to stop it. Former President John Quincy Adams, then a congressman and an ardent abolitionist, feared that the *Princeton* was promoted to members of Congress by the Tyler Administration and Captain Stockton, as he said, to "fire their souls with a patriotic ardor for a naval war."

* * *

"Are you still certain that Captain Stockton is the right man to be in charge?," asked the president.

"Very much so," replied Upshur. "His arrogance will always be a problem, but he has been promoting this new type of warship for years. As you know, he came to us back in '41 with the plans for the ship when I was just starting at the navy department, and we got it funded early in your administration. The screw propeller technology will revolutionize naval ships and warfare."

"He's a good friend and supporter, but a peacock, for sure," said the president, glancing down at a newspaper spread out on his desk. "Some of his quotes here in the New York newspapers make even me cringe. The ship, he says, is 'invincible against any foe' and the biggest advancement in warfare 'since the invention of gunpowder.' Really?"

"The captain is not one prone to understatement, that's for sure," said Upshur. "The sea trials have gone well so far. The ship is now in Philadelphia for installation of the two large deck cannons. After some more sea trials, Stockton will then bring her here to Washington City sometime in February to be seen by Congress and the Navy Department."

"I want all of our people talking about this, emphasizing it, starting now," instructed the president. "Get all of the information out to our newspapers."

"I will make sure of that, but I suspect that publicity is an area where Stockton will leave no stone unturned."

"We show off the ship to the country, make sure that Congress will approve more of them, and then we move forward with our Texas plan," replied the president, with a self-assured nod of his head.

"Exactly," agreed the secretary.

Young Tyler scribbled out his notes on the sheets of foolscap on his lap and then announced the next agenda topic.

CHAPTER 16

January, 1844— "A good 1844 to you, my friend! How was Christmas in Rhode Island?" asked Monty, as he held out his hand and greeted Ben in front of their favorite café for breakfast.

It was a cold Saturday morning. A few months earlier, the third member of their trio, Sam, had gotten his wish for a field artillery assignment and had been transferred by the War Department to Fort Washington, located about twenty miles away, on the Maryland side of the Potomac River. Both kept in touch with Sam by letters and hoped to see him in the spring when he would get a few days of leave and come to the city.

"Excellent!," responded Ben, "And a happy new year to you! All was well in Ohio, I hope?"

"It was."

The two were seated and a waitress soon arrived. "Two fried eggs, bacon, and a biscuit for me," requested Monty.

"I'll have hotcakes and ham," said Ben.

"And coffee!," a jovial Monty added, "For both of us, lots of coffee, please."

"You should be in a good mood," observed Ben, "From what I'm reading in the newspapers, this new year may end with you working for our new president."

"A long way to go before I can even think about that," Monty cautioned. "Who knows if Senator Clay will win the election and, even if he does, whether he would want me to come back and work for him. We have kept in touch some since he left the Senate in '42, but most of the prominent Whigs have lined up behind him this time and there will be many interests to appease in handing out staff appointments."

Monty noticed that Ben was sitting on the edge of his seat. He could feel the table shake slightly from the vibration of Ben's right leg underneath. It was a nervous tic that he had noticed before and usually meant that Ben was excited about something.

"It is definitely going to be a very different new year for me," said Ben. "The Navy Department has assigned me to a ship."

"That's great!," replied Monty. The shaking leg is better than a barometer, he thought, pleased with himself for having sensed the coming good news. "It's what you've been wanting for some time. Get out of an office here and be on the water. Which ship is it?"

"It's the new one, the *Princeton*. She's in Philadelphia and New York getting some final fittings and doing sea trials. She'll be here in February and I will join her crew then."

"That's not just a ship," crowed Monty, "The *Princeton* is *the* ship. Everyone in Congress has been talking about it for weeks. Congratulations! What a plum assignment. I understand that she has some fancy steam engines that the enemy can't attack and two of the biggest cannons ever made."

"So she does. I worked on getting the plans approved back in '41 and have been involved on and off with her construction since then. I'm excited about it."

"Supposed to be the model for a new fleet of warships, if Congress will put up the money," said Monty.

"Sounds like you know more about her than I do."

"Doubt that. I do know that her captain, Stockton, is very politically connected."

"Yes, he is," replied Ben. "From a prominent New Jersey family. As rich as Croesus. Has done some shady things in the past. Arrogant and strong-willed. At least that is his reputation, from what I've seen and heard. He was the driving force in getting the ship built and has funded some of the costs himself."

"Could be a difficult man to work for."

"I guess I'll find out in a few weeks."

"You'll be able deal with him, I'm sure. What a great career opportunity! I guess in a few years I'll be calling you Admiral Geddis. Has a nice ring to it."

"You are ever the optimist, my friend," replied Ben. "There are more important things going on in the country these days than my new job. Did you see the articles in the newspapers about Tyler and Texas annexation? I already hated the man, and now this. What's the inside word?"

"I did see them. Very disturbing," said Monty. "Those slave-owning bastards will not stop until they control everything and, with Tyler, they have their greatest advocate in the President's House. He is pushing this hard. Sees it as the way for him to get elected to a term of his own later this year. He wants us to swallow all of Texas, and bring it into the Union as a slave state. The rumor is that he wants to move quickly because the Texians are deep in debt and the British are offering them a loan to bail them out, conditioned on the abolition of slavery within their borders."

"Wouldn't that be something?" replied Ben. "A free Texas nation on our southwest border. Slaves would race to it, to freedom. It would be the death-knell for slavery in the deep south. We would then be a step closer to abolishing it entirely. I despise the British, but good for them."

"Except that Tyler and his crowd won't stand for it. Annexing Texas will keep that from happening. They are surely behind all of these articles in the papers favoring annexation. Not only will it expand slavery in our country, it will give the slavers control of the Senate. Once Texas is in the Union, as huge as it is, who knows how many more states they will try to carve out of it, giving them even more votes in the Senate."

"Annexation will make the slavers stronger than ever," said Ben.

"It would be a travesty. We'd never get rid of slavery," said Monty. "It needs to be ended. Now, not later."

"You're sounding a lot more like me these days," replied Ben. "What happened to the Mr. Union at All Costs and Mr. Gradual Emancipation that I first met a couple of years ago?"

"You know my views have been shifting. We've talked about it before. I tell you, that slave auction in Alexandria really did it for me. Seeing the evil of it first-hand. I'm glad I mustered enough nerve to do something."

"You did a noble thing. Buying that slave woman and freeing her. I can't remember, what was her name?"

"Delores. And thank you. Wasn't much, but it was something."

"Yes, how could I have forgotten her name? I'm sure that she thanks you every day of her life. What you did, and what the folks on the Underground Railroad are doing, are great, but they are drops in the bucket. We need bolder action. The slavers need to be sent a stronger message." Ben continued, "Do you think Tyler can really pull off annexing Texas?"

"I hear from my friends on Capitol Hill that this thing is much further along than they had ever thought was possible. Secretary of State Upshur has been lobbying senators to support an annexation treaty and the word is that he has the thirty-five votes needed to get it affirmed, including some Whigs and some northern Democrats. Sam Houston and the Texians are all for it. Upshur is portraying bringing Texas into the Union as being in the national interest, rather than solely in the sectional interest of the South and an expansion of slavery, which anyone with any brain at all knows is the real motivation."

"Damn Tyler!," declared Ben, emphatically, but in a hushed tone, not wanting anyone sitting around them to hear what he was about to say. "What was that stupid slogan that the Whigs ran on in 1840, 'Tippecanoe and Tyler too?' Harrison and Tyler. Well, Harrison is dead and we've been left with Tyler. We need to be done with him. No more Tyler! He *has* to be stopped."

Monty noticed a rush of redness to Ben's face, and a protruding vein on the side of his freckled forehead that looked as though it was going to pop. His friend could be emotional, but he had never seen him like this before. Where was Ben going with this, he wondered?

"That's what I'm saying," Monty calmly responded, hoping to settle Ben down. "I don't think he can be. Looks like he's going to have the votes in the Senate to get the treaty approved."

"If there were no President Tyler, there would be no treaty, right?," asked a very serious Ben, staring at Monty.

Monty became alarmed. He can't be going *there*. Ben had talked about it before, he recalled, but those were just jokes, he had assumed. "Probably not," he said to a still red-faced Ben. "What are you saying?"

"I mean if he were dead."

"Well, if Tyler were to die in office," said Monty, "there is no vice president and, under the law, the president *pro tem* of the Senate would then become the president."

"Who is that?," asked Ben.

"Senator Willie Mangum of North Carolina. He is a Whig and a supporter of Senator Clay. He would definitely oppose Texas annexation, as does Clay."

"Well then, we need to make Mr. Mangum our president."

Oh my God. He *is* going there! Maybe if he didn't take him seriously, Monty speculated, Ben will move on to something else.

"And just how might we do *that*?," asked Monty, as sarcastically as he could.

The waitress arrived with their breakfast. "Who has the hotcakes?, she asked.

Ben nodded, "Right here. Looks great, thank you." He waited until she had gone, and checked to make sure no one else was within earshot before responding to Monty, in barely a whisper. "For Christ's sake, Tolliver, for a college boy, you can be dense sometimes. I'm tired of waiting for others to act. Tyler needs to be killed. If others won't do it, then we need to. He should have been taken out back in '41. We saw that mob scene when they hanged him in effigy. That should have been the night. I'm sure someone in the crowd had a plan to do it, but they lost their nerve and Tyler got lucky. If he had been done away with then, the country would be in much better shape now. Don't you agree?"

"Well, yes." Now he could no longer avoid addressing the topic directly. Monty whispered, "Are you serious? You want us, you and me, to kill the president of the United States?"

"Dead serious. And you know my feelings about that. He isn't, or shouldn't be, the president. He's really only the acting president. This expansion of slavery is ten times, a hundred times, worse than all of the things he has done before."

"I can't disagree on that."

"Monty, we are at a fork in the road," said Ben. "We take one route, and we're closer to eliminating this evil. We take the other, and it grows. And that is a road we cannot take. Annexing Texas will forever change the character of our country. You just said it. The slavers will be in charge. No one elected Tyler to do that. He needs to be stopped, before it's too late!"

Monty took a small bite of his bacon. Most of his food remained on his plate. He had lost his appetite. A couple of ladies walked by the table and he waited for them to pass. "What are we going to do, just walk into the President's House and shoot him? They'll fill us with lead on the spot, or hang us the next day. Maybe both."

"I'm not saying we have to be martyrs. There's got to be a smart way to do it. We just have to figure it out. Are you in?"

The waitress arrived with their bill. After paying it, the two walked out into the frosty January air.

"This conversation certainly took a different turn that I had expected. A lot to think about. We'll talk soon," Monty said to his best friend.

* * *

Despite the cold temperature, Monty decided to walk back to his boardinghouse. It was Saturday, he had no plans, and plenty of time. Could he really be pondering this? Assassination of the president. Treason. The more he tried to get it out of his head, the more it consumed his thoughts.

As he walked, he came upon a dray, hitched to a single horse, and parked in front of a market. A White man stood near the back of the wagon; the rear gate was down and a couple of crates had been loaded. Monty observed a Black man exit the market, carrying another crate, and headed for the wagon. He had seen this scene many times. The Black man, he felt sure, was enslaved to a slaveholder in nearby Virginia or Maryland, and had been hired out to one of the restaurants or hotels in the city. He was likely a kitchen worker and he and the White man, probably an overseer of the enslaved staff, were picking up food for Saturday evening's dinner menu. When the Black man placed the crate on the gate of the wagon, the gate gave way and the crate fell to the street. Monty heard the sound of glass breaking.

"You damn fool!," shouted the White man. He shoved the Black man out of the way and bent over and looked into the crate. "All broken!" In an instant, he reached into the wagon and pulled out a whip, and lashed the enslaved man once across the back of his legs, causing him to crumble to the ground in pain.

"Didn't mean to do it, master," said the man, tears in his eyes from the pain. "Gate broke. Forgive me."

"I'm done with you, George! What happened last week, and now this. I'll be sending you back to your owner in Loudoun County. He can deal with your clumsiness. Can sell you down river, for all I care. Let's see how you like picking cotton in Mississippi."

"No sir, not that! I can make it up to you. Please, give me another chance," the man pleaded.

"Too late for that. Clean that stuff up."

Monty took it all in. He felt a rage rise up inside him, something he had not felt since that day in Alexandria with Delores. How many times, he wondered, was the same scene, or much worse, being played out across the South today? And every day? He thought more about his breakfast with Ben. The best and surest way to kill anything, he knew, was to lop off its head. Perhaps Ben was right. Maybe Tyler, the slaveholder-in-chief, had to go.

CHAPTER 17

January, 1844— Monty pulled out his pocket watch. He was now ten minutes late. Unlike him. Ben would understand, he was sure. When they talked a couple of days ago, he had told Ben that he willing, even eager, to go forward with what they had discussed at breakfast the other day. Maybe eager was too strong, given the nature of the matter. Determined. Yes, he decided, that was a better word. Both had arranged to leave work early for this afternoon meeting. It was a relatively mild day for January, with some fog and mist lingering in the air since the morning. A gentle breeze blew through the trees in Lafayette Square. He pulled up the collar of his black frock coat and pushed down his hat a bit, making his face less visible. He had brought along a walking stick. As he rounded a corner, he saw a familiar figure.

"Sorry, it took me a while to get a carriage and, as you suggested, I had the driver drop me off a couple of blocks over and walked from there," said Monty, as he took a seat next to his friend on a bench. It may have been overly cautious, he thought, but taking steps to make sure that as few people as possible saw them coming together at this location was probably a wise move.

"No problem." Ben replied. They then quickly got down to business. "So, what did you find out?"

"Nothing good," responded Monty. "If Tyler has any plans to leave the President's House any time over the next few weeks, no one in the Senate knows anything about it. He's not scheduled to come to Capitol Hill and there are no official events elsewhere in Washington City on his calendar, from what I'm told. I have one source who knows a senator who is a close friend of Tyler and, according to him, Tyler won't leave the city until Easter, when he goes to his home in Virginia. The Texas treaty will be a done deal by then."

"That's what I'm hearing, too," replied Ben. "Folks in the Navy Department say he's so hated, by Whigs and Democrats alike, that he doesn't socialize around town. He's only close to his Virginia cronies, and they always come to visit him."

They both looked toward the president's residence, officially called the Executive Mansion, a block directly to the south of where they were sitting. "If the bastard won't leave there," said Monty, "then there is where we'll have to do it."

"That's why we're here. Let's get this done," said Ben, referring to the purpose of their meeting. "You go first and walk to the left when you get to the fence surrounding the grounds. I'll wait a couple of minutes and then go to the right, and we'll meet back here." Monty nodded, stood, and started walking.

The circular stroll around the perimeter of the mansion's grounds took about half an hour. They took note of the distances, the people, the size and location of the trees, the landscaping, and the handful of structures that they could see from graveled walkway. As Ben and Monty passed each other halfway, both looked away, not making eye contact.

"See anything of note?," asked Ben, as they met back at the bench.

"Unless you saw something that I missed, the only two daytime guards are the ones posted at the main entrances, one on the north side and one on the south."

"That's all that I saw."

"And we know that there's now at least one guard posted at the North Portico at night," Monty continued. "Congress appropriated money for that after the mob event that we saw back in '41."

"His office is on the second floor, with a lot of people coming and going all day," said Ben. "We could get inside during the day. That would be easy enough. I'm a Navy officer and you work for the Senate. We present our cards and ask for a meeting. People show up there and do that every day. Sometimes they get to see him; sometimes not. We're not deadbeats. They won't toss us out. At worst, they'll tell us to come back another day. But any daytime attempt to kill him in there is going to be a suicide mission, and the odds of getting to him first are pretty low."

"Agreed," replied Monty. "If we want any chance of surviving this, we're going to have to break in at night. Kill him in his bed. He's a widower, so he should be alone. I'm thinking that we'll need to stab him, to avoid the sound of a gunshot and waking up others in the house."

"Agreed. That's probably the only way."

"From what I just saw," said Monty, "there's too much open ground to cover from both the north and south sides, even at night. To the west, there is a lot of activity around the War

Department building. So, that's out. Safest approach is probably from the east side. The stables are there, but also plenty of trees and shrubs that we can use for cover."

"We'll need to do it when it is darkest," said Ben. "I looked at the almanac and the new moon in February is on Sunday, the eighteenth. So, a couple of days on either side of that would be best."

"That should work. I am sure that the treaty will not be submitted before then. I know the layout inside fairly well from going to meetings between Senator Clay and Van Buren and Harrison, but that was a few years ago," replied Monty. "I'm sure there are some floor plans in the Library of Congress that I can take a look at and figure out the best entry point, and the best way out."

"It's risky, but I can't think of a better way," said Ben. "We only have a few weeks to act, but we can do this. Will just take a lot of work. If we fail to prepare, we are preparing to fail."

"Don't tell me . . ." said Monty.

"Of course, it's a Ben Franklin saying. You gave me the damn book."

Monty grinned. "So I did. Wonder if ol' Ben would approve of its use with our enterprise?"

"Maybe so. He was involved in a revolution that changed the head of the government, right?"

"I suspect he may have a problem with our means to that end," said Monty. "But enough of him. We are agreed on what we discussed about the timing of things afterward?"

"Correct. Not a good idea for either one of us to stay in Washington City, but leaving right away and at the same time would attract suspicion. You'll leave your Senate job a couple of weeks after it's done and go back to Ohio, and I'll wait a couple of months and resign my commission in the Navy and head back to Rhode Island."

"We have some time. Let's sleep on all of this and think it through some more," said Monty.

The two men got up from the bench and started to walk away in different directions.

"Hope Tyler is not a light sleeper," Monty muttered to himself. Were things going too fast, he wondered? Could this plan really work, or were he and Ben fools to even try it?

CHAPTER 18

February, 1844— "Really, you want me to go with you?," an incredulous Monty asked Ben. "Won't it be like two Daniels in the lion's den? Us among the Tyler Administration's slaveholders and Texas annexation proponents. Talk about a strange mix. We *are* plotting to kill the president. Remember?"

"What's that old Chinese saying, know thy enemy? Think of it as an intelligence mission to obtain some information that will help us in our plan." Ben continued, "This is Captain Stockton's party to promote the *Princeton* to Washington City's high society. Paying for it himself, I'm told. The ship will arrive here in a few days. The invitation is addressed to Lieutenant Benjamin F. Geddis and Guest. Stockton is my new boss and I have to go. It would look suspicious not to. I choose you to be my guest. Besides, you have been around these political folks and know how to act around them, much better than I, and you can keep me from embarrassing myself."

"Can't have you doing that. I'll go."

* * *

As they exited their carriage in front of Gadsby's Hotel, Monty and Ben could not help but think that they looked sharp, with Monty in his best dark suit, white shirt with a high collar, paisley bowtie, and a velvet maroon vest, and Ben in his dress uniform, a tight-fitting dark blue coat with tails, two vertical rows of gold buttons on the chest, a high embroidered collar, gold epaulets, and dark striped slacks. The room was mostly filled as they entered, with Stockton holding court at its center. Monty recognized a few cabinet members and senators.

They were greeted by a commander, the officer rank above Ben's rank of lieutenant, who introduced himself to Ben, unsmilingly, as Thomas Fenwick. Of average height, with a high forehead, short dark hair, a narrow and pointy chin, and dark eyes that seemed to bulge out of their sockets, no one would accuse the man of being handsome. His naval uniform, similar to Ben's, helped draw attention away from his unflattering features.

Ben saluted. "Lieutenant Benjamin Geddis, sir."

"Ah, yes, the new man," said Fenwick. His tone bordered on rudeness. "I saw your name on the new officer list earlier this week. You will have a lot to learn, very quickly. Captain Stockton has high expectations of all his officers. We won't have much time until the *Princeton* gets underway. We will be having a meeting tomorrow at ten at the Navy Department. Be there."

Ben introduced Monty. Fenwick gave him a slight nod and a pro forma handshake before quickly moving on to welcome those arriving behind them. Ben explained to Monty that, as a commander, Fenwick would be second in command of the ship, and his direct superior.

"Not a very friendly chap," observed Monty.

Ben nodded in agreement. "He's been with Stockton for a few years. Extremely loyal to the captain. I've heard that he is humorless, and difficult to deal with. I can now vouch for that."

The light from the gaslit crystal chandeliers in the main banquet room at Gadsby's seemed to twinkle as they walked into the crowded room. A large table was full of delicacies—meats, cheeses, fruits, and breads. White-coated servers with trays of wine and champagne circulated around the room. Monty and Ben grabbed some champagne as one walked by. A string trio in a corner of the room played soft music.

"We knew that your new boss, Stockton, was rich," observed Monty, "but this is something else." He started to point out to his friend some of the senators and other prominent people in the room. Almost all Democrats, he commented, with only a token presence of Whigs.

"Who is that older lady over there with all of those people around her?," asked Ben.

"That would be Dolley Madison, widow of the late president," said Monty. "She was quite the socialite when she lived in the President's House. After her husband died a few years ago, she moved back here from Virginia. She's now in her seventies, and is still the life of any party. Come on, I'll introduce you."

"You *know* Dolley Madison?," asked a disbelieving Ben.

"I used to work for Senator Clay. I know people. I thought that's why you invited me."

The former first lady was wearing one of her trademark turbans, this one cream colored, with hints of her still dark hair showing underneath. She had on a pine green dress, with a white collar, topped off with a long red shawl. She looked matronly, but younger than her years. Monty and Ben took the last sips of their champagne, ditched their glasses, walked toward her, and waited for the surrounding crowd to thin out. At the appropriate moment, Monty caught her eye, took her hand, and gave it a kiss.

"Why, Mr. Tolliver, what a pleasure to see you!"

"The pleasure is all mine, Mrs. Madison. You are radiant, as always."

"You are too kind. How is my old friend, Senator Clay, these days? I have not seen him since he left the Senate. When was that, about two years ago? I see from the newspapers that he is keeping himself quite busy."

"Yes, ma'am, he left here in '42. The senator is now touring in the deep south, I believe."

"Touring, or campaigning?"

"Both, I suspect, probably more of the latter."

"Well, I hear he may well be coming back here as our president next year." Gently grabbing Monty's arm, she whispered in his ear, "I wouldn't want this room full of Democrats to know it, but I don't think that would be such a bad thing. A gentleman and a charmer he is, our Mr. Clay. I have known all ten of our presidents and I think he would make a fitting addition."

"Thank you, I will pass your kind words on to him when I next see him." Monty looked toward Ben. "Mrs. Madison, I would like to introduce my good friend, Lieutenant Benjamin Franklin Geddis, who will be joining Captain Stockton's staff on board the *Princeton* when it arrives in a few days."

"Benjamin Franklin, you say?" Turning to Ben, she continued, "A name to be proud of. I also knew Dr. Franklin. I was in my teens living in Philadelphia during his last years and I made his acquaintance a few times. Talk about your charmers. But then, oh my, I am really dating myself. He passed away more than half a century ago."

Ben reached out, as Monty had done, and planted a kiss on her hand. "Mrs. Madison,' he said, "what an honor it is to meet you. Thank you for saving Mr. Stuart's portrait of President Washington."

"You are very kind, my dear young man. One never knows how one will react in the midst of a crisis. I suppose that is what I will be remembered for." Shifting topics, she continued, "This *Princeton* sounds like quite a warship. If my Jemmy had something like it during the late war, perhaps the British would never have reached Washington City and burned it, and that wonderful portrait would not have needed to be saved."

"Likely so, ma'am. I am looking forward to serving on the *Princeton*, and with Captain Stockton."

"I chatted with the captain earlier," she replied. "Seems rather full of . . . er, a confident man, shall we say."

"That is certainly his reputation," responded Monty.

"Been a lot of them in this town, for a long time," she said. "Always need to keep a close eye on them."

Realizing that others were waiting to speak with this American legend, Monty and Ben politely excused themselves and moved on.

"Did you really say to her," asked a grinning Monty, "'Thank you for saving Washington's portrait?' Are you in primary school?"

"I was nervous. She's Dolley Madison. It was all that I could think of."

"She sure liked your name. Dr. Franklin. I think I shall have to start calling you that."

"Much better than having the name of a southern plantation owner, Mont-gom-er-y."

They both chuckled.

They moved on and spotted another server with a tray of champagne glasses. As they took two from his tray, Monty came face to face with the one person that he had spied across the room earlier, and was most hoping to avoid—John, the president's son. He doubted that this encounter would go any better than the last conversation they had at the horse races back in the spring, but he forced a smile and extended his right hand. "John, Monty Tolliver. Used to work for Senator Clay. Pleased to see you again."

"Yes, Monty, of course I remember. Those were difficult times. Nice to see you under more pleasant circumstances, celebrating our country's newest warship," he said in his Tidewater Virginia drawl.

"I would like to introduce you to Lieutenant Benjamin Geddis," said Monty, "who has been assigned to the Princeton and will be serving under Captain Stockton when the ship arrives here." He then thought of the awkwardness of the encounter, with himself and Ben deep into plans to kill the young man's father.

"A pleasure, sir," said Ben, shaking hands.

"My father's administration is so fortunate to have Captain Stockton, a true patriot, leading its efforts to modernize the Navy. This will enable our country to do some great things." Turning to Monty, the presidential offspring continued, "Monty, I recall from when we last met, I think it was at the National Course races, that you now work on the staff of the Senate. I hope you can use your influence with some of those old windbags to give us the funding we need to have a fleet of *Princetons*."

"I am not involved with the political side of the Senate any longer, but will do what I can," a smiling Monty said, unconvincingly. He recalled what John had said to him at the races several months earlier, that his father had some big cards to play against the Whigs. It was now clear to Monty what he had meant—bringing Texas into the Union.

May as well try to get some information from him, Monty decided. "Sorry to see that your father is not here. Is he out of the city?"

"Oh, no. He's just worn out. Worked himself to the bone today. The people's business always comes first with him, as I am sure you know."

"I'm sure it does. Please give the president my warmest regards."

Thankfully, John simply nodded, did not comment further, excused himself, and moved on.

"That was uncomfortable," commented Ben to Monty.

"What a braggart he is," replied Monty. He and Ben, Monty pondered, had a card of their own that they would be playing. And soon.

At that moment, a man approached Ben and extended his hand. Ben had noticed him speaking to other naval officers at the party. "Lieutenant, I am Thomas Gilmer, about to be your new boss. The president has appointed me to be the new secretary of the Navy." Another Virginia drawl, noticed Ben, as he saluted him, not knowing if it was appropriate. Gilmer, not seeming to know if it was or not, returned the gesture.

"A pleasure to meet you, sir, er, Mr. Secretary, if it is not too soon to call you that."

"I think that's fine but, Lord knows, I am not an expert on protocol. Will you be on the officer staff of the *Princeton?*"

"Yes sir, proudly so," responded Ben.

STAN HAYNES

"This is an exciting time for our Navy. Our president has some big plans."

"Yes, it is. So I have heard. Glad to do my part, sir." Ben introduced Monty and Gilmer also shook his hand.

"Y'all be well," said the secretary to be, as he moved on to another naval officer that he saw nearby.

"He sure is working the room," said Monty. "It's like he gets a prize for each man in uniform that he talks to."

Ben was aware from the newspapers that Gilmer had been named by Tyler to be the new secretary of the Navy, but knew nothing about him. Monty filled him in. Gilmer, he told Ben, was a congressman from Virginia and was one of a small group of informal advisors from Tyler's home state whom the president relied upon heavily for advice. The Virginia cabal, as the press called them. Gilmer was the leading advocate for the president in the House and, in 1843, at Tyler's request, he had launched the administration's public relations campaign for the annexation of Texas by writing a widely-published letter arguing that bringing Texas into the Union was in the national interest, in that it would expand the market for northern manufactured goods, increase the nation's wealth, thwart British imperialism, and that excitement over expansion would bring the country together and lessen sectionalism. When Tyler's first choice to fill a vacancy at the head of the Navy Department was rejected by the Senate, he named Gilmer to the post in early 1844, and his confirmation was all but certain.

"Does he know anything about the Navy?" asked Ben.

"Probably not," said Monty, "but when has knowledge of their department ever been a job requirement for a cabinet member?"

"And we have Tyler as our president. Nothing like the incompetent leading the clueless," replied Ben. "Change will be coming soon, my friend. You and I will see to that."

The din of conversations throughout the room was interrupted by the high-pitched sound of the tapping of spoons on crystal glasses. Captain Stockton raised his glass, turned slowly in a circle to catch the eyes of all of his guests, and bellowed, "A toast to the United States of America, may she ever be strong!"

"And to you and the *Princeton*, who will keep her so!" responded Gilmer, followed by a round of applause throughout the room.

Stockton continued, "President Tyler was not able to be with us, but we are glad to have here his son, John, and so many members of his administration. I would like to announce tonight that, when the *Princeton* arrives here soon in Washington City, we will be offering an excursion on the Potomac, to demonstrate her innovations, speed, and firepower, and you are all invited. I am very pleased to state that the president has accepted my invitation and will be on board."

There was another burst of applause from the crowd.

"A toast to the president!" someone shouted, and glasses were raised once more.

Ben's face suddenly looked pensive.

"Dr. Franklin, is something wrong?" asked Monty.

"Wrong? Nothing is *wrong*," said Ben, his face now breaking into a smile. He grabbed another couple of glasses of champagne from a passing server, handed one to Monty, and clinked the tips of the glasses together. "Don't you see what this means? This changes everything."

CHAPTER 19

February, 1844— Ben and Monty left the party, hailed a carriage in front of the hotel, and directed the driver first to Ben's boardinghouse. "Come in with me," Ben said to Monty. "We need to talk more about our plan and figure this out."

"It's late and we've both had a lot of champagne," said Monty. "Can't it wait until tomorrow?"

"Tomorrow it is. Come here after work."

"See you then," said Ben as he unlocked the front door of the house and headed down the long hallway to his room at the end.

* * *

The next evening, shortly before seven, Ben answered the knock at his door and let Monty in. They immediately got down to business. "You heard Stockton at the party last night. This is perfect. We don't have to break into the President's House. Tyler will be on my ship for hours. I will have easy access to him and I can kill him then."

"I heard him. But what do you mean by 'I,'" replied Monty. "We're in this together. I'm sure I can get my hands on an invitation to Stockton's party on the *Princeton* and be on board. If we decide to do it there, we will do it together."

"No need for that. I can do it alone."

"It will be a suicide mission."

"I realize that." said Ben. "The only thing you can accomplish by being on board is that both of us would get killed."

"We already have a plan. One where the goal is for both of us to escape and live through it. We've studied the floor plans of the Executive Mansion that I got from the Library of Congress and figured a way in and out, and across the grounds, that we think will work. Why not stick with that?"

"I know, but we can't be sure we can get to Tyler there without being discovered first," said Ben. "Suppose the floor creaks, a dog barks, or something else happens, and someone inside is awakened, or the guard at the north entrance hears something and comes inspecting? We'll be arrested, or shot, before we make it to the bedroom. We fail and the bastard survives. The only reason we decided to do it there is because he was not leaving the mansion anytime soon. Now we know that he's leaving, and when. And what a gift to us. He's coming to *my* ship. I can walk right up to him and do the job."

"Don't you think Tyler will have security guards with him when he is on board?," asked Monty.

"Probably not. We know that he usually travels without any."

"I am not going to agree to any changes in our plan," said Monty, "unless there are strong odds of you surviving. Tell me about the plans for this excursion."

"Stockton had a meeting with the officers this morning and filled us in some more on what he said last night. It's set for February 28. He said all of the dignitaries will board the *Princeton* at Alexandria, around noon. They will first get on a steamship upriver and be ferried there. More than three hundred are expected, he said. We head downriver to Mount Vernon and turn around there. He is ordering an extravagant meal to impress everyone. He wants to show off the big cannons on the deck, so he is going to have one of them fired, three times, the last time at Mount Vernon. Then back upriver to Alexandria. The whole thing should last about five hours."

"I know those cannons are huge. What happens when one of them is fired?," asked Monty.

"Can't say for sure, but I've seen and heard smaller ones fired at sea and the noise is deafening. The whole ship shakes and there's a thick cloud of black smoke for a few seconds. These are the largest cannons ever placed on a ship, so I am certain that the noise and the smoke will be much greater."

"Isn't Fort Washington near Mount Vernon?," asked Monty.

"Yes. Across the Potomac, on the Maryland side," replied Ben. "Maybe a little bit to the north."

"I think I see a way to do this with both of us surviving. You don't need to be a martyr." said Monty. "We need to pay a visit to our friend Sam at Fort Washington, and I need to see some people to make some plans."

CHAPTER 20

February, 1844— It was a Sunday afternoon, another cold day in February. Monty went up the steps and opened the door to the rowhouse. Much larger than it looks from the outside, he thought. On the right, he peered into a large dining room with a long narrow table, about twenty chairs around it. A bigger boardinghouse than his, he thought. He walked past the stairway on the left, unbuttoned his coat and took off his gloves and hat, passed a couple of numbered rooms, and then came to an open door. Beyond it, he saw a pleasant-looking lady, who appeared to be in her forties, wearing a long apron and giving directions to two kitchen workers.

"Excuse me, ma'am, would you be Mrs. Sprigg?" he asked.

"I sure am. All of my rooms are full until the spring," she responded, appearing annoyed.

Monty had walked past this block of five large row houses countless times. Known as Duff Green's Row, they stood two blocks east of the Capitol, on First Street. Mrs. Sprigg's boardinghouse, the fourth one in from Pennsylvania Avenue, was known around town as the Abolition House, due to the handful of abolitionist Whig congressmen who resided there, along with a few lobbyists for northern abolitionist societies, and a couple of reporters from abolitionist newspapers. Monty remembered that the abolitionist Theodore Weld had told him a couple of years ago to have the enslaved woman he had purchased and freed, Delores, come here for help. Now, it was he who needed help from one of the residents. He had discretely asked around and was told whom he needed to see.

Monty reached out and handed Mrs. Sprigg his card, explaining, "Oh no, I am not looking for a room."

"What can I do for you, Mr. Montgomery Estes Tolliver, Deputy Clerk, United States Senate?," she asked, reading the card.

"I am here to see one of your boarders, Mr. Jeremiah Turner."

Monty noticed her face begin to lose its sternness. Was it, he wondered, due to the fact that he worked for the Senate, or the mentioning of Turner's name? Although he had thought that she would first send a servant up to Turner's room with his card, she did not. Perhaps Turner accepted all callers. "Mr. Turner is on the third floor, Room Nine," she said. "You can go on up."

The knock on the door was answered by a Black man, in his fifties, with mostly gray hair and wearing spectacles. Monty knew that Turner was the Washington-based reporter for *The Colored American*, a New York City newspaper. He had been in the city for a couple of years covering the abolitionist movement and its lobbying of Congress. Turner sometimes wrote, Monty had heard, under the *nom de plume* of Libertas. But it was another rumored activity of Turner that had brought Monty to his door. He introduced himself, and was invited to take a seat at a small round table covered with piles of books and papers. He kept his coat on, as the fire in the small fireplace was almost out.

"Come on in. Excuse the mess, I'm working on an article for next week's paper. What can I do for you?" said Turner. "Did you say your name is Tolliver?"

"Yes, sir, it is." Monty hesitated, not sure how to broach the subject, finally deciding to be direct and blunt. "Mr. Turner, I am a Whig, originally from Ohio, and I used to work for Senator Clay. I now work in the clerk's office of the Senate. I have heard . . ." he hesitated a bit, and then continued, "that you have ties to the Underground Railroad and I was hoping that you could help me. I need to get someone safely to Canada, in a couple of weeks."

He watched Turner stare at him intently, no doubt, he believed, suspicious that he could be a law enforcement agent trying to entrap him into an admission of criminal activity. "I don't know what you're talking about," Turner responded curtly, testing Monty.

"Please, Mr. Turner, I will swear on a Bible, my intentions here are honorable and I need your help."

"In my experience, folks with dishonorable intentions don't mind swearing on a Bible. Means nothing to them."

"Maybe so. But would they venture out on such a cold Sunday afternoon, to the room of a man with such a pitiful fire?," responded Monty, rubbing his hands together and glancing at the last few glowing embers in Turner's fireplace. He hoped that the attempt at humor would ease his host's concern over his intentions.

It seemed to work. Turner let out a small laugh, and his face then became serious, which Monty took as a sign of trust.

"What if I do know something about this, what did you call it, Underground Railroad?," asked Turner. "How would *you* know when a slave is going to run away? What have you done, gotten a slave girl pregnant? Now feeling guilty, and want to get her to freedom?"

"No, no!" responded Monty, "Nothing like that. It's complicated. The person that I want you to help is not a slave, and he is not of color. He is a friend. I cannot reveal the details, but he will be a wanted man by the authorities for what he will do for the abolition cause and will need to get safely out of the country. This is the only way."

"Interesting," said Turner, stroking his unshaven chin, and having decided to fully trust his visitor. "A white man traveling on the Underground Railroad. That's something new. I have never thought of these services being used, or needed, by anyone other than my people. When and from where would your friend be starting his journey?"

"End of February or early March, from Prince George's County, in Maryland. He will be traveling on horseback."

They talked some more. Monty gave as few details as possible. To his surprise, Turner did not demand to know his friend's name, or what he would be doing that would necessitate the need to escape.

"The less I know, the better. That is how we operate. Your friend will need to avoid going through Washington City and Baltimore," explained Turner, now speaking like the like the expert on human smuggling that he was, and having already formulated a plan. "The larger the city, the greater the chance of being observed and caught. The best route is to go east, cross the Chesapeake Bay to Maryland's Eastern Shore, and go north from there. Tell him to make his way to Deale, on Herring Bay. He'll need to wait for a fishing steamer, the *Kathryn*, to come into the dock, and ask for the captain. The ship is there twice a week. I will get the word out and he will be expected. Make sure he tells the captain that Libertas sent him."

"Thank you, sir."

"Fair enough, but I do have one condition. You must tell your friend, Mr. Clay, if he comes back here in a position of power, and I hear that he may well be, that we need some real support from him. Denouncing slavery, as he has done in the past, without action, accomplishes nothing. Understood?"

"Agreed, and will do." responded Monty, "Much appreciated."

The two shook hands. As Monty made his way down the stairs of the boardinghouse, he let out a sigh of relief that the conversation with Turner had gone well. One less thing to worry about. As he crossed the street, he stared intently at the Capitol, directly in front of him. If this plan is successful, he thought, what a den of chaos that place will be in a couple of weeks.

CHAPTER 21

February, 1844— "It looks like sketches of medieval castles that I remember from my books in primary school," said Monty to Ben, as the massive fort on a hill overlooking the Potomac River came into view.

"Kind of," replied Ben, "except those castles didn't have cannons pointed out in all directions."

The twenty-mile trip on horseback from the city had been an arduous one—crossing the Navy Yard Bridge over the Anacostia River and, once in Maryland, following stagecoach roads and paths south until the bleak-looking stone and brick structure finally came into view. The cold February weather did not make the trip any easier, but at least there was no snow or rain. The third horse they had brought along, with a saddle and a saddle bag, did not slow them down too much. During the long ride, Monty and Ben discussed the history of the fort and its strategic location. Completed twenty years earlier, in 1824, Fort Washington was America's main defense against an enemy attack by water on the nation's capital. Its predecessor, Fort Warburton, had miserably failed to stop the British fleet during the War of 1812 and had been blown up, on the order of its own commanding officer, to prevent the enemy from occupying it.

Monty and Ben made the journey to Fort Washington to conduct reconnaissance and to meet with their good friend Sam Shipley, now a captain in the Third U.S. Artillery, and who was stationed there. Arriving in the early afternoon, the two gazed up and down the Potomac to get the lay of the land and the water. They were standing where the river began to widen on its downstream path to the Chesapeake Bay. Less than a mile away, to the southwest and around the bend on the Virginia side, on a high bluff and barely visible, was George Washington's Mount Vernon.

Ben stared at the river. "It's doable."

"Definitely so," replied Monty.

Both men committed the area's geography to memory. As planned, they then walked to a tavern a few hundred yards from the fort's outer walls, took a table in the back corner, near the fireplace, and ordered a couple of ales.

They had not seen Sam for a few months, since he had been transferred from the War Department to the fort. Ben had written to Sam recently to share the news of his appointment to the *Princeton*, and Sam had written back with his congratulations.

"Swill," said Ben on taking a first sip of the brew.

"Not good, but it's not terrible. Bad ale, after the long ride we had today, is better than none at all," countered Monty.

Within a few minutes, Sam arrived, wearing a military uniform, as were several others in the tavern. He quietly pulled a chair up to the table. "So, what's so urgent?," he asked in a hushed tone, "and why all of the secrecy?" The message, marked confidential, that he had received from Monty three days ago from the weekly courier to the fort from Congress had been brief and cryptic, stating only when, where, and whom to meet, and to tell no one. Monty's job in the Senate had its perks. He had arranged through a friend who worked in the congressional mailroom for his private message to Sam to be slipped into the pouch. There was no small talk; they got down to business.

"Do you *really* believe in the abolition cause?," Ben asked Sam, knowing the answer.

"Of course, I do. You know me. How many times have we talked politics? We need to get rid of slavery."

"We all agree on that," said Ben, adding, "We've recently heard some news that, if it happens, will embolden the slave power in the South and make abolition all but impossible. And we intend to do something about it."

Monty turned up his tankard, took the last sip of his warm ale, and looked into Sam's eyes. "Can we take a walk outside?," he asked.

The cold winter air hit their warm faces as they walked out of the tavern and down a path toward the river. "Tyler has really done it now," said Ben.

"What else can he do?," responded Sam. "He's already betrayed his party, and run the economy into the ground. At least he will be gone in less than a year's time."

Monty looked around, to make sure no one was within earshot. "Unfortunately, he can still do a lot of damage over the next few months, and he's plotting to get elected in November. The word in Washington City is that Secretary of State Upshur is in the final stage of negotiating a treaty to annex Texas and bring it into the Union as a slave state. Tyler thinks Texas will be his path to get nominated by the Democrats this summer, or to head his own third party, and get a full term of his own."

Sam looked shocked. "Just what we need. More of Tyler, and another slave state. And a huge one. If all of this is true, what can be done about it?," he asked.

"Put a stop to it," said Monty.

"How?"

Ben and Monty stared at Sam. "We're going to kill him," said Ben.

"And we need your help," added Monty.

"You can't be serious," said Sam, "What are you going to do, walk into the President's House and shoot him? You'll never get close to him and they'll kill you first."

"We thought about that, breaking in at night, but we decided that it's too risky to try anything there," said Ben. "Away from there, it's a different story. Much easier and safer to get close to him. My boss, Captain Stockton, has invited Tyler to a cruise on the *Princeton* Wednesday next, along with other dignitaries, and the president has accepted. The ship will leave from Alexandria, and come right down here, before turning around at Mount Vernon."

Monty pointed toward the river. "On board, he will be accessible and vulnerable, and we have a plan."

"He *is* the commander-in-chief. I am a captain in the United States Army. Are you asking me to help you kill him?"

They walked farther along the path, downhill, toward the dock on the Potomac. The fort's two small steamboats, used to patrol the river, were covered by canvas tarps. Monty and Ben explained their plan to their friend, who listened attentively. It was a risk, they knew. He could arrest them himself, or have them arrested, charged with treason, and thrown in the stockade of Fort Washington as prisoners. But they believed that Sam would react differently and that, based on their prior conversations, there was in him a calling higher than country, a moral one. They knew that bringing Texas into the Union as a slave state would be anathema to Sam.

"Not really," said Monty, "We just need some help from you after it's done." They explained what they needed from Sam, who listened attentively.

After thinking about it for longer than Monty and Ben had expected, Sam agreed to his role. The three friends walked back uphill toward the tavern and shook hands. At the hitching post, the reins of the extra horse that they had brought, a chestnut gelding, were handed over to Sam, who headed toward the fort's stables, as Monty and Ben mounted up for the long trip back to Washington City.

"I never doubted that he would help us," said Ben, as they settled into their saddles.

"Nor did I," said Monty, "I think we are getting all of the pieces of the puzzle in place to get this done."

CHAPTER 22

February, 1844— The bed sheets were soaked with sweat, despite the below freezing February temperature outside. The quilt had been kicked to the floor. Nothing new, sighed Monty. Almost 3:00 a.m. It was another night, the third in a row, of little to no sleep. Was this right, he kept asking himself? Could it be morally justified? Can taking the life of one man, a political assassination, be justified for the greater moral good? A stopping of the expansion of slavery in the United States. He recalled his history lessons from school. The Roman senators who killed Julius Caesar apparently thought so. Would God, if he really existed, condone it? "Thou Shall Not Kill," he remembered from the Ten Commandments. But what if thousands of enslaved people, if not those living now, at least their children or grandchildren, could be brought closer to freedom by a single death? Ben seemed to have no reservations or, if he did, he didn't let on. Why was this so difficult, Monty thought to himself? Was it too late to back out now?

Beyond morality and religion, what about democracy? He believed in America, in free elections, in majority rule. Wouldn't killing the president, he thought, be repugnant to every belief that he held dear? "What are the facts?," he mumbled to himself. He rehashed them in his mind for the hundredth time. Tyler was hell-bent on annexing Texas into the Union and his secretary of state, Upshur, was dotting the I's and crossing the T's on a treaty, and had apparently gotten two-thirds of the Senate on board to make it a reality. It could all be a *fait accompli* in a couple of weeks. Now was the time to act. If not, with Texas a state, the South would have the upper hand and control of the federal government. Limiting the expansion of slavery, not to mention getting rid of it where it existed, would be a lost cause. This was not what the people had voted for in 1840, Monty thought. President Harrison, if he were alive, would not be pushing this. Tyler was a usurper, a pretender, not the duly elected president. The Constitution states that upon the president's death, the powers and duties of the office devolve on the vice president, not that he *becomes* the president. Tyler should be carrying out the policies of the deceased president, Harrison, and of the voters of the Whig Party who elected him. He had run on the Whig ticket, hadn't he? Despite this, he had used the veto power in '41 to thwart the will of the majority of the voters in the election, and had betrayed his own party. The party had rightly kicked him out. He was power-hungry, now using Texas as a way to try to get a term of his own. This was dishonorable, Monty told himself. This man deserved no sympathy. His death would restore the rightful order of things, as they had been intended by the American people in 1840.

By acting now on this plan with Ben, Monty reasoned, a true Whig, the president *pro tem* of the Senate, Senator Mangum, would become the president, or at least the acting president. He would never send the Texas treaty to the Senate for ratification. There would be a presidential election in a few months, in November, and then the voice of the people could be heard.

It was decided. Monty rolled over onto his stomach, burying his face in his moist pillow. He was not backing out. The plan would go forward.

* * *

Ben lay half-awake on his bunk on the *Princeton*, trying to get some rest after his shift on duty. It had been three days since the ship had arrived and his formal addition to the officer roster. The ship was docked at Alexandria. Out of the corner of his eye, he saw his roommate, Lieutenant Nathaniel Travis, whose shift would begin in a few minutes, donning his uniform.

"I'm not sure how much more cleaning we can do," complained Travis. "The ship is new and already looks spotless to me. But the captain and Fenwick keep saying to do more."

"Agreed," replied Ben. "The men sure were grumbling about it on my shift. I understand that the president will be aboard in a few days, but really, what do they expect? It's not like Tyler is a king, although he tends to act like one."

"Well, that's what we do, right? Follow orders, whether we like them or not," said Travis, as he put on the coat of his uniform and opened the door of the cramped officer quarters. "See you in a few hours."

Ben was glad to have some time to himself. He tried to sleep, but could not. He finally gave up and went to the small desk in the quarters. It was more of a flat board to write on than a desk.

He sat down and buried his face in his hands. Inside of a week, it would be done. Was he ready for all of this, he wondered? Giving up life as he had known it up to now? Never seeing his family, nor his friends, again? Ever. This had been his idea. He had started it. He needed to be strong and get these doubts out of his head. Monty seemed to be all in. This is the right thing to do, he kept telling himself. Striking a blow against slavery. Yes, a man would be dead, at his hand, but it would be for the greater good. Tyler does not have clean hands. He has this coming to him.

He went over the plan again in his head. Several times. What if something went wrong, before or after? He could be killed in the act. If not, he could be captured and tried. They would hang him, for sure. He knew the risks.

Ben noticed his hands shaking. He was anxious. Could he get through this? Yes, he resolved, he had to, and he would. He reached into the small drawer underneath the desktop and pulled out a sheet of paper and an envelope. He had been putting off writing a letter to his parents explaining his actions and saying goodbye. He gathered his thoughts and dipped the quill in the ink. "My Dearest Parents," he began. Once it was completed, he read it over a couple of times, was satisfied with it, addressed the envelope, waited to make sure all of the ink was dry, and then sealed the letter inside.

CHAPTER 23

February, 1844— Ben stared at the whitewashed bottom of the bunk above him. This was the day, February 28. Some early morning light was just beginning to filter in through the small window in his cramped officers' quarters on the *Princeton*. Once in a while, the docked ship swayed ever so slightly. His roommate's snoring had been annoying, but he knew that he would not have slept much anyway. If all went as planned today, he would be the first presidential assassin in American history and, by sunset, would be on his way to a new life in Canada. He thought about the planning with Monty over the past few weeks, and of their visit with Sam. He was comfortable with the decisions that he had made. Family was his main regret. He had, of course, said nothing to them. Would they be ostracized and vilified? Hopefully, the letter that he had written to his parents and given to Monty, with instructions for it to be mailed in a few days, would ease their concerns and help them understand the reasons for his actions. As a boy, they had taught him that the Declaration of Independence meant what it said, that all men are created equal; that slavery in the United States was evil, a stain on the country's honor, and should be abolished. He was acting to further that goal. He swallowed hard and extricated himself from the tight bunk space, ready to begin the day.

* * *

Monty got dressed early and left his boardinghouse for a walk. He skipped breakfast. Nervousness killed his appetite and he was in no mood to sit and make small talk with fellow boarders. The cold air hit his face as he went down the porch steps. The winter sun had just risen over the horizon, the day dawning clear and crisp, the rain from last evening having stopped. It looks like the weather will cooperate, he thought. He noticed a couple of one-horse carriages pass by, empty inside, but their drivers moving along at a good clip. Unusual, he thought, for this early in the morning.

A man on the sidewalk in front of him shouted to the driver of a third empty carriage, "Where's everyone going?"

The driver slowed and shouted back, "It's *Princeton* day. Every carriage in the city is booked. Gotta pick up the rich folks and get them to Greenleaf's Point by ten."

I will see you there, thought Monty, as he rehashed the plan for the morning in his mind. He would go to the dock at Greenleaf's Point, a peninsula at the confluence of the Potomac and Anacostia Rivers, where a large steamboat was waiting. Washington's elite, including the president, would board there and be ferried six miles down the Potomac to Alexandria, where the *Princeton* awaited. Monty would get to the dock early and observe Tyler's arrival. The man had better show up, he thought, suddenly worried. No, calming himself after a second, the president wouldn't miss this day for the world. Monty would see if there were any security guards or police with or around Tyler. Unlikely that there would be. Through his job in the Senate, he had obtained an invitation to the day's festivities. He would get on the steamer to Alexandria, looking and listening all the way. At Alexandria, he would not board the *Princeton*, but would stand on the dock at the spot that he and Ben had discussed. If nothing was amiss and if Monty had observed no unexpected risks, he would raise his hat above his head and wave it, a signal to Ben. If the plan needed to be aborted, his hat would remain on his head.

Two hours later, Monty was one of the first to arrive on the dock at Greenleaf's. On a bench, someone had left a copy of the *National Intelligencer* newspaper from a couple of days earlier. He picked it up. An article on the excursion was featured prominently on the front page. Between three and four hundred of "the cream of Washington society," he read, were expected on the *Princeton* to see firsthand "this splendid and unequalled specimen of our naval ingenuity, and to witness something of the performance of her formidable battery." Beginning at half past nine, carriage after carriage arrived, depositing well-dressed men and ladies, their finest attire covered by winter coats and hats, who then queued up on the dock in front of the steamer and had their invitations checked by two seamen before being permitted to board.

Shortly before eleven, a gate closest to the dock was opened and a handsome black carriage, with two chestnut horses, pulled up. This one has to be Tyler's, thought Monty. A young Black man riding next to the driver got down, opened the carriage door, and helped out a young lady, followed by a young man, whom Monty recognized as John, the president's son. The lady, he speculated, was Priscilla, the wife of one of Tyler's other sons, Robert, and who served as the official hostess for the widowed chief executive. A tallish and trim man in his fifties then emerged from the carriage, his distinctive aquiline nose leaving no doubt, even from the distance that Monty was observing, that it was Tyler. The president, a spring in his step, walked over to a group of a half dozen men standing nearby, heartily shook their hands, and there were broad smiles all around. Monty recognized Secretary of State Upshur and Secretary of the Navy Gilmer, the latter of whom had only been in office for a couple of weeks, and whom he had met at Stockton's recent party. The group then joined the president's family and all walked toward the steamer. Monty looked around. No noticeable police or security.

To Monty, Tyler looked like a man brimming with confidence, a man about to show all of those who looked on him as a caretaker, as the Accidental President, that this day would be his opening salvo in the campaign of 1844 and his election to a term of his own. A man who would today show the nation, indeed, the world, a demonstration of American naval superiority. A man who would soon submit his Texas annexation treaty to the Senate and who was positive that no opponent, domestic or foreign, would dare to interfere. A man for whom this bright and sunny Wednesday in February would be a day of triumph.

After the president and his entourage were aboard, Monty got in line and had his invitation checked.

The steamer pulled away from the dock twenty minutes past its scheduled time of eleven, riding low in the water, due to the heavy load of passengers. A quick stop was made at the nearby Navy Yard, where a Marine band boarded. As the ship slowly chugged along, Monty spotted Dolley Madison surrounded by a crowd, as usual. Despite her age, he knew that she would not miss this event, a highlight of the winter's social events in Washington City. He caught her eye and blew her a kiss. She smiled at him and batted her eyelashes. Still a flirt, even in her seventies. Good for her, he thought.

Monty went to an upper deck and came upon Captain Stockton, encircled by a group of men. He recognized one as Senator Thomas Hart Benton of Missouri, a Democrat, in office for ages, who had been the right-hand man in the Senate for Jackson and Van Buren during their administrations. Benton and Senator Clay, Monty recalled, had sparred a lot over the years. "I tell you," he overheard Stockton say to Senator Benton, "it is not only the propeller system and engines that are revolutionary. The two cannons are equally so. The art of gunning for sea-service has, for the first time, been reduced to something like mathematical certainty."

"It sure sounds impressive, captain. A ball weighing more than two hundred pounds, you say, shot downrange, with precision, for up to five miles? If your ship can do that," replied the Missouri senator, "then the administration will have my vote for a fleet of them."

Stockton put his left hand on Benton's shoulder, heartily shook the senator's right hand, and looked up at the clear blue winter sky. "On this glorious day, you will see it with your own eyes." Stockton then moved on, no doubt, Monty thought, to lobby more members of Congress on the wonders of his new ship.

By noon, the *Princeton* came into view. As the steamer got closer, a reflection of the warship's three masts and rigging could be seen shimmering on the calm waters of the Potomac. All of her crew were on deck, in dress uniform, standing at attention. The Stars and Stripes flapped in the gentle breeze from her stern. The flags of other nations were also on display. Stockton had invited several members of the Diplomatic Corps to this show of American military power. Of the two nations of most interest to the Tyler Administration, Mexico and Great Britain, the Mexican minister, General Juan Almonte, had accepted, but the British minister, Sir Richard Pakenham, had declined. As the steamer circled the ship for all to get a good view, Monty saw the two massive twelve-inch bore cannons on the deck that everyone had been talking about. At the stern, the Oregon was mounted and, at the bow, the larger Peacemaker.

A ramp was placed from the hurricane deck of the steamer to the *Princeton*. The president, his family, and his cabinet were the first to cross, as the band played *The Star Spangled Banner*. Captain Stockton stood at the end of the ramp, greeting the arrivals. It was hard to tell, Monty thought, who looked prouder, Stockton or Tyler. Still no sign of any police or security near the president. None of Stockton's sailors hovered around him. The president was among friends and supporters. No need for protection. Everything looked good, Monty decided. The plan was a go. When he saw that no one was watching him, Monty exited the steamer from the other side, and walked to the wharf, where hundreds of people had assembled to watch the sendoff. Finding the spot that he and Ben had discussed, he stood there while the rest of the passengers crossed over to the *Princeton*. He spotted Ben near the bow, standing in a row of four officers.

When he was sure that Ben was looking in his direction, he raised his hat high above his head and waved it. Ben nodded. Message received.

* * *

Ben had been all over the ship that morning. Though the *Princeton* was still new, he had to admit that the constant cleaning that the crew had done over the past few days had made her look even better. Every board on the deck had been scrubbed and every piece of metal had been polished. Below deck, the temporary walls that created the quarters for the seamen and junior officers had been removed, creating a large open area that was as wide as the ship, and extended almost her full length. A long table, with more than a hundred chairs surrounding it, had been placed on one side of this room. For the past two days, Ben had helped supervise receipt of the deliveries, brought in mostly from Philadelphia, for the feast that was to be served. Stockton had bragged to his officers that much better-quality food and drink was available there, and made sure all knew that he was footing the entire bill himself. Hams, turkeys, fruits, breads, cakes, and cheeses of every kind. And crates of wine and champagne, lots of champagne, known to be the president's favorite libation.

That morning, Stockton had updated Ben and the other officers on the day's schedule, which was little changed from what he had told them a few days earlier. Anchor up at Alexandria shortly after noon. Down the Potomac to just past Mount Vernon, part with sails unfurled, and part without sails, the latter to demonstrate the power of the ship's innovative engines and screw-driven propeller. Three firings of the massive cannons, the Oregon and the Peacemaker, one or both, were planned. Two would occur when heading downriver and the third at the turn at Mount Vernon, to be made in honor of George Washington. It was this third firing that Ben cared about most. It was the key to the plan. There would be a feast for the guests with two seatings, ladies first, and then the men. Ben and the other officers had been instructed by Stockton to mingle with those on board, to tout the features of the ship and, without explicitly being told by him to do so, to laud its captain. Just in case the implication from Stockton was not enough, Commander Fenwick had later told the officers, more than once, to miss no opportunity to sing the praises of the captain. The ship should be back to Alexandria by five or six in the afternoon.

As the *Princeton* began to unfurl her sails and slowly glide on the water, Ben heard three loud cheers from the crowd assembled on the wharf, knowing that Monty was somewhere in its midst. It was a melancholy moment for him. He reflected on the fact that, after today, he would never see his good friend again, nor anyone who had been part of his life. Canada awaited. The twelve smaller cannons on the ship, forty-two-pound carronades, six on each side of the deck, were fired twenty-six times in slow succession, an honorary salute to each state in the Union. When the sails were fully down, the band played *Hail Columbia*, and the grand excursion was under way.

Mingle, Ben remembered. Failure to do so would likely draw attention to him from Stockton and the other officers. That was the last thing he wanted. He walked about the deck and introduced himself to a stout, dark-haired man who appeared to be in his forties. "Congressman George Sykes, from New Jersey," came the reply. "Pleased to meet you, lieutenant. This is a proud day for our country! A grand ship this is!" A stiff breeze kicked up, causing the sails to become full. The man pulled up the collar of his topcoat.

"Yes sir, it is. So proud to have been assigned to her," said Ben. "You must go below later and inspect the engines. A marvel, they are."

"I had the good fortune of seeing Captain Stockton last evening at his hotel," said the congressman. "Impressive man! He expressed to me his nervousness that something may go amiss today, worried about so many ladies on board. Rubbish, I told him! If this ship is half as good as I have read about and heard, he should sleep like a babe."

"Indeed, he should."

"I hear there is quite an assortment of fine wines below. One of my weaknesses. I believe I will go down and partake," said Sykes, shaking Ben's hand, as he turned to go below deck. "A pleasure to have met you. Our nation is so fortunate to have young men such as you."

"Thank you, sir." I doubt he will feel that way about me tomorrow, mused Ben.

Ben heard a familiar voice, coming from the stern. It was Commander Fenwick, addressing all within shouting distance. "Ladies and gentlemen, we will be firing the Peacemaker in about ten minutes. Gather around then at the bow and witness a demonstration of the *Princeton's* firepower."

Although not an artillery officer, Ben was familiar with the process required to safely load a naval cannon for firing. For the Peacemaker, it took four seamen and an officer. A wet swab on a large pole was inserted to mop out the barrel, to make sure there were no embers left from prior firings. A gunpowder cartridge, enclosed in canvas, was inserted down the barrel, followed by cloth wadding, and then was rammed tightly in place. This massive cannon could hold a charge of up to fifty pounds; one of twenty-five would be used for today's demonstration. Then, the cannonball, weighing more than two hundred pounds, was lifted and rolled down the barrel, followed by another piece of wadding. The Peacemaker was mounted on a turntable and, once loaded, the in-charge officer, Lieutenant Hunt, would perform the mathematical calculations needed for direction and elevation, taking into account the wind and the roll of the ship, to accurately reach the target. Once done, the turntable was locked in place. Through the small touch hole in the cannon's base, a rod was inserted to prick the gunpowder cartridge and then, through a porcupine quill, fine gunpowder was poured down the touch hole, which was topped by a flint mechanism, with a lanyard of several feet attached to it. When all was set, the lanyard was pulled from a safe distance, the flint sparked, and the cannon roared, propelling the ball to its destination.

After a few minutes, Ben walked toward the bow to witness the firing. There, he almost walked into Dolley Madison. He wondered if she remembered him. He extended his hand, and she hers. "My apologies, Mrs. Madison. Benjamin Geddis, I had the pleasure of making your acquaintance at Captain Stockton's recent party at Gadsby's."

"Yes, yes, lieutenant, you are Mr. Tolliver's friend. Is he aboard? I saw him on the steamer this morning."

Dammit, why would he have let her see him on the steamer, wondered Ben, worried over how to explain Monty's absence. He thought quickly. "Unfortunately, no, I saw him but for a fleeting moment. He got a message in Alexandria and shouted to me from the steamer that some urgent matter had come up in the Senate and he had to get back to the city."

"Heavens, I can't imagine what that would be. Half of the Senate is on this ship!" replied the former first lady, but seeming to accept his explanation.

"Do you plan to watch the firing of the Peacemaker?" inquired Ben.

"I am hesitant. Is it wise for an old lady such as me?"

"You most assuredly should. It will be the highlight of the day. With your permission," Ben offered, "I would be happy to stand by you and we can experience it together." He noticed that the artillery seamen had almost completed the loading of the cannon.

She hesitated for a moment, and then a broad smile came across her face, "Let's do it," she said.

At that moment, Commander Fenwick shouted, "One minute to firing!"

The president and most of his cabinet had walked over and stood behind Captain Stockton, who was closest to the artillery crew. A look of eager anticipation, Ben noticed, was on Tyler's rugged face.

"Let's move back a bit," Ben said, as he grabbed Mrs. Madison's hand and led her toward the rear of the large crowd that had gathered at the bow of the ship. "A sailor's tip," he said looking directly at her, "Open your mouth as wide as you can," and demonstrating. "It lessens the pressure on the ears."

Stockton, of course, gave himself the honor of pulling the lanyard and firing the Peacemaker. The whole ship shook and the noise was deafening. A cloud of thick black smoke engulfed the area surrounding the cannon, and lasted for several seconds.

The widow of the former president tightly squeezed Ben's hand, her mouth agape. Pretty good grip strength for someone her age, he thought. Many in the crowd followed the flight of the ball down the wide Potomac, landing about two miles away. "There, did you see it skip on the water before submerging!" exclaimed one man. Ben glanced over at Tyler and his cabinet, who were backslapping each other like excited schoolboys.

"We survived!," Ben said to Mrs. Madison. "That wasn't so bad, was it?"

"How exciting! I wish my Jemmy could have seen it. Thank you, lieutenant, I would not have had the courage to watch it without you."

"Glad to have been of service," he responded, as some of her friends came up.

"Heavens, Dolley, where have you been? Are you alright?," asked a middle-aged lady, a worried look on her face.

"Oh, Frances, calm down. Lieutenant Geddis here has been taking good care of me," looking at Ben and giving him a wink.

He left her safely in the care of her friends and decided to go below to check out the preparations for the feast. As he walked along the deck, he smiled. Dolley Madison, he realized, had just winked at him. And then, a darker thought. It would be the last moment of happiness in his life for some time. A nice memory to have. "Focus, focus!" he said, mouthing the words under his breath. He made his way down the wooden steps at the stern of the ship leading below deck. The food was still being spread out on the large table. He spotted President Tyler, who had already made his way below, a glass of champagne in hand, engaged in lively conversation and laughter with two striking young women and an older gentleman.

He asked a fellow officer if he knew to whom Tyler was speaking. "That would be David Gardiner, a wealthy state senator from New York, and his two daughters. They are in Washington City for the social season. Rumor has it," said Ben's colleague, whispering, "that the president is infatuated with the dark-haired older sister, Julia, and recently proposed marriage, but was rejected."

"Interesting," replied Ben, also in a hushed tone, "and here I was under the impression that he was still a grieving widower. How old is she, half his age?"

"Oh, way less than that. Twenty-three, I heard."

"Some of his children are older," replied an amazed Ben. He felt a sense of relief that the young lady had rejected Tyler's proposal; perhaps she would not be as grief-stricken by what Ben had planned in an hour or so. Focus, he thought again to himself, irritated that he had let emotions slip into his head. There was a cause that had brought him to this day, and it was much bigger and more important than the sadness of one person. He made his way back up to the deck and noticed that the river had widened, with the Virginia and Maryland banks on either side more distant than before.

The voice of Captain Stockton resonated again over the crowded deck of the *Princeton*. "Ladies and gentlemen," he shouted, "our afternoon repast is set to begin. Ladies, please make your way below for the first seating. Gentlemen, it will then be your turn. We will have two more firings of the Peacemaker, the last as we make our turn at Mount Vernon, in honor of our first president, George Washington."

There was a round of applause and the ladies started toward the stern to go below deck. Now was the time for Ben to begin his preparations. He went below and, as the ladies began seating themselves, walked down the narrow hallway that led to the officers' quarters. Once in his small room, he reached into the drawer that held his clothes, next to his bunk, pulled out what he needed, and put it in the inside pocket of his uniform.

CHAPTER 24

February, 1844— Captain Sam Shipley awoke in his bunk in his quarters at Fort Washington at a very soldierly five o'clock. A quick breakfast in the officers' mess was followed by morning reveille and flag raising in the fort's large center court. He looked up at the clear blue sky and felt the gentle winter breeze. For the end of winter, he thought, it looked to be a good day to be on the water. What would this day bring, he wondered? What had Monty and Ben gotten him into? After doing some paperwork at his desk, he walked over to the enlisted men's barracks.

"Good morning, Sergeant O'Reilly," he said to the head of one of the artillery platoons under his command. "I need to take one of the small steamers, make it the *Monroe*, out on patrol at midday. Please have a couple of the men get the tarpaulins off, clean her up, and the boiler heated. Have her ready to go at noon."

"Yes, sir," responded the sergeant, "How many men will you want to accompany you?"

"None," said Sam. "just a routine patrol. I can handle it alone. The *Princeton* will be coming by us on its way to Mount Vernon this afternoon and I want to make sure none of the ships following her get too close and cause any trouble, at least not while she is on the river in front of us. There are sure to be gawkers."

"Yes sir. I heard from some of the officers that the president will be on board. Good to take extra precautions."

"I understand that he will be, and I agree. And sergeant," added Sam, "you can keep this between us. Not a formal order from above, just something that I think is appropriate."

"Consider it done, sir. We can't be too careful where our commander-in-chief is concerned."

Sam left the barracks and walked out of the main fort to the nearby stables. He found the stall of the chestnut gelding that Monty and Ben had left with him last week. Rubbing the horse's soft nose, he checked him over, and went into the tack room and saw that the saddle and saddlebag were where he had left them. He bridled and saddled the horse and led him into the woods just south of the fort and tied him there, surrounded by hay that he had earlier spread on the ground. That should, he was sure, keep the horse satisfied for a good while. He then made his way back to his desk and pretended, with difficulty, to do some work. It seemed like time was standing still. He was anxious over the events to take place the coming hours. Was he up to it, he wondered? Finally, he heard the bell from the chapel inside the fort toll twelve times. He walked down the steep hill toward the river. Halfway, he saw puffs of smoke coming from the smokestack on the small steamer that had been prepared, per his instructions. A lone seaman was loading more coal into the bin next to the boiler as Sam stepped aboard. The man turned and saluted.

"She's all fired up and ready for you, sir. Enough coal here for about six hours. Equipment all in the storage locker, as you requested—filled water canteens, signal flags, rope, you name it. The tarpaulins are stored there also."

Sam returned the salute. "Thank you, seaman. Dismissed."

Sam eased the ship away from the dock. The paddlewheel turned faster as the engine slowly picked up steam. He squinted at the bright sunlight reflecting off of the placid Potomac and headed toward the main channel. Once he rounded a bend in the river and was away from a view from the dock, he opened the duffle bag he had brought along and got out what he needed, exchanging his officer's coat and hat for a dark blue peacoat and a black wool knit cap. He pulled out two tarpaulins from the locker and draped them over both sides of the ship, covering its name and number. He looked around. Had he forgotten any-thing? The flag! How could he have forgotten that? He quickly pulled the Stars and Stripes from the pole in the ship's rear, and steered the ship to mid-river, about a mile upstream from Mount Vernon, to await the *Princeton*.

* * *

Monty watched the crowd depart the wharf in Alexandria and decided to stay in town. No sense in going back to Washington City. Any news from the *Princeton* would arrive here first. He wondered how people would react to the death of the president. Outrage at first, he was sure, but then maybe there would be a realization over time that it was for the good of the country, especially if this Texas mess was stopped by it. He thought about Senator Clay. Would this help him in the upcoming campaign?

Yes, he believed it would. He had not done this for Clay, and the senator knew nothing about it. But there was a risk. If Monty's fingerprints were ever found on the events of this day, even though he had not worked for Clay for almost two years, it could bring Clay down. The Democrats would try to hang it around Clay's neck and argue that he had been complicit in the assassination. He was sure that he had been careful, confident that only Ben and Sam knew of the plot.

He decided to walk over to Duke Street. It was there that the slave auction had taken place, almost two years ago. That was the day that had changed his views on slavery, and which had led to this day. He wondered about Delores. Did she make it to Canada? Was she having a good life? It had to be better than the enslaved life that she would have faced had he not intervened. Did she still think of him? He hoped so. He walked by 1315 Duke Street. The same sign, Kephart and Company, was above the door. He saw a couple of people go in and out, but it was otherwise quiet. Fortunately, there were no slave auctions scheduled for today. That was not something that he ever wanted to witness again.

Monty's worries then shifted to Ben. Would Ben be successful in his mission and, with Sam's help, get away safely? Would his trip go smoothly? Would he get to Canada? Maybe, he speculated, Ben and Delores would pass each other one day on the streets of Montreal, or Toronto, not knowing that their lives were intertwined through him. The thought brought a slight smile to his face.

He walked back toward the dock and stopped in a café, mostly to get out of the cold air for a while. He ordered some lunch, but ate very little. It was going to be a long afternoon of waiting.

CHAPTER 25

February, 1844— Ben watched as the ladies enjoyed their meal, and as the men stood about and chatted, most with drinks in their hands. He scanned the cabin and observed President Tyler and Secretary Upshur engaged in conversation. He walked over to another officer standing behind them and made pleasantries, in a successful attempt to eavesdrop on some of the conversation.

"Did you see the look on the Mexican minister's face after the firing of the Peacemaker?," said Tyler.

"Indeed, I did," replied Upshur, "General Almonte was more than suitably impressed. I don't think we will be having much trouble from our friends to the south when the news of our treaty breaks."

"Agreed, but it's the British that worry me more. Shame they are not here."

"Minister Pakenham's failure to show up is surely a snub to our country, and to you. His absence is intended as a statement," said Upshur, "but rest assured he has eyes on board who saw everything and who will report to him."

"I suspect you are right; our message will be delivered. One way or another," said the president. "Stockton has put on quite the show today. A good man. We were right to put him in charge of rebuilding the Navy. I can't wait to see the headlines in the newspapers over the next few days. We can definitely move forward with our plan, and quickly."

"You are right about that, sir. I was up late last night looking over the treaty. It is almost finished. I'm thinking another week or so and we can have it signed by the Texians and submit it to the Senate."

"Excellent!," replied Tyler.

Ben noticed the ladies had finished eating and had begun to leave the table. The Marine band was set up in a corner of the cabin, softly playing patriotic airs and other popular tunes. Fenwick was walking around the room, going up to several groups and pointing toward the stairway up to the deck. "Second firing in five minutes," he kept saying, over the din of conversations. Most men complied and headed up, while many of the ladies stayed in place.

"No more for me," Ben overheard one lady say to another. "My ears are still ringing from the last one."

"Men and their weapons!" replied her friend, as she rolled her eyes. "The size of guns fascinates them. The bigger, in their view, the better. Seen one, seen them all, as far as I am concerned."

Ben went up on deck and saw that all of the dignitaries were in the same place as before, with Stockton directly behind the cannon and Tyler and his cabinet members just to his rear. He stood back, at a distance, watching. This will work, he thought. No problem getting into position next time. He looked toward the mid-section of the ship and memorized the scene. His escape route. A couple of minutes later, there was a loud roar, the ship shook, a cloud of black smoke, and the second cannonball of the day was propelled out of the Peacemaker and sent speeding on its trek down the Potomac. Ben counted the seconds until the smoke began to clear and he could see Stockton and Tyler again. Fifteen. Should be enough time.

The excitement once again over, the crowd meandered below and the men's turn at the table began. Stockton was seated at the head. The president was at his right, with Postmaster General Wickliffe next to him. To Stockton's left sat Senator Woodbury of New Hampshire, and then Secretary of State Upshur. Ben, definitely without an appetite and his stomach churning from nervousness, stood nearby, and tried to look important by making sure that the seamen doing the serving quickly replenished the food and drink. In one corner near the table, empty bottles of wine and champagne, about forty so far, were neatly stacked on their sides. "There are the dead men," one of Ben's fellow officers joked to him as he walked by, pointing to the bottles, and adding, "and their number will surely grow." Well into the devouring of the turkey, ham, breads, and cheeses, Stockton rose, and got the attention of all. Ben took it all in. The captain looked to his right and raised his glass, "A toast to the President of the United States! His foresight and determination have given our country this great ship," he bellowed. Glasses were raised and there was applause from all at the long table and those surrounding it. "Three cheers for the President!," someone shouted, and the cheers were robustly given. Tyler looked as proud as a peacock. He stood, thanked all, and raised his glass and offered his own toast, "To the three big guns—the Peacemaker, the Oregon, and Captain Stockton!" Stockton's face beamed.

The meal ending, Fenwick made the rounds announcing to all the third firing of the Peacemaker. Ben saw Stockton and some of Tyler's cabinet members head up the stairs to the deck. He followed, at a discrete distance. The moment was at hand. His stomach churned more. He looked up and to the ship's starboard side and, on a high bluff, could just make out the cupula and roof of Mount Vernon. He got into position a few feet to the left and to the rear of Stockton, directly behind the spot where Tyler had stood last time. He again went over in his mind the plan that he and Monty had discussed a dozen times. He would position himself squarely behind Tyler and, as Stockton ignited the Peacemaker, he would raise his pistol and fire it into the back of the president's head. Amid the sound and fury of the cannon, with the cloud of black smoke engulfing the immediate area, and with all eyes trying to follow the ball's flight through the air, Ben and Monty had figured that Ben would have, before the fate of Tyler was discovered, about fifteen seconds to make his escape. The earlier firings had confirmed that estimate. He would slowly move a couple of steps backward, then run toward mid-ship, strip off his uniform coat and his boots, and toss them, along with the gun, into the Potomac. He would then jump off the ship's side and start swimming toward Fort Washington. Sam would be nearby, watching through his spyglass aboard his steamer, and would head Ben's way. In the frigid late February waters of the Potomac, Ben and Monty thought he would have about ten minutes before hypothermia set in. Maybe, with his experience from swimming in the cold waters of Rhode Island, he could last a couple of minutes more. Sam would get him aboard and steer the steamer to the secluded spot that they had selected just south of the fort during Ben and Monty's recent visit. The horse that they had brought and left with Sam would be there, saddled and tied. A quick change into the dry clothes in the saddlebag, and off he would go, headed east toward the Chesapeake Bay, to Deale, to begin his route via the Underground Railroad to Canada.

CHAPTER 26

February, 1844— Ben's heart pounded. He was in position. The Peacemaker was pointed down the wide channel of the Potomac. He looked up. The sun was bright and there was no wind. The sails were all furled and the ship was running smoothly, solely on the power of the unseen engines. In front of him and to his right, he saw Stockton, less than ten feet away, his foot again resting on the cannon's carriage. He unbuttoned the coat of his uniform and patted his loaded pistol. The artillery crew of four seamen and Lieutenant Hunt were in position on both sides of the cannon. Just to his left, Ben saw the backs of the heads of Secretary Upshur and Secretary Gilmer. Next to them was Gardiner, the man whom he had learned earlier was the father of the lovely Julia, the new object of Tyler's affections. Others stood to their left and to their right. Behind him, more than a hundred more, mostly men, looked on. But where was Tyler? An anxious Ben scanned the scene. Just then, Stockton said, in a loud voice, to the surrounding crowd, "Folks, just waiting for the president." He pointed to an officer standing near the foremast. "Lieutenant, go check on his status."

"Yes sir, captain" came the reply, and the lieutenant hurried toward the stern and the stairs leading below deck.

"Everyone enjoying the day?," asked Stockton to the crowd, filling the time.

Ben heard replies of "Splendid!," "Wonderful!," "Top notch!," and "The Brits are quaking!," among others.

Stockton looked up at the clear blue winter sky. "God has given us a perfect day," he loudly said to all. "We and our country are truly blessed!"

After a couple of minutes, the lieutenant returned. "The president is detained below," he reported to Stockton. "He said to proceed without him."

"Are you sure?," replied Stockton, unable to hide the dejection on his face.

"Quite sure, sir."

One person on the deck was even more disappointed than Stockton. "The bastard!" murmured Ben under his breath. His mind raced. How could Tyler not be here? He should be standing directly in front of Ben right now. What to do? All of this planning for naught. This could not be happening. Within a few seconds, he had decided on an alternative plan. Tyler, he resolved, was not getting off this ship alive. To hell with what he had promised Monty. Ben's life was no longer important. He would sacrifice himself to accomplish his mission. As soon as the smoke from the firing of the Peacemaker cleared, he would go below, find the president, and shoot him in the head at point-blank range. Hopefully, he would then have time to reload the pistol and use a second bullet on himself before being subdued. If not, he knew what the consequences would be and was willing to face them. He looked to his right and saw Stockton raise his right arm to begin the firing process.

CHAPTER 27

February, 1844— "Lieutenant, can you hear me?" Ben felt someone gently slapping his left cheek. He opened his eyes. The man's voice sounded familiar, but the face was a blur. "Praise be to God! You had us worried, young man." Ben raised his hands to his throbbing head, and rubbed his eyes and forehead. He tried to speak. No words came. After several more seconds, his vision improved slightly. He looked to his left and realized that he was lying on a mattress, at floor level. The coat of his uniform had been removed and he was covered by a blanket. The man was seated next to him. He could make out a ceiling above, and heard loud footsteps on a wooden floor all around him.

"I'm Congressman Sykes, lieutenant. We spoke earlier on the deck. Remember?"

A few words finally came out, no louder than a whisper. "Yes, from New Jersey," said Ben, "What happened?

"The Peacemaker exploded on firing," replied Sykes. "A terrible tragedy. We found you lying unconscious by one of the carronades. You were blown back by the force of the blast and must have hit your head on it. We brought you here, below deck. A doctor on board checked you out. No bleeding or wounds that we can see. Here, take a sip of water."

Ben lifted his head slightly and put his lips to the offered canteen. He felt the refreshing water slide down his parched throat.

"How long have I been out?"

"About twenty minutes."

"Were others injured?," he asked.

"I'm afraid so. At least eight dead, Secretary Upshur and Secretary Gilmer among them. Probably twenty wounded. Some severely."

Ben began to notice more of his surroundings. He could see that he was but one of several people lying on mattresses on the floor of the cabin of the ship, where only an hour or so earlier Stockton's grand feast had been served. His senses improved. He recalled his mission. His last memory was one of being anxious and upset. He could see the scene in his mind. Tyler, what about Tyler? He remembered that Tyler had not been there. "What about the president?," he inquired of Sykes.

"A miracle!" responded the congressman. "He was here, below deck, and was out of harm's way. I saw him on the steps not a minute before the explosion and we were both headed up. I thought he was right behind me, but Providence kept him here and safe."

"A miracle indeed," murmured a disappointed Ben.

He heard the rustling of a lady's dress approach, its wearer taking a seat in an empty chair by his mattress, next to Sykes. He looked up and saw a familiar face. A soft hand reached out and caressed his hand. "Mrs. Madison," said Ben, "so glad to see that you are unharmed."

"I stopped by a couple of times earlier to check on you. Wonderful to see that you are now stirring. How are you feeling?"

"Like someone took a sledgehammer to my head, but nothing serious otherwise, as far as I can tell. I hear that I am one of the lucky ones."

"An unimaginable tragedy," she responded. Ben noticed some tears form in her eyes. "I cannot speak of what I have seen."

Just then, an officer, whose name Ben could not recall, walked by and announced, "We put in at Alexandria in fifteen minutes. Ambulances will be waiting to transport the wounded."

* * *

Over the next several days, newspapers described in detail to the nation the devastation of the explosion on the *Princeton*. A "Most Awful and Lamentable Tragedy," read the headline in the *National Intelligencer*, one of Washington City's leading papers. "Horrible Accident! Great Gloom in Washington," proclaimed the *New York Herald*. The Peacemaker had exploded near its breech on one side during its third firing of the day, near Mount Vernon, shooting chunks of iron, some weighing more than a ton, across the deck. There were eight fatalities and almost thirty wounded. The press did not spare the gory details and there was a melancholy fascination among the public about them. Virgil Maxcy, a former American diplomat to Belgium, was killed instantly, his body mutilated, losing both arms and a leg. The chest of Commodore Beverly Kennon, a high-level official in the Navy Department, was crushed from a chunk of the cannon. He died within minutes, likely of suffocation. David Gardiner, from New York, who had been aboard with his two adult daughters, one of whom was the object of President Tyler's affections, also died within minutes. Two Cabinet members, Secretary of State Abel Upshur and the recently-appointed Secretary of the Navy Thomas Gilmer, fell side-by-side where they were struck, Upshur likely dead before he hit the deck, and Gilmer shortly thereafter. Blood flowed from their ears, but their bodies otherwise appeared uninjured. Three others, an enslaved man of President Tyler, named Armistead, and two seamen on the cannon's artillery crew, lost their lives. Twenty feet of railing on the starboard side of the ship was blown away and numerous hats were seen floating in the water. Initial reports, later determined to be unfounded, were that several people had been blown overboard and drowned. A senator hit his head on the deck and was unconscious for a few minutes. Several members of the ship's crew likewise had head injuries, as well as broken bones, cuts, and bruises. Fortunately, there were two doctors on board who tended to the injured as the ship made its way back to Alexandria.

Captain Robert Stockton, the man nearest to the base of the cannon during the explosion, amazingly survived with no serious injuries. The heat from the blast singed off much of his facial hair, his face and hands were burned, and a piece of shrapnel went through one of his legs. Dazed and confused, he was taken below to his quarters by some of his crew, where his wounds were dressed. He then returned topside to oversee the aftermath of the tragedy on his beloved *Princeton*. "Would to God that I had alone been slain," he cried out, "and all of my friends saved!"

The life of President Tyler, the newspapers reported, had been spared by a song. As he was heading up the steps to the deck to watch the third firing of the cannon, according to the papers, he decided to stop and listen to the singing of an old song that was one of his favorites from his youth. As it ended, he heard the blast from above, thinking, as did the others below deck, that it was the routine firing of the cannon. Minutes later, people rushed down the steps from the deck and the truth became known. Had he been on the deck, he would have been standing with Upshur and Gilmer, and would likely have met the same fate.

CHAPTER 28

January, 1849— There had been a steady stream of visitors to the small green-shuttered townhouse on the east side of Lafayette Square all afternoon. As he approached the three marble entry steps, Henry Clay tipped his hat to the man walking out. "A happy 1849 to you, Mr. Vice President," he said to George Dallas, from Pennsylvania, of the outgoing Polk Administration.

"And to you, Mr. Clay. Congratulations on your soon-to-be return to the Senate. Our political merry-go-round continues. We Democrats are headed out of power and you Whigs are headed in again."

"Thank you. So it goes. It will turn again in your favor at some point, I am certain. How is our hostess?"

"As spry as ever. Eighty years old and she still has the best New Year's Day open house in the city."

Clay had not seen his old friend Dolley Madison for a few years. Probably, he thought, not since 1842, when he was last in the Senate. Last fall, the Kentucky Legislature had again honored him by naming him to one of the Bluegrass State's seats in the Senate. He would be taking office in early March, when the Whig Administration of the incoming president, General Zachary Taylor, would be taking the reins of the federal executive branch. He had a tenuous relationship with Taylor, another military man with no political experience, nominated by the Whigs as a vote-getter, not for any strongly held political philosophy or beliefs. Just like Harrison, in his opinion. Maybe worse. And that had turned out to be a disaster. At least Taylor's vice president, Congressman Millard Fillmore of New York, was, Clay was certain, a true Whig and one of his supporters.

He walked through the crowded small townhouse and greeted the widow of James Madison, "Dolley, you look wonderful! A Happy New Year to you!," he said, as he took her hand and gave it a kiss.

"Why Henry Clay, what a pleasant surprise! I did not know you were in town already. Is Lucretia with you?"

"Heavens, no. You know well that she had more than enough of the political life in Washington City decades ago. She hasn't set foot here since I was secretary of state. I doubt I will ever get her to leave Ashland again."

"I am so glad that you are returning to the Senate. These are trying times. All this sectional division."

"Thank you, Dolley. That is the reason I decided to come back. I was hesitant to accept, but I am worried about our country. Maybe an old man like me can do some good and help to diffuse the situation before I depart the stage."

"I hope so. You've done it before. Texas and the war with Mexico sure stirred up a hornet's nest."

"That's for sure. We shall see. Each side seems more entrenched in their position than in the past."

"I also read in the newspapers," said Mrs. Madison, "that the nice young man who used to work for you, Mr. Tolliver, has been elected to Congress from Ohio and will also be taking his seat in March."

"Yes, Monty will be coming in as a congressman. I was not aware that you were acquainted with him. Best man that I ever had work for me. Very bright and very capable."

"I am not surprised by that. Yes, I had the pleasure of first meeting him when he was on your staff, and then also a few times when he worked for the Senate. I saw him and his good friend, an officer in the Navy, at some social events around town a few years ago. He served on the *Princeton*. They were both very kind to me. An old lady remembers such things. The last time that I saw the two of them was on that terrible day of the explosion. I was on board that day, you know."

"Yes, I am so sorry that you had to endure that," said Clay.

"I rarely speak of it. That morning, I saw Mr. Tolliver on the steamer from Greenleaf's Point to Alexandria but, by the grace of God, he did not get on board the *Princeton*. I saw his friend later that day on board the warship and he said that Mr. Tolliver had some urgent business to attend to in the city and had to leave. His friend was injured in the explosion. I helped tend to him. I am so glad that Mr. Tolliver did not have to experience that tragedy. His change of plans may have saved his life. I still have nightmares about it. I wish that I had never set foot on that ship. But there I go again, an old lady rambling."

"We never know what fate holds for us. That you found the courage to nurse others in a time of need is not surprising, and is commendable," responded Clay. He grabbed two champagne coupes from a server walking through the crowded living room in the rowhouse, and turned and handed one to Dolley. "A toast to you, Mrs. Madison, on this New Year's Day, and to the memory of your late husband, the father of our Constitution and a great president!"

He mingled with the other guests, who included a handful of current House members and senators, and some cabinet secretaries from past administrations. An almost equal mix of Democrats and Whigs, he noted. It was a display of bipartisanship that was getting rarer in Washington City. Everyone, he thought to himself, loves Dolley. She transcends politics. As he left, Clay pondered the upcoming 1849 session of Congress and the inauguration of General Taylor as president, and whether sectional divisions over slavery had become so divisive that a bipartisan solution was not possible.

As he walked back to his hotel, Clay also thought about what Dolley had said about his former aide. Monty had never mentioned anything to him about having planned to be on the *Princeton* that fateful day, nor of having a friend who had been one of the ship's officers and who had been injured in the explosion. They had been exchanging letters around that time, and since then. Seems like it was something that he would have written about. He would have to ask Monty about it when he next saw him.

CHAPTER 29

March, 1844— Ben lifted up the rope that was strung along the dock at the Washington Navy Yard, crossing underneath it between two seamen, armed with rifles on their shoulders, who stood on either side of the gangway. They recognized him, and he returned their salutes. "Here to pick up a few things from my quarters," he said. From the dock, the *Princeton* showed no visible signs of the tragedy. Still woozy from the concussion he sustained in the explosion two days earlier, he steadied himself as he walked up the creaky wooden ramp. The last forty-eight hours had been a blur. Nothing had turned out as expected. By now, he thought that he would be the most wanted man in America, the assassin of the president of the United States, and on his way, via the Underground Railroad, to Canada and a new life. He would probably by now have been in Delaware, or maybe New Jersey, he guessed. It was a fate that he had been prepared, even eager, to accept. The sound of his boots landing on the deck brought him back to reality. He was still a naval officer, in good standing, his treasonous plot with Monty unfulfilled and undiscovered, halted moments before its execution by an unexpected tragedy.

He did not notice anyone else aboard. He walked to the ship's bow and to the scene of the catastrophe. The Peacemaker was still there. He put his fingers in the gaping hole on the side near its breech. He turned and looked at the carronades that lined the sides of the ship, the first one about twenty feet away, likely the one that he had been thrown into by the force of the blast, and where he had lain, unconscious. The silence on the ship was broken by a squawking sound from above. He looked up and saw two seagulls on one of the upper yards of the foremast. Lowering his eyes, Ben stared at the bloodstains that were still on the deck and walked over and stood over the largest one. "Why couldn't Tyler have been standing right here, dammit," he muttered to himself. It would have accomplished his and Monty's goal, and something good could have come from this. Or maybe something did, he thought. Would Secretary Upshur's death stop, or at least delay, the Texas treaty? He would have to wait and see what happened and get together with Monty and make new plans, if needed. Nothing had changed in his views toward the president. If the annexation of Texas was still likely to be approved by the Senate, he was determined that Tyler needed to be stopped, and he was prepared to do it, whatever it took.

Ben went below deck. The long table from the banquet was shoved to the side. He remembered Washington's elite sitting around it, so gay and celebratory. He had planned for their party to end in death, the death of the president, but fate had intervened and other lives had been taken. He looked over to the area where he had regained his senses, lying on a mattress on the floor, and attended to by Congressman Sykes and Dolley

Madison. Ben made a mental note. Have to make calls on them, or at least write notes, to thank them. One of those things his mother had instilled in him as a child.

He walked back to the narrow hallway that led to the officers' quarters and went into the small room that he shared with Lieutenant Travis. This was the purpose of his visit, to make sure that he did not leave any incriminating clues about the assassination plot. He thought there were none, but, paranoid, he wanted to make certain. There was enough light coming in from the small portal window that he didn't need to light a candle. He looked at his small writing desk, with nothing on it, and opened the three drawers underneath. Some writing paper, and a couple of navy manuals. He glanced at the handful of books that he had brought on board only a week or so earlier and put on a shelf, to make it look like he had intended to stay for a while. He looked around for the coat of his uniform. It was not there. When he had regained his senses after the explosion, he noticed that his coat had been taken off of him. He had his service pistol in the pocket. They'll turn up later, he thought. Satisfied that there was nothing in his quarters that could lead to discovery of the plot, he opened a small canvas bag and tossed some of his clothes in it. He would need to show the seamen when he left that he had picked up something.

Back in the hallway, he noticed some muffled voices coming from behind the closed door of Captain Stockton's quarters. He crept closer, to the edge of the door. He had been in the room only once during his brief time on the ship's staff. A couple of nights before the explosion, just before lights out, Stockton had invited in all of the officers. He had pulled out a bottle of sherry and some small glasses from a cabinet, and offered a toast to a successful Potomac excursion.

"I already burned the letter," he heard someone state, barely above a whisper. He recognized the voice as Stockton's.

Another voice, again barely audible. "The men know nothing." This one, he was sure, belonged to Fenwick. Ben's interactions with Fenwick had been terse, ever since they had first met at Stockton's party a couple of weeks earlier. Once aboard the ship, Ben had quickly realized that Fenwick was protective of Stockton and leery of any newcomers to the officer staff.

Ben heard the captain's voice again, slightly louder than before. "The president will say it was an accident. Ericsson is not a fool."

Then the sound of footsteps. Ben took giant steps, on the toes of his boots, down the hallway. He heard the creaking of a door's hinges. Can't look back, he told himself. He made his way quickly through the large room where the feast had been served. Just as he approached the steps, he heard it.

"Who goes there?," a voice barked.

It was Fenwick. He turned and faced his inquisitor. "Good day, commander. Just came aboard to pick up some personal things." He raised his canvas bag, his prop to support his lie, hoping that it would be convincing.

Fenwick stared at him, icily. "You got what you came for, now leave. The ship is off limits until you hear otherwise from the captain, or from me. Understood?"

"Yes, sir." Ben breathed a sigh of relief. He made his way up the steps to the deck, and walked to and down the gangway.

"Carry on. Good day," he said to the two saluting seamen as he stepped back onto the dock, making sure that they noticed his bag.

There was no carriage at the stop where he had been dropped off. Rather than wait, he decided to walk to the next one. His heart was pounding. Did Fenwick suspect that he had overheard the exchange in the captain's quarters? A letter? Burned? Ericsson? What was that about? He recalled that Ericsson was the Swedish inventor who had designed the engines and the propeller on the ship, and one of the cannons, the Oregon. Was this information that he could use, if his and Monty's plot were ever discovered? Maybe, he thought. Maybe not. As he continued to walk, he thought he heard some footsteps at a distance behind him. He turned around and looked. No one there. He hastened his pace. Perhaps it was his head injury playing tricks. Probably just imagining things, he told himself.

CHAPTER 30

April, 1852— Henry Clay heard the faint knock on the door to his suite at the National Hotel. It was quickly answered by his servant, James, who took a folded note from the bellman. The senator, on this pleasant April afternoon, had been having a day better than most, able to leave his bed and sit, surrounded by pillows, on the sofa in the parlor, reviewing letters from well-wishers. He had been confined to the hotel for almost four months. A couple of weeks earlier, President Fillmore had come by for a chat, as had several others who had known the senator over his long career. Clay loved people, and being around them. His confinement was torture to him. So long as he felt up to it, and his health varied from day to day, he appreciated having some company. When James handed the senator the note and he read it, a slight smile came to his face. "Yes," Clay said, looking toward to the bellman, "Give me ten minutes."

"James," instructed Clay, "find me a clean shirt and get my favorite frock coat from the wardrobe, the blue one."

"No clean shirts, senator. Waiting for them to come back from downstairs."

"Then the cleanest dirty one will have to do. And get a comb and work on my hair. It's a stringy mess, I'm sure."

James grinned. He knew what this meant. A lady was about to visit.

Ten minutes later, there was another knock on the door and the bellman motioned into the parlor room a tall, fair-skinned woman. Mary Ann Hall wore an emerald green dress, with more than enough petticoats and crinoline underneath to make a statement, and mutton sleeves. Her red hair was worn up and was topped with a tasteful matching green hat.

"Mary Ann!" said Clay, in an animated tone, "So good of you to drop by. How long has it been, ten years?" Unable to stand without difficulty, he reached for her hand and gave it a kiss.

"At least. I read in the newspaper that you were cooped up in this place and just had to stop by and see how you were doing," the soft-spoken guest replied.

With a discreet signal from his boss, James knew that it was time to excuse himself, go outside, enjoy the spring air, and get in a smoke.

"Business is good, I hope?," queried Clay.

"Yes, thank you. As you well know, it usually is when Congress is in session."

The senator had once been a customer of Miss Hall. Like many politicians of his era, and others before and since, Henry Clay had vices. In the prime of his career, in addition to drinking and gambling, his had included visiting Miss Hall's establishment during the long sessions of Congress for the services offered.

The two talked for several minutes, at times interrupted by Clay's coughing, but nonetheless enjoyable for both. They discussed mutual acquaintances. Mary Ann asked about Monty Tolliver, the senator's former aide and also a prior customer. "I know that he left for a while and then returned a couple of years ago as a congressman. We haven't seen him since he's been back. I hope he is doing well, such a pleasant young man."

"He may have a lady friend back home in Ohio. Not sure." offered Clay.

"Well, *that* never stopped you," chided the madam.

"Now, now, Mary Ann, you will remember I told you that my Lucretia hated living in Washington City. Couldn't stand the fancy dinners and the parties. She's a Kentucky girl. She did her duty when I was secretary of state under ol' John Quincy and, since then, has left me on my own when I have been here. Such a good woman, an excellent mother and grandmother. And has an excellent mind for business. She runs the farm. Don't know what I would do without her. But a man has certain needs when he is away from home for an extended time."

"And my staff and I are pleased to be able to be of service. Mr. Tolliver," Mary Ann continued, "was always a favorite of my younger sister, Elizabeth. Liz tells a story of the last time she was with him; he was in a bad state. It was a few months after that terrible explosion on the Potomac several years back. Poor fella could hardly focus on the task at hand and fell asleep. Before Liz could stir him, he said 'How could I have gotten into this?,' and mumbled something about 'President Tyler and Princeton.' That was the name of that ship that blew up, the *Princeton*, right?"

"Yes, yes, it was the *Princeton*" confirmed Clay. "I am sure he was just having a bad dream. I have kept in touch with Monty over the years. In fact, he stopped by just a couple of weeks ago and seemed to be doing fine."

"That is good to hear," said Mary Ann. "I hope I did not betray any confidences by telling that to you."

"I think that your story is safe with me." Clay then smirked a bit, and added, "You know, dead men tell no tales."

"Oh, senator, I can tell by our talk today that there is a lot of life left in you yet. I promise you that I am going to be sitting in the front row of the gallery the first day that you get back to the Senate."

"You are ever the optimist, Mary Ann. A good disposition to have. I am afraid that I seem to be losing mine."

With a knock on the door, James reappeared. Clay gave him a nod. Mary Ann knew this was a signal that it was time to go and got up from her chair. The senator reached out and briefly held her hand in his. "Your visit has made my day." She leaned over and gently kissed the senator's forehead and she was on her way.

After James had shown her out, Clay released the coughs that he had been suppressing. That was an interesting story that she told about Monty, he thought. Monty had never said anything to him about the *Princeton* and that fateful day, or anything about the explosion. He thought some more. He then vaguely recollected that someone had mentioned something to him about Monty and the *Princeton*. Who was it, and what had they said? He hated how age and illness had affected his memory. Maybe it would come to him.

CHAPTER 31

arch, 1844— Monty knocked on Ben's door. No response. It was mid-afternoon on Friday, two days after the explosion. Maybe he's sleeping, he thought. Probably what he needs. Just as he was about to turn away, he saw the knob start to slowly turn.

"You look a lot better than you did the other night," said Monty. In truth, Ben did. Amid a mass of people and confusion, Monty had been at the dock at Alexandria when the *Princeton* had arrived. Ben had been one of the first escorted off of the ship, along with the other wounded. Some were on stretchers, but Ben was able to walk, although slowly and unsteadily. Monty had noticed that Ben looked dazed, as if he was in shock. As the line of the wounded passed by Monty, Ben had muttered to him, barely above a whisper, "Banged my head. Nothing serious. Give me a day or so and come by." He had then been escorted away and helped into a waiting ambulance by some uniformed Navy men.

Ben eased himself down and sat on the edge of his bed, while Monty sat on a stiff wooden chair. "I'll be alright. More frustrated with what happened, than with my head. I can't believe it." said Ben. "Tyler was not there for the firing. The bastard. I had just decided that I was going to hunt him down on the ship and get the job done. That's the last thing that I remember."

"We knew that things could go wrong, but not this. What a tragedy, and not just because it spared Tyler's life." said Monty. "Eight people dead. The city is basically shut down and is in mourning. The funeral procession is set for tomorrow."

"I just wish it was Tyler's death that was being mourned."

"If the crowds that were at the President's House today are any indication," said Monty, "there are going to be a lot of people on the streets tomorrow."

"You went there today?," asked Ben.

"Yes, the Senate shut down just before lunch for the viewing and the other clerks went over as a group. I thought it would look suspicious if I declined. The caskets were lined up in the East Room, five of them, Upshur, Gilmer, Maxcy, Kennon, and Gardiner." Monty continued, "The upper portions were open and covered with glass lids. You could see them from the neck up. There was no evidence of the explosion on their faces, except for Kennon, whose was covered. The rest looked peaceful, like they were sleeping. It took more than an hour to get through the line."

"I guess Tyler decided that the other three, the two dead seamen and his slave, didn't merit first class honors. No fancy eternity boxes for them," said Ben.

"Would you have expected otherwise from him, especially for his slave?" said Monty. He then picked up a newspaper sitting on a table next to Ben's bed and perused the lead article about the explosion. "Tyler certainly is not putting any blame on Stockton for the explosion." He continued, reading from the paper, "Listen to what he told Congress. 'It affords me much satisfaction to say that this painful event was produced by no carelessness or inattention on the part of the officers and crew of the *Princeton*; but must be set down as one of those casualties which, to a greater or less degree, attend upon every service, and which are invariably incident to the temporal affairs of mankind.'" Monty added, "Seems a bit premature, don't you think?"

"One thing I am sure of. Stockton won't take the fall," said Ben. "Believe me, from what I've seen during the short time I've been on his staff, he's a fighter and knows all the right people. There is no way he's going to let himself get blamed for this."

"I can't think Congress will be in a mood to fund any more ships like the *Princeton*," said Monty. "So much for showing off our new military might to the world. After this, I don't believe anyone is much afraid. I'm sure the Brits are laughing at us."

"Have you heard anything from Sam?," Ben asked.

"Nothing. I'm sure he was in position and just went back to the fort when he figured out what had happened. Probably not a good idea to try to contact him until things calm down and we're sure that no one was aware of the plot."

"I saw a small steamer on the Maryland side of the river a few minutes before the explosion. Pretty sure that it was Sam."

"What's going on with you and with the ship?," asked Monty. "Are you on leave?"

"Yes. The ship is not going anywhere for a while," replied Ben. "I actually felt steady enough on my feet this morning that I took a carriage down to it. Just wanted to make sure that I didn't leave behind anything incriminating in my quarters."

"Find anything?"

"Nothing that should worry us."

"I'm surprised that you were able to go aboard today."

"I was too. There were just two guards from the ship posted at the gangway, who know me. Told them I just needed to pick up a few things. The Peacemaker is still there, mounted on the bow. Huge hole on one side. Blood stains all over the deck. Commander Fenwick, who I have told you about, was the only one I saw aboard."

"He's the one I saw at the party at Gadsby's, right?," interjected Monty.

"Correct. Stockton's lackey. He said to stay off of the ship until I hear from him or Stockton. Can't imagine that will be anytime soon." Ben continued. "I did overhear something said between Fenwick and Stockton, behind the closed door of the captain's quarters."

"Do tell," inquired Monty.

Ben yawned. "Probably nothing important. I can tell you about it later."

Monty noticed that Ben did appear to be tiring. "If you say so. You should probably get some rest," he said, as he stood up from the chair and shook hands with his friend. "Stay well, Dr. Franklin. I'll stop by in a couple of days. Get word to me, if you need anything before then. We will have to see what the repercussions of all this are on the Texas treaty."

"Hard to say which way it is going to go, with Secretary Upshur dead," replied Ben.

As he walked down the hallway from Ben's room to the front door of the boardinghouse, Monty was pleased to have seen Ben and with the extent of his friend's recovery from the head injury. But, he lamented, it was a visit that he had never wanted to have. How he wished that Ben had been able to accomplish his mission and, by now, would have been on his way to a new life in Canada.

CHAPTER 32

ay, 1852— "Senator, a gentleman at the door to see you," said James.

"Someone else dropping by to view the corpse before it stiffens?," said Clay, with a wry smile. "Who is it?"

"Says his name is Mr. Dickins, sir. From the Senate,"

"Oh, it's Asbury. Give me a minute and you can send him in." Clay roused himself in bed. He looked at his reflection in the small handheld mirror that he kept on the nightstand. "It will have to do," he grunted to himself.

Asbury Dickins was one of those behind-the-scenes people who made Congress work. He had been secretary of the Senate since the mid-1830s. Clay had worked closely with him during his earlier stint in that body.

"Senator, I bring best wishes from your colleagues. It pains them and me to walk by your desk on the Senate floor and see it empty, day after day," said Dickins, in his Tarheel accent. He pulled a large envelope out of the leather satchel he was carrying. "Earlier this week, a resolution wishing you a speedy recovery was passed unanimously. Here is a copy signed by all of your fellow senators."

Clay perused the document. "Well, that's something!" He continued, half in jest. "Even all of the Democrats? When was the last time anything got through the Senate without *any* dissent?" He then hesitated, choked up by emotion. "Tell everyone . . . Asbury . . . how much I appreciate this . . . I am afraid I may have seen the last of that beloved chamber."

"If those hallowed walls could talk, they would say that yours were the best speeches ever delivered there," said Dickins.

"You flatter an old, dying man."

"When the history books are written, it will be verified, I am sure."

"What is that quote from Napoleon," replied Clay, as he chuckled a bit. "History is just a set of lies that have been generally agreed upon?"

"No lies, sir, in your ability to capture and hold an audience with your words," said Dickins.

He then pulled another envelope out of his satchel, which contained a few pages. "I also came across these recently," as he handed it to Clay. "Found these in the bottom of a desk drawer, underneath some other papers. There are a couple of pages of notes, written on your Senate stationery. Appear to have been written in '44, judging from the other documents. There is a newspaper article about the schedule for the *Princeton* excursion on the day of the explosion in February of that year. There is also a page torn from a map book. I know you were not in the Senate in '44, but I thought, since it is on your stationery, that it may belong to someone in your family, or on your staff. I did not want to throw them out without first checking with you."

Clay put on his spectacles and held the pages near his face. In the notes, he could make out the words Greenleaf's Point and Alexandria, with some times written next to them, and some other words that were difficult to read. The page from the map book showed a section of the Potomac River, with Mount Vernon and Fort Washington circled.

"Thank you for bringing these, Asbury. I will keep them. I think I know who they belong to and I can see that they are returned."

As his guest stood up to leave, Clay asked him again to make sure that his Senate colleagues knew how much he appreciated their gesture.

Alone, propped up in his bed, he looked at the notes again. He knew whose handwriting this was. He had seen it every day for years. The notes were written by Monty Tolliver.

CHAPTER 33

arch, 1844—It was a dreary and cold Saturday morning. Fitting weather for the occasion, Monty thought. He was not sure why he had come. Genuine sympathy for the victims, he decided. This was, after all, a national tragedy, despite the fact that it had thwarted his plot with Ben. He looked toward the President's House, where the funeral service for five of the victims of the *Princeton* explosion in the East Room would be ending soon. According to the newspapers, the procession would start from there sharply at noon. A cavalry squadron would lead the way, followed by General Winfield Scott, the commanding general of the United States Army, and then five hearses, each pulled by a single black horse. Behind the hearses, the president and his cabinet would join in the somber journey, then members of Congress, and then the justices of the Supreme Court. They would be followed by diplomats and other dignitaries, and then more military units.

Monty turned and looked down Pennsylvania Avenue toward the Capitol. People lined both sides of the street, several deep, as far as he could see. As he stared into the distance, he heard the man next to him ask, "How far to the cemetery?"

"About three and a half miles," he responded.

As the procession began to slowly pass in front of him, Monty noticed the black crepe bands on the left upper arm of all of the participants. He moved to the back of the crowd and followed the hearses for a couple of blocks as they made their way down Pennsylvania Avenue. He noticed that all of the shops were closed. Most were draped in black. It was Saturday, what would normally be their busiest day of the week. The crowds on both sides of the street stood almost motionless. Where had they all come from, he wondered? The men were stoic. Many of the women dabbed their eyes with handkerchiefs; some openly sobbed. The muffled beat of the drummers in the procession added the gloomy tone, as did the sound of a cannon being fired in the distance, at one-minute intervals.

After the cortege passed the Capitol, it would make a turn onto E Street, and the five bodies would be placed in the Public Vault at Congressional Cemetery, where they would be temporarily stored until the families made arrangements to move them for permanent interment. Monty watched as the dignitaries passed by him. He got only a brief glimpse of President Tyler, riding in a carriage with his head bowed. He recalled the last time that he had stood along this street in similar circumstances. It was almost three years earlier, in April of 1841, for the funeral of President Harrison, the death that had put Tyler in the presidency, and which led to all of the political turmoil of the past few years. He had seen enough, he decided, although only half of the entourage had passed by him. As he turned to leave, one thought stuck in his mind. How he wished that this had been Tyler's funeral.

CHAPTER 34

arch, 1844— "Mr. Tolliver, sir, someone here to see you," stated one of the stenographers in the clerk's office of the Senate.

"Do you know who it is?" Monty asked.

"He says he's with the police. I didn't catch the name."

Monty gulped. Seated at his desk, he ran his fingers through his hair. It was Monday, late in the morning, five days since the explosion. Could this be about the Tyler plot, he wondered? Couldn't be. Nothing had happened. The plot had been aborted before it began by the explosion. He had talked to Ben. All was good. "Tell him I will be out in a minute." Have to act normal, he told himself. He composed himself and walked from his small office in the back to the counter in the main clerk's office.

"Good afternoon. I am Monty Tolliver, what can I do for you?"

"Mr. Tolliver, I am Detective Patrick Lawrence with Washington City Police. Is there a place where we can talk privately?

"Certainly," said Monty. Not a good start, he thought. He motioned to a small adjacent room, which was used for reviewing documents. He closed the door behind them.

"I spoke this morning with Mrs. Edwards, the proprietor of a boardinghouse on F Street, and she told me that you are a friend of one of her boarders, Lieutenant Benjamin Geddis. Is that correct?"

"Yes, I am a friend of the lieutenant."

"I am afraid that I have sad news. Lieutenant Geddis is dead."

"Oh my God," gasped Monty. He steadied himself, barely able to seat himself in one of the chairs located in the room. He felt tears well up in his eyes. "Are you sure?"

"Unfortunately, quite sure. He was found in his room."

"How?," Monty asked, as the tears started to run down his face.

"I suspect a burglary. The room was ransacked. My thinking is that the thief thought the room was not occupied and the lieutenant surprised him, they fought a bit, and he fell back and hit his head. A mortal injury. The thief went in and out through a window."

"When did this happen?"

"Late Friday night, we believe, or early Saturday morning. When did you last see him?"

"A few days ago. Let me think. It was the day before the funeral for the *Princeton* victims. I went to see him there, in his room. I guess it was on Friday, in the afternoon."

"Yes, it would have been," replied Lawrence. "The funeral was on Saturday. I understand from Mrs. Edwards that he was an officer on the *Princeton* and that he sustained a head injury in the explosion, is that correct?"

"Yes, he had a concussion."

"He having any problems from that?"

"He was recovering well when I saw him. Lucid. Just a bit wobbly on his feet. He said that he was not planning to attend the funeral because of that."

"Had you been to his room before?"

"Yes, often. He was my best friend."

"Do you know of anyone who would want to do him harm?" asked Detective Lawrence.

"No, not to my knowledge."

"We have had a few similar break-ins over the past several weeks. His room was on the ground floor, at the back of the house, and had a low window that was easily accessible from the outside. I suspect the thief did not know that it was a board-inghouse and thought that no one would be on the first floor at night."

"You're saying it was totally random?"

"Appears to be. Unless we get evidence otherwise. I under-stand that he was not married. Do you know anything about his next of kin?"

"Ben was from Rhode Island. His parents are still there, in Newport."

"Would you happen to know their names and address?"

Monty thought of the letter that he still had in his room, the one that Ben had written and sealed in an envelope addressed to his parents, which he was to have mailed to them after the assassination of Tyler. "Yes, I do have their names and address somewhere. I can get that to you."

"That would be appreciated. We will ask for that from the Navy, but it could take some time for them to respond. I would like to get a letter out to them as soon as possible."

"I can get that to you."

"Mr. Tolliver, since you are familiar with his room, I would like you to inspect it with me. Perhaps you will notice something different, clues that may be of help in finding the killer."

"Willing to help in any way I can."

"How about later this afternoon, around five."

"That's fine. I will meet you there."

After Detective Lawrence left, Monty went back to his office and closed the door. He sat at his desk and buried his face in his hands. Tears flowed. This could not have happened, he thought, not to Ben.

CHAPTER 35

arch, 1844— Monty walked down the long hallway to the back of the house, as he had done countless times before. The landlady unlocked the door, excused herself, and he and Detective Lawrence walked into the room. The open curtains on the two windows let in some dim late afternoon light from the winter sun, but it was not until the detective lit two small oil lamps that the items in the room came into focus. Monty's eyes were immediately drawn to the large dark circular stain on the rug directly in front of them. The spot where his friend had died. He wanted to cry. Be strong, he told himself.

"Watch your step. Walk around it," said the detective, nonchalantly, as though it was a puddle of mud in the middle of the street. Kind of disrespectful, Monty thought. "The back window there was open. The rest is mostly as we found it."

Monty scanned the room. The drawers of the chest of drawers had been pulled open, one having fallen to the floor, and their contents rummaged through. He noticed a couple of Ben's favorite shirts. The doors of the wardrobe were open, the clothes there also disturbed, with some on the floor. Beside the unmade bed was a night table. He took a few steps toward it.

"May I?" he asked.

"Yes, please feel free to touch anything you'd like. We've looked at it all already."

He picked up a folded newspaper, *The Liberator*, an abolitionist paper that he knew Ben had subscribed to. Underneath it, there were two books, *The Pathfinder* by James Fenimore Cooper and *The Old Curiosity Shop* by Charles Dickens. He recalled that he and Ben had discussed some of Dickens' prior books, and that Ben had enjoyed them more than he had. Underneath them, he spotted a smaller book, which he picked up, *Quotations of Benjamin Franklin*. It brought a tear to his eye.

"I gave this to him," Monty said to the detective. "You know he was named after Benjamin Franklin."

"I had assumed so. Please feel free to keep it, as it was a gift from you."

"Are you sure?"

"Quite certain, yes. We will not need it for our investigation. Something you can have to remember him."

"Thank you." Monty shoved the small book in the outer pocket of his coat.

"Other than the ransacking, anything you see here that looks out of the ordinary?"

"Nothing jumps out at me. Sorry."

"Do you know if he kept anything of value here?"

"Not to my knowledge. Ben lived frugally. Not one to buy fancy things or to keep money sitting around."

"I figured as much. Would fit with my theory that the perpetrator thought the room would be unoccupied and that he was looking for valuables elsewhere in the house."

"Only one person did this?"

"Probably. Possibly two, but unlikely, in my opinion."

"I almost forgot." Monty retrieved a piece of paper from one of his pockets, unfolded it, and handed it to the detective. "The names of Ben's parents and their address in Rhode Island."

"Thank you. One of the worst parts of my jobs. Notifying the next of kin. Especially in a case such like this."

CHAPTER 36

December, 1844— Monty sat on the bench just inside the front door of a diner on B Street, keeping his hat and gloves on. He may as well have been outside. The cold December air came in whenever customers opened the door, which was frequently. He was looking forward to this Saturday morning breakfast with Sam, although not the circumstance that had brought it about. He had seen Sam only once since the explosion and Ben's death ten months earlier, when Sam had been able to get a couple of days of leave during the summer to come to Washington City for a visit. Their meeting then had been melancholy. They both talked about Ben and reminisced about the times that the three of them had spent together. Sam had seemed somber and distant, Monty thought, but then, he had likely been the same. Letters with Sam had been less frequent than Monty had hoped, from both of them. Maybe Ben, he realized, had been the glue that had held them together. This meeting would likely be their last for some time. Sam had written a few weeks ago that the Army was transferring him out of the area and that he would be passing through the city this weekend. He wanted to meet for breakfast today to say goodbye, suggesting the place and time.

Monty reached his hand into the lining of his coat and felt the inside pocket, as he had done three or four times since he left his boardinghouse. It was still there. Of course, it was. Why, he wondered, did he need to keep checking?

Another burst of cold air came in as the door opened and Sam appeared. The two greeted each other and had to wait a few minutes to be seated at a table. They both ordered coffee. Sam decided on the pancakes and bacon. Monty went with eggs, sunny-side up, and ham.

"You are looking well," said Monty. "Tell me more about your news."

"I'm on leave now and headed to Pennsylvania to spend Christmas with my family. From there, I will report in January to my new assignment, which is at Fort Moultrie in South Carolina."

"I've seen that name in War Department bills that have come before the Senate," said Monty. "It's near Charleston?"

"Correct. Just outside the city. I will be stationed there, but will be working on the construction of a new fort, Sumter, that's being built in Charleston Harbor."

"I've seen that name in Senate bills also. A lot of money is being spent on it, as I recall."

"Definitely. Sumter is going to be an engineering feat," said Sam. "A fort built on a man-made island in the middle of the harbor. They started it about fifteen years ago, dumping huge boulders on a shoal underneath the water, and adding rocks, sand and dirt. Once the island is completed, construction of the fort will begin and I will be involved in that, and with the design and placement of the artillery."

"I am excited for you. Good for your career, although I regret that it will make it much more difficult for us to see each other. We've been through a lot together."

"Thanks, we sure have. I'm looking forward to it, although not at all happy about moving to the heart of slavery. It's bad enough what I see around here. I'm sure it is much worse there."

"Undoubtedly, it is," said Monty. "We tried to do something about it, but failed. Damn that terrible day."

The waitress arrived with their breakfast. "Looks good," they both said in unison, thanked her, and asked for some more coffee.

"We do have one thing from the past that we need to discuss," said Monty, as he reached into his pocket and pulled out an envelope. "This is the letter that Ben left with me, addressed to his parents, and which I was to have mailed to them a few days after the deed was done, when Ben was to have been safely on his way to Canada. Obviously, I did not mail it, given what happened. I have been torn as to whether to open it, and did not want to do so without your input and without you being present. What do you think?"

Monty noticed that the mention of Ben's name brought a look of sadness to Sam's face. Sam hesitated before responding. "I believe that Ben would want you to know his last words to his family. He entrusted you with the letter, and the two of you were in this thing from the beginning. You had no secrets. You should open it. If you want to share it with me after you read it, that is up to you."

"That was my inclination, but I wanted to hear it from you." He gently tore open the top of the envelope and pulled out the letter. As he began to read it, tears formed his eyes, then made their way to his cheeks by the time that he got to the end.

"Please, you also," said Monty, as he handed the letter to Sam. Sam also shed tears as he read Ben's words:

My Dearest Parents,

By now, you will have heard the news. I deeply regret the dishonor that will undoubtedly be brought on you and our family by what I have done, and of which you had no knowledge. Please know that I have acted alone and with the sincere belief that my decisions were made in the best interest of our country.

Tyler has committed many transgressions since fate placed him in the President's House, but his impending treaty to annex Texas into the Union goes far beyond what he has done before. As a boy, you taught me that the Declaration of Independence means what it says, that <u>all</u> men are created equal, and that slavery is an evil that must be removed from our country. Hopefully, my deed will arrest its growth and will hasten its demise.

I will now try to build a new life elsewhere. I will not contact you further, for fear of imperiling your safety. Do not cry for me. I have done this with full knowledge of the consequences. Thank you for your love and for the values that you instilled in me. Let Robert know that he is the best brother that I could ever have hoped to have, and give my best to the rest of the family. I will think of you always.

Your loving son,
Ben

"Just like Ben," said Monty, as Sam handed the letter back to him. "Taking all of the responsibility and not implicating us, even to his parents."

"Anything further from the police on their investigation of Ben's death?," asked Sam.

"No. As far as they are concerned, it was from a burglary gone bad. The last I heard, they had no suspects and no leads. I sometime wonder, with the timing of it, whether his death had something to do with our plot. But I have no proof."

"Doubtful. Probably just a random act, like they have concluded. It happens," said Sam.

"I will be sure to write to you if something new turns up."

The waitress came and took away their empty plates. They declined more coffee and Monty paid the bill. "My treat," he said to Sam. "A going away present."

"So, what about your future?," asked Sam. "Staying around here?"

"Probably not. I have been giving it a lot of thought. I think it is time to move on, to go back to Ohio. Probably in a few months. Maybe try to start a family."

"Sounds like a good plan."

As they made their way to the front door of the diner, they walked by a large fireplace, with flames blazing. Monty paused, pulled out Ben's letter and the envelope, ripped them into several pieces, and dropped them into the flames. Sam looked on. Monty paused to make sure the pieces were fully consumed by the flames.

"Rest in peace, Dr. Franklin," he said, as they moved on toward the exit.

CHAPTER 37

June, 1852— "How is he today?," Monty asked James, as the door to Suite 32 was opened.

"He had a rough morning, Mr. Tolliver, but is doing somewhat better this afternoon," replied James. "He has been looking forward to your visit."

Monty found Clay where he had been the last time, in his bed, propped up with pillows. He was staring at an empty corner of the dimly lit room.

"Monty," said the senator, moving his eyes to the doorway. "It is good of you to come again. I know that you are a busy man."

"Never too busy to see you, sir."

"I was just lying here thinking about the day you were sworn in as a member of Congress. I was so proud. Not that long ago, but so much has happened since."

"March 4, 1849. I remember it well. The same day that you returned to the Senate. It was a bittersweet day," responded Monty, "Personally rewarding for me, but another Inauguration Day with another man inferior to you taking the oath of office as president."

"I will leave that judgment to others," Clay chuckled, "but if there is one thing that our Whig voters have shown over the years, it is that they love a man in uniform, never mind if he knows a whit about what's going on in the country and has a plan to deal with it. First it was Granny Harrison in '40 and then ol' Taylor in '48."

* * *

The race for the Whig nomination for president in 1848 had pitted Clay against General Zachary Taylor as the two frontrunners, with Senator Daniel Webster of Massachusetts and General Winfield Scott of Virginia also in the contest. Out of office, Clay had returned to Kentucky to practice law after his 1844 loss. Shortly thereafter, the Mexican War began, an outgrowth of the annexation of Texas, which he had opposed. The man who narrowly had beaten Clay in the election, President James Polk, had pursued the war to a favorable conclusion in less than two years. The war was also a personal tragedy for Clay, with one of his sons and namesake, Henry Clay, Jr., a West Point graduate, having been killed in combat in 1847. Taylor, who was generally unkempt in his personal appearance, was dubbed by his men and the press as "Old Rough and Ready," and he and General Scott were the two main military heroes to emerge from the war. Taylor was a southerner, born in Virginia, eventually settling in Louisiana. A large slaveholder who had never opposed his region's "peculiar institution," he had much support throughout the South. Although the Kentuckian Clay was also a southerner and a slaveholder, he had long denounced the institution and had worked over his political career to bring about the gradual emancipation of enslaved people. He drew his support in 1848 mainly from the North.

At that year's Whig nominating convention, held in Philadelphia, Clay trailed Taylor by only fourteen votes on the first ballot, with Scott and Webster far behind. Taylor went on to win the nomination on the fourth ballot. The apolitical Taylor, who bragged that he had never before voted in any election, portrayed himself as a man above political ideology. He went on to beat the nominee of the Democratic Party, Senator Lewis Cass of Michigan, in the general election and became the nation's twelfth president.

* * *

As Monty spoke with Clay about his first day in Congress and Taylor's inauguration, he recalled to the senator his having met another Whig that day, who was seated next to him at the ceremony, and who had made an impression. The tall and lanky Illinoian, Abraham Lincoln, was leaving Congress as Monty was joining it. Serving only one term, Lincoln had agreed not to seek reelection, in keeping with the wishes of local party leaders in Illinois, who rotated their candidate for the seat every two years. After Taylor's inauguration, Lincoln would be heading back to his home in Springfield to resume his law practice.

"Mr. Lincoln sure had a lot of nice things to say about you," said Monty to Clay.

"Yes," said Clay, "Although I was not here during his term, he sent me several wonderful letters before and after he was elected, telling me how much he supported my policies. A true Whig. I've had my eye on him for a while. Lincoln is the type of young, smart, self-made man that we need more of in Washington City. Stupid policy of the party in Illinois to put a new man up as its candidate in each election. How are we ever going to develop leaders with one-termers? I hope they come to their senses and that Lincoln will come back here someday."

"He is a character," said Monty. "I remember him telling me a funny story, in his homespun way, during Taylor's dreadful inauguration speech. The tale was about him leaving the bustle of Washington City for quaint Springfield."

"Do tell."

"It went something like, 'A visitor came to Springfield to deliver some lectures and was directed to the mayor's office to see if a permit was needed. The clerk there inquired as to the subject matter of the lectures. The visitor replied that they concerned the second coming of the Lord. Don't waste your time, said the clerk. If the Lord's seen Springfield once, He ain't coming back.' We both laughed so hard I thought one of the ushers was going to toss us out."

Clay laughed aloud, coughed a bit, and his face then turned serious. "Monty, I love a good joke, have told more than my share, but we both know why I wanted to speak with you. You avoided it at our last meeting. I assure you, our conversation will not leave this room, and will go with me to my imminent grave."

The senator then called for his servant, who was in the parlor room, to come in. "James, Mr. Tolliver will be staying and watching over me for a while. Go out and enjoy this nice summer day."

"Yes, sir, thank you. When do you want me to come back?"

"An hour."

"Better make it two," interjected Monty. He had a long story to tell.

"And James," added Clay, "on your way back through the lobby, please stop in the restaurant and get me another bottle of Kentucky bourbon. Old Crow, if they have it."

The two of them now alone, Monty swallowed hard, having decided to be open and truthful with this man whom he admired and trusted.

"I will tell you about the Tyler plot but, first, I want to know how you found out about it. It has been eight years and, to my knowledge, no one else has discovered it. I have lived in fear of it becoming known. Still have nightmares about it to this day. I had thought I was in the clear, having been in Congress for three years now, and no one having asked me about it, nothing being published in the press, and not having been threatened or blackmailed."

"Before I got into politics," said Clay, "I was a trial lawyer. A damn good one, if I say so myself." He coughed a few times, brought his handkerchief to his face, and then continued. "A lawyer builds a good case with evidence, bit by bit. Some pieces of information about you came to me, mostly in the last couple of months, from different sources, while I have been cooped up here. Alone, they meant nothing but, together, they made me suspicious. I have nothing else to do here but sit and speculate, and I'm pretty sure I've put this together correctly."

"Well then, counselor," said Monty, "please continue."

"You and at least two accomplices, friends of yours, devised a plot to assassinate President Tyler. You planned for it to take place on the *Princeton* when he was aboard on that tragic day in 1844. You acted as a lookout that morning on the steamship that ferried the passengers to the warship, when it was anchored at Alexandria, and you scouted the scene there to take notice of any security around Tyler, and that nothing was amiss. You then signaled one of your friends, an officer on the *Princeton*, that all was well, and did not board the ship. He was then to have done the deed during the excursion, but the cannon exploded before he could carry it out. It was planned that, after killing Tyler, your friend would to row or swim to Fort Washington, where another accomplice awaited to get him safely away. How did I do?"

"Pretty accurate," replied Monty, amazed at how much Clay had put together. He then began to fill in some of the details for the senator, not mentioning the names of his accomplices. No need for Clay to know anything about them. As he spoke, Monty had a strange sense of relief. He was unburdening himself with things he had not discussed with anyone, other than Sam, for eight years. Perhaps, he wondered, this would help him get rid of the nightmares.

"Sounds like a well-thought-out plan," said Clay. "I figured out the plot, but one thing still has me stumped. What was the motive? I hope it was not to benefit me in the 1844 election."

"It was not. Striking a blow against slavery, by stopping the annexation of Texas, was the motivation. My friends and I talked politics constantly. We couldn't stand Tyler from the time he took office, calling himself the real president, his betrayal of the Whig Party, the bank vetoes, his Virginia cabal, the tariff vetoes, you name it. But it was his annexation treaty that put us over the edge and led us to take action. We couldn't sit by and allow a doubling the amount of slave territory in the Union without trying to stop it. The planning was mainly with one friend. He was an abolitionist and I was increasingly leaning in that direction. We knew that Tyler would be submitting the treaty to the Senate within a few weeks, and that Secretary Upshur had likely lined up the votes to get it passed. With Tyler dead, Senator

Mangum would have taken over as president, and we knew he would never submit the treaty. Would our killing of Tyler have benefitted you politically in the 1844 election? Probably so. But that is not what moved us to act."

"And all that you had hoped to prevent has now come to pass," responded Clay, who remained almost upright in his bed, propped up by pillows, and coughing intermittently. His voice became raspier the more he spoke, but was still understandable.

"It certainly has. Despite how much I have been haunted about it for eight years, if I had it to do over again, and if I knew it would have been successful, I would still take the same actions. With Texas in the Union, the slaveholders have taken control of our government. We fought an unnecessary war, at much cost. We now have these new territories, New Mexico and Utah, that could end up as more slave states. Despite your efforts in 1850 and the compromise you forged, the country is more divided now than ever over slavery. I do not have a good feeling about the future."

"Monty, I share your concerns," responded Clay. "I fought my political opponents hard over my career, but assassination can never be the answer in a republic. Where would it end? Would someone have then killed a President Mangum? It would lead us down the road to anarchy. We have our Constitution. God knows that I couldn't stand Tyler, and I that detested that despot Jackson even more, and would not have shed a tear if either one of them had taken his last breath while in office. But death by natural causes and death by murder are totally different."

"Apparently Jackson didn't think the same about you. Didn't he say after retiring that the only two regrets of his life were that he did not shoot you, and did not hang Calhoun?"

"I'm told it was said in jest, although with him, one can never know. The old buzzard."

"You fought two duels against political opponents," said Monty. "Tried to kill them. You told me the stories."

"Please, you're comparing apples and oysters. Those were matters of personal honor. There were rules and everyone was a willing participant. I was but a young man at the time of the first one, in the Kentucky Legislature. My opponent called me a demagogue to my face. What was I to do? Let it stand, unchallenged? I missed him, but he got me with a minor wound to the thigh. The second one was when I was secretary of state. That old coot, Senator Randolph of Virginia, said I was corrupt in getting appointed to the office. Even said that I cheated at cards. Couldn't let that go by. We both missed, although I did put a hole in his coat."

"Good that all of you were lousy shots," said Monty, chuckling. He noticed that Clay did not pick up on the attempt at humor.

"Dueling days are now over," continued the senator, "but, back then, if John Tyler said you were a liar and a cheat, he'd be fair game for a duel about honor, provided that he was put on notice and accepted a challenge. But if he annexed Texas, that's a political disagreement. You can't assassinate a man for a difference of opinion over policy."

"Every rule has its exception," said Monty. "Early 1844 was a moment in time when the death of one man could have changed the course of history, for the better, and improved the lives of thousands of slaves then, and maybe millions in the future."

"How would the lives of slaves in Texas be any different now, if you had succeeded?," asked Clay. "They are now slaves in the

State of Texas with annexation, and would have also been slaves in the Republic of Texas without annexation."

"Maybe not," responded Monty. "We were aware then of stories in the newspapers that the British were considering a loan to the Texians to alleviate their huge debts, and were going to use it as leverage to have slavery abolished there."

"Is that what you would have wanted, a British ally on our southwestern border? Isn't Canada on our northern border enough? Would that have been in the best interests of the United States?," replied Clay.

"We will never know, but I am certain it would have helped the slaves."

"You are right that history would have been changed, for the better, had your plot been successful," said Clay. "No Tyler, no annexation, no Mexican War, and no new territories to further divide us. You know that I lost my son, Henry, in that damn war. At the Battle of Buena Vista. He was one of the lights of my life. His death hit Lucretia particularly hard. She has never been the same. But a laudable end can never justify tainted means."

"Respectfully, sir, your personal loss makes me even more convinced that my position was the correct one. I had the pleasure of meeting Henry when I was working for you. A fine man. His life, and those of thousands of soldiers like him, lost in a war caused by annexation."

Monty then shifted to a new argument. "Tyler wasn't even the real president. He should have just been a caretaker."

"Future presidents will die in office and their vice presidents will face the same situation. History will judge whether Tyler was a usurper, or whether he acted appropriately. Our Founding

Fathers left some ambiguity in the Constitution. It was not his taking on the trappings of the office of president, but the arrogance of the man in betraying the party that elected him, for what he saw as his own political benefit, that galled me. But that is solved with ballots, not bullets."

Same old Clay, thought Monty. On his deathbed, and he can still turn a phrase.

They both heard a knock at the door, followed by the creaking sound of it being opened. "Senator," said James, "should I come back later?"

"No, James," said Clay, "come on in. I think Mr. Tolliver and I are about done with our conversation."

James appeared at the doorway to the bedroom, holding a bottle and displaying it. "Your bourbon, sir."

"Excellent. I see that they did have the Old Crow. My favorite," said Clay, his face more animated. "Could you pour two glasses for my friend and me?"

James went into the parlor, opened the bottle, poured some of the golden-brown liquid into two glasses, and took them to Clay and Monty.

"A toast," said Clay, raising his glass and looking at Monty. "To a good friend, and to agreeing to disagree."

"I hope that you do not think less of me for my views on this subject," said Monty.

"Nonsense. If men did not disagree, we would have little to talk about. Fate intervened and your plot was never carried out. Nothing happened. More of a topic for a Saturday afternoon debate on the town square. I can hear the introduction now. Can the assassination of the president ever be justified? Mr. Tolliver for the affirmative, and Mr. Clay for the negative."

"Except that I would never be fool enough to debate you in public."

"At least I now know that my suspicions were correct, and that I have not totally lost my ability to think. Now that we have gotten that matter out of the way, I hope that you will come back soon and keep an old man company. I have enjoyed our visits."

"Most assuredly, I will. However, the Whig convention opens on Thursday in Baltimore and I need to go there for a couple of days. I will stop by when I get back."

"I had forgotten that the convention is this week. The days are a blur for me. What is today?"

"Monday, June 14," said Monty.

"I hope you are a Fillmore man," said Clay, "The president has been good for the country. He signed into law the recent compromise that I worked on for so long. Millard is a decent and kind man. Been to see me here a couple of times over the past few months. He did not have to do that. I have given him my endorsement, if that is worth anything these days."

Monty agreed, "In a perfect world, Fillmore would not be my first choice, but he is our best option now. Much better than either of his opponents. His men asked me to go to Baltimore to see if I can sway some of the Ohio delegates to him."

"Damn that Webster," said Clay. "Always making himself a nuisance."

Monty stood up to take his leave. "We shall see how things turn out in Baltimore. I'll stop in next week and fill you in."

On his way out of the National Hotel, Monty saw Clay's son, Thomas, in the lobby, who was on his way to visit with his father. Thomas, a decade older than Monty, had arrived in the city a few weeks earlier, hoping that his father would be well enough to escort him home to Kentucky. Clay's doctor had ruled that out, so Thomas had decided to stay for the duration. Thomas and Monty were acquainted from Monty's days on the senator's staff. They exchanged greetings. "I think he has had a good day," said Monty, "We talked quite a bit."

CHAPTER 38

February, 1845— Monty had been lying in bed and staring at the ceiling of his room for a while. *What is it about remembering sad events on their anniversaries,* he wondered? *Why do we feel a need to relive them?*

It was February 28, 1845, one year to the day since the explosion on the *Princeton* and only a few days until the first anniversary of Ben's death. He had cursed that fateful day a thousand times. Had things turned out as planned, Tyler would be dead and Ben would be safely in Canada, living a new life. Senator Mangum would have become the president and would have never pursued the annexation of Texas. Senator Clay would likely have been elected this past November to succeed him and, perhaps, once he was in office, Monty could have convinced him to take some real action to rid the United States of slavery. A forced gradual emancipation. A ban on expansion of slavery into the territories. At least something.

Instead, he reflected on all that had happened over the past year. Hope, and then despair. Everything that he and Ben had wanted to prevent by killing Tyler had now occurred. The slave power was ascendent in the country. Tyler's Texas annexation treaty had failed in the Senate in June 1844 by not getting the necessary two-thirds vote. In fact, it had failed miserably, with only sixteen votes in favor and thirty-five against. The rejection was due, in large part, to a letter that Upshur's replacement as secretary of state, John Calhoun, had written to the British minister to the United States, which had been included with the treaty documents sent to the Senate and which had been leaked to the press. In the letter, Calhoun, a South Carolinian and former vice president, berated the British for their promotion of abolition in the Republic of Texas and admitted that annexation by the United States was being done primarily to protect slavery in the South, and to thwart British abolition efforts in Texas. Northern support for annexation had evaporated with the publication of Calhoun's letter. Given the failure of the treaty, Monty had decided not to pursue any additional action, on his own, against Tyler.

Months later, however, a persistent Tyler had turned defeat into a victory. After the Democrats nominated a pro-annexation candidate for president in the summer of 1844, James Polk of Tennessee, Tyler gave up his quest for a term of his own and endorsed Polk. He had then gotten annexation passed, in the waning days of his administration, by a joint resolution of Congress, which required only a simple majority of both houses. It was a done deal. All that remained was a vote by Texians to accept the terms of the treaty, set for the coming fall, and Texas would be admitted to the Union as a slave state, likely by the end of the year. In a close election, Polk, a southern slaveholder, had beaten Clay and would be replacing Tyler in the presidency.

The outcome of the election, though narrow, was viewed as an endorsement by the electorate of annexation. The new president, Monty was certain, would surely push the slave agenda as much as Tyler had during his time in office. It all turned his stomach.

Monty looked over at the books on the shelf next to his bed. Where is it, he wondered? He got up and went over to the shelf. Today is an appropriate day to look through it, he decided, ashamed that he had not done so after the detective let him take it from Ben's room a year ago. He found it. Dark blue cover with a gold title and a thin spine. *Quotations of Benjamin Franklin.* He sat on the bed and opened it to a random page and scanned the sayings. "He that speaks much, is much mistaken." "When in doubt, don't." He turned the page. The quote at the top brought a tear to his eye. "A true friend is the best possession." When he turned to the next page, a folded piece of paper fell out. He opened it and recognized Ben's handwriting. The date of March 1, 1844, was written at the top. Underneath, Ben had written, on four separate lines, "Overhead Fenwick and Stockton on ship today. They said a letter was burned. Said Tyler will call it an accident. Said Ericsson is not a fool."

Monty was disgusted and angry with himself. Why had he not looked through this book a year ago? Or any time since then? Did the information in this note have anything to do with Ben's death? Why was the note in this book? Could Ben have foreseen, if something happened to him, that Monty would end up with the book and find the note? If so, why would Ben think something could happen to him? One thing was certain. He needed to take this information to Detective Lawrence.

CHAPTER 39

arch, 1845— "Thank you for seeing me. I am not sure if you remember me."

"Of course, I remember you, Mr. Tolliver," said Detective Lawrence, as he stood up from his desk. "It's been, what, about a year? I see a lot of tragedy in my job, but your friend's death was particularly troublesome for me. Such a fine young man. Serving his country."

"Any progress on your investigation? On finding who may have done this?"

"We had a suspect in some of the other burglaries that were going on in that area at the time. But he was killed, stabbed in a bar fight, a few months ago. No similar burglaries around there since then, so we're pretty sure that he was the one. Based on that, we have closed the case."

Monty pulled a small book out of his coat pocket and put it on the detective's desk. "Do you remember letting me take this when we met at Ben's room?"

Lawrence glanced at the book's title, *Quotations of Benjamin Franklin.* "Yes, he was named after Franklin, as I recall."

"I have new evidence and I would like you to reopen the case."

"What evidence?," asked the detective.

Monty explained how he had not opened the book until recently, and showed the detective the note from Ben that he had found in it.

Lawrence fumbled in a pocket for his eyeglasses, put them on, and perused the note. "And why do you think this had anything to do with his death?," he queried.

"Timing, for one thing. It was written on the day of, or the day before, Ben was killed. And the contents. Letters are burned for a reason. So no one will know what was written. It obviously refers to the explosion on the *Princeton.* I remember that Ben mentioned to me, after the explosion, that he overheard on the ship something said by Stockton and Fenwick. He gave me no details, but if they suspected Ben overheard them talking about something they wanted kept secret, they may have killed him over it."

The detective stroked his chin. "I know Stockton was the captain of the ship. I seem to recall that Fenwick was one of the ship's officers and that we talked to him."

"Correct, he was second in command."

"Who is this Ericsson?"

"He is an inventor who designed the ship."

"Are any of these people currently living in Washington City?"

"Not to my knowledge," replied Monty.

"Mr. Tolliver, I understand what you are saying. There may be something to it. But I am going to need more than this to reopen an investigation that we have closed. Even if I could reopen it now, I don't have the resources or the authority to investigate outside the city."

"If you can't, then I will. I need to find the truth. I owe it to Ben. May I look through your file?"

"I don't see the harm in that, assuming I can put my hands on it. Let me go look around. I know where it should be. Remind me again of the month?

"March," replied Monty.

"You can wait here."

A few minutes later, the detective returned with a folder in his hand. "We're in luck. Doesn't appear to be a whole lot in it, but you can take a look. I can't let it leave the office. There's a room down the hall that you can use. Bring it back to me when you're done."

"Will do. Thank you, detective."

Monty looked through the pages in the file. Fortunately, the handwritten notes were mostly legible. Ben's landlady and two other boarders in the house had been interviewed. They had seen and heard nothing. According to the landlady, the front door had been locked from the inside that evening and had remained so until morning. The outside and inside of the house had been inspected. The only evidence of entry was the ground-level window at the rear of the house, in Ben's room, that was found to be opened. The ransacking of the room was noted and described. One weapon was found, a pistol, in a half-opened drawer, noted to be the one issued to Ben by the Navy. He read through the additional few pages. There was a summary of Monty's conversation with the police, noting his friendship with Ben and that he had visited Ben in his room two days after the explosion, a Friday, in the mid-afternoon. It was noted that he had stated that Ben had sustained a head injury in the explosion and that he was still having some lingering minor symptoms. The only other interview that was conducted was with Commander Thomas Fenwick, identified as Ben's immediate superior officer. Fenwick had also advised that Ben had sustained a concussion during the explosion on the *Princeton* and that he had, a couple of days later, on Friday, in the early evening, checked up on Ben at home. Fenwick's statement noted that he had brought to Ben his pistol and the coat of his uniform, which had been separated from him in the aftermath of the explosion. The manner of death, as stated by Detective Lawrence in his report, was listed as a fatal head injury sustained during a burglary.

Monty put everything back in the folder and walked down the hallway to Lawrence's office. "Thank you, detective," he said as he returned the file. "Anything I can do to get you to change your mind about reopening the investigation?"

"I'm afraid not. Bring me a witness who can testify that it was something other than a burglary gone awry, and we can talk." He added, "See anything of interest in the file?"

"Not sure, maybe."

As he rode his horse back to Capitol Hill, Monty pondered Ben's pistol. Why would a burglar not take a pistol? Wasn't that something that could be sold on the streets, or of use in committing other crimes? It made no sense, he thought. And what about Ben's note? What was there about the explosion that Stockton did not want known? Did Stockton and Fenwick know that Ben had overheard them talking on the ship? He reminded himself of what Ben had said about Fenwick. Ben couldn't stand him. Monty recalled Fenwick's rudeness when he had been introduced at Stockton's party a few weeks before the explosion. According to Ben, Fenwick was Stockton's right-hand man, and was protective of him. The notes from the police investigation stated that Fenwick had gone to Ben's boardinghouse early Friday evening, a few hours after Monty had visited. That made Fenwick the last person known to have seen Ben alive and put him at the scene hours before Ben's death. Could Fenwick had gone back later, opened the rear window, and killed Ben? On his own, or ordered to do so by Stockton? And what about Ericsson, whose name was also in Ben's note?

Monty was determined to get some answers, and knew he would have to do it himself. Fortunately, his job in the Senate gave him some useful connections. He called upon an acquaintance in the Navy Department, who agreed to do some research for him. A few days later, over lunch, the acquaintance came through. Captain Stockton was not currently assigned to a ship and was on furlough, believed to be at his home in New Jersey. Fenwick had resigned from the Navy in the spring of 1844, a couple of months after the explosion. His whereabouts were unknown. Ericsson, according to the last records that the Navy had on him, was working at a foundry in New York City.

"Think this through, Tolliver," Monty muttered to himself. Seems suspicious that Fenwick would have left the Navy and disappeared only weeks after Ben's death. Can't confront Stockton, at least not yet. Gotta start with Ericsson, he decided. What did Ericsson know? What would he be "a fool" to say? Monty remembered having read in the newspapers that Ericsson and Stockton had a falling out just before the explosion, rumored to be over Ericsson's belief that Stockton had taken all of the credit for the *Princeton* when he brought the ship to Washington City, and not mentioning Ericsson's substantial contributions.

If anyone has information that would be helpful, Monty was sure that it would be Ericsson.

Monty's boss was understanding. The next week would be busy, but then the Senate would be in recess a few days for Easter and Monty could then take some days off. Some personal matters to take care of, he had stated, and no one pressed him for specifics.

CHAPTER 40

arch, 1845— Monty had never traveled much. Other than Ohio, he had been to Kentucky, and to Indiana a couple of times to visit family. He had passed through Pennsylvania when going to and from Ohio and Washington City, and had ventured into Maryland and Virginia briefly a few times. This was his first trip to New York City. The overnight train ride was more cumbersome than he had thought it would be. Three transfers in route, in Baltimore, Philadelphia, and Trenton, with some waiting time in each city. Finally, in the early afternoon, the chugging locomotive came to a stop at the station in Manhattan. Monty grabbed his bag and walked out into the cold and sooty air. He looked up. No sun. It was hard to tell if it was cloudy, or if the sunlight was blocked by the smoke from all of the trains. He walked over to a line of hacks, the drivers patiently waiting for arriving train passengers. "How long to get to Hogg and DeLamater Ironworks on West Thirteenth Street?," he asked the first one in the line.

The man quickly folded the newspaper that had half covered his face. "About twenty minutes. Hop in."

As the carriage headed south toward lower Manhattan, Monty was amazed by the size of the city and by the activity on the streets. Block after block of buildings, and people everywhere, rushing about. When the rig slowed at intersections, he heard different languages being spoken. His driver weaved between wagons and carts that seemed as if they had purposely been left in and along the road as obstacles. This place makes Washington City look, he thought, well, insignificant. He remembered having felt that way about Dayton when he had first seen the nation's capital. Everything is relative, he decided. Monty's rig finally made its last turn—west onto Thirteenth Street. He saw several smokestacks, with black smoke billowing from them, and the North River just beyond. The scene reminded him of his father's foundry back in Ohio, but on a much larger scale. The sign on top of one of the buildings read Hogg & DeLamater Ironworks. Sure hope that Ericsson is here today, he said to himself. He had not sent ahead word of his arrival, concerned that the Swede, who, according to everything Monty had read about him, had a volatile personality and would likely try to avoid a meeting.

Monty walked into a long red brick building with an office sign above the main door. "Good afternoon. My name is Montgomery Tolliver," he said to the young man sitting at a desk. "I am here to see Mr. John Ericsson."

The startled man, not much more than a boy, stood up, almost as if at attention. Before he could respond, a well-dressed man in a suit came out of an office just behind the desk and extended his hand to Monty. "Sir, I am Cornelius DeLamater, the owner," said the friendly-looking man with chin whiskers, who appeared to be in his early-thirties. "I could not help but overhear. You are looking for Mr. Ericsson? I'm sorry, I did not catch the name."

"Tolliver, Montgomery Tolliver. From Washington City. Yes, I am here to speak with Mr. John Ericsson, whom I understand is in your employ."

"Please come into my office." said the gentlemen, motioning for Monty to follow him. Once both were seated, he continued, "Is John expecting you?"

"He is not. My journey from Washington City is on short notice to me, and based on information that I only recently received." He handed DeLamater his card. "I should note, sir, that my business is of a personal nature. I do work for the United States Senate, but my visit is not related to government matters."

"I am relieved to hear that," said DeLamater. "John, as you may know, does not have good relations with the government. I doubt that he would agree to see you if your visit was in any official capacity. May I inquire as to the specific nature of your inquiry?"

"It concerns his past work with Captain Robert Stockton of the Navy. I am looking into the death of a close friend, who was an officer on one of Stockton's ships. I have just a few questions for him."

"Very well. Walk with me, Mr. Tolliver. John is usually in our research and design building," said DeLamater, as he led Monty out of a back door and toward another building, nearer the river. "I can introduce you. Beyond that, it is up to John. I should warn you that he is often a temperamental man. He may refuse to speak with you."

"I am aware of that, and understand."

"John is an inventor, a genius. I have known him since he came here from Sweden several years ago. Like many brilliant men, human interaction is not one of his strong points. But he is a good man at heart."

They walked into a large building, three stories tall, the inside of which was mostly open space. Spread around the large floor were a dozen or so boilers, engines, and other mechanical devices that Monty could not identify, in various states of assembly. Several workers hovered over them. There were lifts, reaching to the roof, with chains and pulleys, to move the heavy metal pieces into place. DeLamater motioned Monty through a doorway to the right and, in the room beyond it, he saw a man hunched over a draftsman's table, pencil in hand, and surrounded by papers and books. His spectacles were on the tip of his nose. The man looked up as they entered, but only for a second, and continued his work. He appeared to be maybe fifty, Monty thought, with a strong chin being his most prominent feature. He was balding, but had very little gray in his remaining black hair, which covered most of his ears, and he had bushy side whiskers.

"Good afternoon, John. A gentleman, Mr. Tolliver here, has come from Washington City to see you and would like to have a few words."

"I have no interest in speaking to anyone from that place. You know my thoughts on that, Cornelius."

"I do, but he tells me that he is here on a personal matter, not government business. Please give him a few minutes, John, as a courtesy to me. I will leave the two of you to talk," said DeLamater, as he backed out of the doorway.

"Mr. Ericsson, it is an honor to meet you. I have read much about your inventions," said Monty, hoping to soften up the Swede with praise. "I will only take a few minutes of your time."

"I *am* busy. Only a few minutes. What can I do for you, Mr. Tolliver?"

"I am here about Captain Robert Stockton," said Monty. The mention of Stockton's name produced an icy stare from Ericsson.

"Stockton. Are you a friend of Stockton?"

"No, not at all."

"Good. Any friend of his is no friend of mine."

"Mr. Ericsson, I will get directly to the point of my visit. I had a friend who was an officer on the *Princeton*. He was killed shortly after the explosion last year and I suspect that it had something to do with the explosion, and that Stockton may have been involved."

"Ahh, the *Princeton*," said Ericsson. "One of my proudest achievements, which Stockton took all the credit for. He is a showman. An egotist and a liar. I would not put much past him, although I have to say I never figured him to be a murderer. Quite possible, though."

"I understand that you were not in Washington City at the time of the explosion," said Monty. "Is that correct?"

"Only because the captain excluded me. The scoundrel. When the *Princeton* left New York for Washington City, we had agreed that I was to accompany him. I spent most of two years working on the design and supervising the ship's construction. At the appointed time, I was at the dock at the end of Wall Street, with my bags. The ship passed by without as much as slowing down. Stockton intentionally left me behind. Once in the capital, he touted the ship as his own creation. Referred to me in a letter to Congress as merely a 'good mechanic' who had done some work on her. Only after the tragedy did he seek to involve me as, what is the word in English for it, a scapegoat?"

"Correct. How so?"

"A few days after the explosion," Ericsson continued, "Stockton told the Navy Department's Board of Inquiry that was investigating it to request my testimony. He was trying, I was certain, to set me up for the blame. He declined to appear before them himself, allegedly due to his injuries from the explosion, which I understand were not serious. I refused. I responded to them how I would have appreciated an invitation from Captain Stockton a week earlier, *before* the explosion. Then, I might have been able to render good service and valuable counsel. Too late, after the fact, I advised them."

Monty was surprised at how much, and how freely, Ericsson was talking, and to a total stranger. He had not been expecting this, having thought that getting information from the thin-skinned inventor would be difficult. It was, he thought, as if Ericsson's pent-up resentment and anger toward Stockton finally had an outlet, a release valve.

"Do you think Stockton could have prevented the explosion?"

"Absolutely. What is your American legal term for it? Negligence? It was all his fault, and the government covered it up. He and his friend President Tyler saw to that."

"What could he have done?"

"The Peacemaker, the cannon that exploded, was the only thing on the *Princeton* that was Stockton's creation. The rest of it, the ship's design, the screw propeller system, the boilers, the collapsible smokestack, even the other big cannon, the Oregon, were all my inventions. They all worked to perfection. His small contribution caused the tragedy. It was defective."

"How so? I thought that the two large cannons were basically the same?," asked Monty.

"Similar, but not the same. I had a belief, Mr. Tolliver, that cannons could be made of wrought iron, instead of the traditional molten iron. It is lighter, allows for a bigger weapon, and hence a larger and more damaging projectile. While I was still living in England, I designed the Oregon, a twelve-inch bore wrought iron cannon. I supervised its forging in Liverpool and brought it with me when I came to this country. I designed it to be of the maximum safe size and weight. A wrought iron cannon, you have to understand, is made of multiple pieces, heated and beaten into a solid unit. The longer and thicker the cannon is, the less likely a homogeneous unit can be achieved, causing an increased risk of cracks developing at the seams."

"I see," said Monty. "It's not made as one solid unit, but in pieces joined together."

"Exactly." Ericsson continued, "I had the Oregon tested at a beach on the New Jersey coast. After multiple firings, it developed small cracks near its breech. I determined that the cracks could be arrested, and future ones prevented, by heating iron rings and shrinking them over the base of the weapon. I used two of these at each key point, one above the other. Together, they were more than three inches thick. It worked perfectly. We fired it more than a hundred times, with no evidence of any increased cracking."

"And what about the Peacemaker?," asked Monty.

"That was Stockton's. He wanted his own cannon on the *Princeton*. Unfortunately, he does not possess the mechanical ability to design anything more complicated than a wheelbarrow. He copied my design for the Oregon but, of course, his cannon had to be bigger. It was longer and a foot thicker at its base, making it less likely that it could be properly forged. He had it made at a foundry here in New York. He had it tested at sea, mounted on a ship, and it also developed small cracks upon multiple firings. Stockton had metal bands put on the cannon's base, knowing that I had put bands on the Oregon. But, not understanding metallurgy, he used metal strips and welded them onto the base."

"How was that different from your solution for the cracking?"

"I had molten metal formed into solid rings and, while still hot, placed them at intervals on the base of the cannon, and then put second rings on top of them. When cooled, they shrank and provided a secure bond with no weak points. Stockton's welded strips were just that, strips, with two ends. Points of weakness. And he did not double them. They did nothing to arrest the cracks. Read the study of the Franklin Institute in Philadelphia concerning the explosion, if you can find a copy. They confirmed this. Of course, Stockton and his friend President Tyler managed to have that report buried and no blame for the tragedy attributed to Stockton. 'Just an unavoidable accident,' Tyler told the country."

"How do you know that Stockton was aware of a problem with the method that he used to deal with the cracking?"

"I wrote to him and told him so. I explained how my solution of dealing with the cracks on the Oregon was effective and had solved the issue, and that what he had done with the Peacemaker would likely not be so. I strongly suggested that any demonstration firings of the *Princeton's* ordnance while in Washington City, especially with civilians on board, be done using the Oregon, instead of the Peacemaker."

Monty could not believe his ears. A letter from Ericsson to Stockton warning him of a problem with the Peacemaker. It had to be *the* letter. The one that had been burned and that Ben had overheard Stockton and Fenwick talking about. A letter over which they may have been willing to kill Ben, to forever silence him for having knowledge of its destruction.

"Do you know when you wrote this letter, and would you have a copy of it?"

"Sometime in late January, or early February, of last year. I do not keep copies of my letters, Mr. Tolliver. I am an engineer, an inventor, not a man of letters. Copies of sketches and designs I keep. Not correspondence."

"I believe that your letter to Stockton was burned by him and suspect that my friend's knowledge of it may have led to his murder." Monty continued, almost pleading. "Would you be willing to come to Washington City to give a statement to the police, or send them an affidavit stating what you have told me today?"

"I will not," responded Ericsson, with a firmness in his voice. "These matters occurred more than a year ago. I have moved on. I made a decision then not to publicly accuse Captain Stockton. A decision I have come to regret, but nonetheless one that I made. The man has wronged me, then and since. Due to him, my claim to the government for reimbursement for the two years that I spent working on the *Princeton* was denied. The whole matter has left a bitter taste in my mouth for anyone associated with the government. My hurling of accusations at Stockton now would only, I am certain, be viewed as revenge against him over these financial matters, and would not be believed. I do not need that. Stockton is a powerful man and he is not one to react well to criticism."

Monty was dejected at hearing the words, but he saw the basis for Ericsson's reasoning. He had gotten much more information from the Swede than he had anticipated, and was glad that he had made the trip to New York. But he could not force the man to do something against his will. He decided not to press the matter.

Monty extended his hand to Ericsson. "I understand your position. You have been most helpful and I thank you for your time. Perhaps in the future our paths will cross again."

"Perhaps. Pleased to have been of help," responded the inventor, as he pushed his spectacles up on his nose and went back to his work. As Monty turned to leave, Ericsson added, "If you can hold Captain Stockton accountable for his actions, Mr. Tolliver, then Godspeed to you. But a word of caution. I know this man. Tread warily. If, as you suspect, he was involved in the killing of your friend, what would stop him from killing again?"

CHAPTER 41

March, 1845— Monty found a hotel in Manhattan about a mile or so from the Hogg & DeLamater Ironworks. He had already decided press forward with his investigation. It was time to pay a visit to Captain Robert Stockton. The fact that the man had escaped any damage to his reputation from the explosion was testament, Monty thought, to his power and influence. Stockton had friends in high places. Ericsson's last words of warning to him rang in his ears. Despite the risk of possible danger, he determined that he owed it to Ben to take the next step. Surely, he was confident, Ben would have done the same for him. At the train station, only a few blocks from the hotel, he purchased a ticket for the first train the next morning to Princeton, New Jersey. He hoped that his information that Stockton was there was still accurate. He decided not to send any message in advance, willing to take the risk that the captain may not be there. He had gotten a lot of information from Ericsson by showing up unannounced. Maybe it would also work with Stockton.

The train trip to Princeton took all morning. Monty grabbed a quick lunch near the station and then hailed a carriage. "To Captain Stockton's home," he said to the driver. "I believe it's called Morven."

"Yes sir, it is," responded the driver. "I've taken a lot of folks there over the years. About the fanciest place in town. Only a few minutes away."

As the carriage passed through Morven's ornate entrance gates, Monty took it all in. There were landscaped gardens, with sculptures, on both sides of the cobblestone driveway. He imagined how beautiful they would look in a few weeks, when spring arrived. In front of him stood an imposing brick mansion, with a large front porch supported by four white columns. He remembered talking with Ben about Stockton being wealthy beyond belief. It was no exaggeration, judging by his home.

Monty's knock on the door was answered by a butler. "Good afternoon," he began, "I am Montgomery Tolliver." He handed to the butler his card identifying himself and listing his job with the Senate. "I would like to know if Captain Stockton is available for a brief meeting."

"Do you have an appointment, sir?," asked the butler, somewhat gruffly.

"I do not. I am passing through town today, having left Washington City a few days ago, and was hoping that the captain could spare a few minutes. It concerns one of his former officers on the *Princeton*."

The butler showed Monty into the parlor, located to the right of the foyer, and asked him to take a seat. A fire burned in the large fireplace on the far side of the room. Monty walked over to it, warmed his hands, and unbuttoned his coat. Although the sun had peaked out of the clouds some during his carriage ride from the train station, the temperature was cool, typical of a March day in the northeast. He took a seat in a plush chair near the fire.

A few minutes later, the butler returned. "The captain will see you, sir. He is finishing his lunch and will be with you in a few minutes."

Monty waited, rehearsing in his mind the tone that he was going to take with Stockton, and how much information he wanted to disclose. Start gently, he decided, and only reveal what he had to. A servant came in and added logs to the fire. It started to crackle. Finally, after about fifteen minutes, a tall gentleman with a rugged face and a full head of dark hair walked into the room. The hair made him seem younger than his years. Monty judged him to be in his mid-fifties. He walked erectly and had the bearing of a military man, Monty thought.

"Mr. Tolliver," said Stockton, reading Monty's card, as he held it in his hand. "I do not recall that we have previously been acquainted. I am not aware of any pending issues that I have with the United States Senate."

"We have not met before, captain. My apologies for stopping by unannounced. Thank you for taking the time to see me. My visit is not related to my work with the Senate. It is of a personal nature. I will only take a few minutes of your time."

"Quite alright. My man, Leonard, advises me that you wanted to discuss one of my former officers on the *Princeton*. Which one?"

"Lieutenant Benjamin Geddis, sir."

Stockton brought his right hand to his face and rubbed his chin. "Lieutenant Geddis, yes, I remember the name. He was with me but for a short time. Can't say that I really knew him. I do recall that he sustained some sort of minor injury in that tragic explosion and that he was the unfortunate chap who was killed a few days later. A robbery, or something similar, I was told. If I may ask, what was your relationship with the lieutenant?"

"Ben was a friend of mine," replied Monty. "I have been looking into his death. I have doubts that it occurred as determined by the authorities in Washington City."

"Kind of late to be doing that, isn't it, Mr. Tolliver? More than a year has passed." At the mention of the possibility that the cause of Ben's death may be other than previously determined, Monty noticed the tone of Stockton's voice change to one of annoyance. "I know nothing of the details of his death," said the captain, "only what I was told."

"What can you tell me about Commander Thomas Fenwick? I understand that he was your second in command on the *Princeton* at that time? According to the police, he was the lieutenant's last known visitor before his death." Stockton, Monty observed, turned his head a bit and seemed surprised at the mentioning of Fenwick's name.

"Correct. Second in command. Fenwick was a first-rate officer." Stockton stood, walked over to the fireplace, warmed his hands, and continued. "He served under me for several years. The explosion affected all of my officers and crew, him more than most. He resigned his commission a couple of months later. Said he needed a change. Maybe head out west. He wasn't sure."

"Do you know where he went, where he may be reached?"

"Are you married, Mr. Tolliver?"

"No, sir."

"Neither was the commander. No wife, no close family. Told me he wanted to be a free spirit, to go where fate may take him. He could be anywhere. I have heard nothing of him since his resignation."

Might as well ask it, Monty decided. "Captain, would you have any reason to suspect that Commander Fenwick could have been involved in the death of Lieutenant Geddis?"

"Fenwick a murderer, is that what you are suggesting?," responded Stockton, now clearly irritated. "Nonsense. He would have had no reason. He knew Geddis no more than I did. As I said, your friend was with us only a short time, only a week or so, as I recall." Monty saw Stockton pull his watch out of the pocket of his waistcoat and glance at it, a clear signal that he was ready to end the conversation. "Is there anything else, *young* man? I do have matters that I need to attend to." He noticed Stockton's emphasis on the word young, as though he were a boy wasting the captain's time. He decided to press the captain a bit further, before he was dismissed.

"Just one more question. Was the cause of the explosion ever determined? I understand that there was an inquiry done by the Franklin Institute that concluded there was some defect in the cannon, the Peacemaker, and that Mr. Ericsson, who worked on the ship's design, agreed with that assessment?"

"The Franklin Institute report?," scoffed Stockton, in a mocking tone. "A bunch of so-called experts looking for an answer when there was none. No attention was paid to it, and rightfully so. Ericsson? I am not aware of, nor do I care, about his opinion. A very disgruntled man, and hostile to me, ever since I opposed his exorbitant request for money from the government for work that he claimed to have done on the *Princeton*, and which I had never authorized. What happened that tragic day, Mr. Tolliver, was, as President Tyler told the country, an unavoidable accident, pure and simple."

"Do you feel that there was anything you could have done, captain, to have prevented it?"

"Sir, are you here to accuse *me* of something? If so, state it," said a now outraged Stockton.

If it were a generation earlier, Monty thought, this irate man would have challenged him to a duel. Good thing that those days were over. He decided that going any further would not be productive. Instead, he replied, "No, captain, just here to get some information."

Stockton, still standing near the fireplace and hovering over the seated Monty, walked over to a table and rang a small bell. Monty stood; he knew when he was being dismissed. Within a few seconds, the butler appeared.

"Good day, Mr. Tolliver. Leonard will show you out." No hand was extended.

The butler dutifully directed Monty out of the front door and onto the porch. "Can I have someone take you to the train station, sir?," he asked.

"That won't be necessary. How far to the nearest carriage stop?"

"About a quarter of a mile, to the left after the main gate. I can have one of the men run you up there."

Monty, still taking in the abrupt end to his conversation with Stockton, looked up at the now mostly clear March sky. He felt he needed some time alone. "Thank you, but I'll walk," he replied. At least the butler, he thought, as he made his way to the gate, had been polite.

* * *

A couple of hours later, Monty was on board a train back to Washington City. As he sat on an uncomfortable seat in the half-empty rail car, he kept going over the meeting with Stockton. The captain readily remembered Ben's name and knew about his death. Unusual, he speculated, for an officer whom he said he hardly knew. The captain's hostility to Ericsson, and to any questioning of the cause of the explosion, was palpable. He was hiding something, Monty was sure. But did the captain have anything to do with Ben's death? He reviewed the facts again in his mind. There was a letter from Ericsson to Stockton warning him that the repairs to the cracks on the Peacemaker were not effective. He had confirmed that with Ericsson. It was information that, if known to the press or the public, would destroy the captain's reputation and career. According to Ben's note, when he was on the ship a couple of days after the explosion, he overheard Stockton and Fenwick talking behind a closed door about a burned letter. Ericsson's name had been mentioned. Fenwick, according to what Ben had told Monty, had seen Ben on the ship that day. Fenwick, according to his statement to the police, had gone to Ben's room the night of Ben's death, giving him knowledge of the layout of the room, and of the rear window. Ben was dead within hours.

Monty mulled over a theory. Fenwick knew that Ben had overheard he and the captain talking about the burned letter, he had gone back to Ben's room that night, broken in through the window, and killed Ben, either under a direct order from Stockton, or under an implicit one. Maybe Fenwick had free rein to do whatever he determined was needed to protect his boss, including murder, had done it on his own, and Stockton just knew, without having to be told. Fenwick's resignation from the Navy a few weeks later, and his subsequent disappearance, were too convenient. Fenwick, Monty suspected, was a killer in hiding. But how, he wondered, was he ever going to be able to prove any of this? Or even make a credible allegation? The authorities had ruled Ben's death the result of a burglary and they were not going to reconsider that conclusion without more evidence. Evidence that Monty did not have.

The next morning, the train finally pulled into the station in Washington City. Monty had reached a decision. It was not one that he was fully satisfied with, but one which he believed was correct. He decided to not go any further, on his own, looking into Ben's death. He had done what he could, but knew nothing could be proved. He would go to Detective Lawrence, let him know what he had found, and any further action would be in the detective's hands.

* * *

Monty sat across from Detective Lawrence's desk. As the man stroked his chin, Monty could tell his decision by the look on his face.

"The information from your trip to New York and New Jersey is interesting. Your loyalty to your friend is admirable. But unless Ericsson changes his mind and agrees to talk to us, or unless Fenwick reappears and can be questioned, I still have no basis to reopen the lieutenant's case."

"But . . ."

"I understand your frustration, Mr. Tolliver. My hands are tied. If we had this information a year ago, when Fenwick and Stockton were still here in the city, and when Ericsson may have been willing to speak to us, my answer would have been different. I am sorry."

Monty decided against any further pleas. He stood up and reached for Lawrence's hand. "Thank you for your time, detective."

As he walked out of the police station, Monty's frustration was directed more at himself, than at the detective. If he had only looked through the Ben Franklin quotation book when the detective gave it to him a year ago and had found the note then. At least a timely and full investigation could then have been done. He felt like he had failed Ben.

CHAPTER 42

*J**une, 1845, to February, 1851* — "Thank you for all of your hard work over the past three years. It has been a pleasure to have known you and to have worked with you. I know that I speak on behalf of the entire Senate in wishing you well."

"Thank you, sir," Monty replied to his boss, Asbury Dickins, the secretary of the Senate. "I am still in awe every time that I am in the Senate chamber. From when I began working for Senator Clay seven years ago, and through my time working here for you, it has been the experience of a lifetime. But it is time to move on, to go back to Ohio, to my family."

It had been more than a year since the failed assassination plot and Ben's death. Monty still had recurring nightmares about the plot. In one, there was no explosion and the killing of Tyler had been successful, but he and his friends were caught, tried, and convicted of treason and murder. That one always ended with he, Ben, and Sam standing on the gallows, with ropes around their necks and hoods over their heads, awaiting the signal from the executioner. In another, on the day before the *Princeton's* excursion, he became overwhelmed at the thought of committing treason and killing the president and frantically tried to back out of it at the last minute. In yet another nightmare, the facts were as they happened in reality, but he began to be followed by strangers, and then anonymous notes arrived implicating him in the failed plot, and threatening to expose him.

Monty was surprised that he had lasted so long in Washington City. Now, in the summer of 1845, it was time to turn the page. He needed a change of scenery. His best friend had been dead for more than a year. His attempt a few months earlier to have the investigation into Ben's death reopened had failed. His next closest friend, Sam, had been transferred by the Army to South Carolina. Monty was now thirty-one years old. His love life was almost non-existent. He felt ashamed of his continued visits, although less frequent, to Liz at the brothel. Politics, with the new Polk Administration in power and the impending annexation of Texas, depressed him even more.

* * *

The trip home to Ohio was uneventful, taking only a week in the pleasant June weather. Prior trips in the winter had taken more than twice as long. Monty followed his usual route, taking the Baltimore and Ohio Railroad to Baltimore and then traveling by stagecoach on the National Road in an almost straight-line westward to central Ohio. The talk at dinner in the taverns along the way focused on the new president, Polk, and whether the annexation of Texas would lead to war with Mexico. Monty was pleased to hear that most who expressed their views had voted for

Senator Clay the previous fall, and were opposed to annexation. Many thought that war was now inevitable. At times, he had imagined himself, while passing a dish of overcooked tavern food, telling his eating companions that he and his friend had come within a hair's breadth of killing Tyler last year and of having stopped annexation dead in its tracks.

In Dayton, Monty's parents, Roger and Elizabeth, were overjoyed to have him back home after seven years of living away. Both were proud of their son's work in the nation's capital, but glad that he had decided to return to Ohio. Monty learned that the family business, Tolliver's Metal Works, a foundry located on the bank of the Miami River, was doing well, employing almost twenty men, making it one of the largest employers in Dayton. His mother updated him on the latest news of his three siblings and their children, proudly advising that she had one more grandchild on the way. Monty and his father discussed and confirmed what they had both broached in letters over the past few months. Roger offered, and Monty agreed to accept, a position at the foundry, as Roger described it, to be the face of the foundry in the community, to pursue more contracts, and to work on expanding the products made and sold. Roger had always preferred the technical side of the work, the metallurgy, and being with and overseeing the employees. Monty's skills from the political world, his father was certain, would be an asset in growing the business.

Over the next couple of years, Roger's fatherly instincts proved to be accurate. Monty thrived in his new position. His likeable personality and his ability to remember names and faces served him well in his new role. He became a good salesman, joining professional and gentlemen's clubs in Dayton and getting to know many of the business leaders in the community. His ideas for pursuing new lines of business, including making parts for weapons for the military, and for railroads, produced new work. The foundry hired five new employees to keep up with the volume.

Those with whom Monty had traveled on his way to Ohio in the summer of 1845 had also been good prognosticators. Within six months of Texas becoming a state at the end of that year, war with Mexico came and, by mid-1847, was in its second year. It irritated Monty every time he picked up a newspaper. He had tried to stop all of this, but had failed. Strong Whig opposition to going to war had ceased once troops were committed and causalities began to mount. Supporting the troops then became bipartisan, despite past differences over how or why the fighting had begun.

While the war was still going on, in the spring of 1847, Monty was called upon by an unexpected visitor in his office at the foundry. The gentlemen identified himself as the chairman of the Whig Party of Montgomery County, the county in which Dayton was located. Monty had avoided becoming involved in local politics since his return home. The man explained that the purpose of his visit was to recruit Monty to be the Whig Party's candidate for Congress in the Tenth District of Ohio in the upcoming 1848 election. The incumbent Whig congressman, the man explained, would be running for governor and the party was in search of a candidate to hold onto the seat. They wanted a fresh face to present to the voters. Several business leaders had suggested Monty, and it was also noted that Monty's prior work for Senator Clay, who had carried the district by a wide margin over Polk in the 1844 election, would be an asset. If Monty consented, the party chairman assured him that he would be the Whig nominee for the seat. Take your time to think about it, the man had said.

Over the next few weeks, Monty pondered the proposition. What about his work at the foundry, which had been going so well? His father had given his blessing to accepting the offer, and had seemed to be sincere, not just because he thought it was what Monty wanted to hear. Roger was willing to take on extra work himself and explained that he could assign some of Monty's tasks to the foundry's bookkeeper, who was eager for more responsibility and who showed promise. Elizabeth also approved, despite knowing that it would mean, if elected, Monty would be away in Washington City for months at a time. Both of his parents, neither of whom had come from any wealth, nor who had much in the way of formal education, told Monty they would be proud to have their son become a member of Congress. But the decision was his to make.

Monty weighed the plusses and minuses of the situation. Yes, he had meaningful experience from working for Senator Clay and for the Senate, which would serve him well. He knew how Congress worked, having seen it from the inside. He had developed relationships there that would be an asset. There were things he wanted to accomplish. He wanted to do something about slavery. Limit it. Get rid of it. But there was another part to his past in Washington City that he had to consider, one that kept him up at night as he weighed the offer from the Whig Party. He had a skeleton in his closet. A big one. He had conspired to kill the president of the United States. To his knowledge, only two other people knew. One was dead and the other, he was sure, would never reveal it. It had now been more than three years. If anyone else knew about it, he felt that he would have been approached, threatened, or blackmailed by now. He satisfied himself that his secret was safe and decided to accept the party's offer.

The local Whig Party chairman was true to his promise. In the summer of 1848, the party met in convention and Monty was unanimously nominated to be its candidate for Congress. In November, he won the election with more than fifty-five percent of the vote, running a couple of percent higher than the Whig candidate in the last election. He went to Washington City for a brief two-week session in March 1849 to open the Thirty-First Congress, including the inauguration of Zachary Taylor as president, and then returned home for almost eight months, when Congress was in a long recess. During that time, he immersed himself in his work at the foundry, knowing that when he left again in December, it would be for an extended period of time. At least six months, maybe more. Business was good. The foundry received a contract to make several cannons for the Army, and also for rifle parts. Some orders from two Ohio-based railroads had also been received.

Professional success, unfortunately, was coupled with frustration in his personal life. When he had visited Dayton over Christmas in 1843, he had met a local woman, Theresa Bennett, the daughter of the owner of a local dry goods store. Over the three or four times that they were together then, Monty realized that she was different from any of the women he had previously courted. A potential wife. He had never felt that way before. Six years younger than he, Theresa had auburn hair, blue eyes, and an infectious smile. She was intelligent and well read. Although he had promised to write her after he returned to Washington City, he then became involved in the plot to kill Tyler. Not thinking it was wise to pursue romance while plotting to assassinate the president of the United States, he chose not to write her. Then, with his grief over Ben's death, and his frustration over how things had turned out, he further delayed contacting her. By the time he finally arrived in Dayton in mid-1845, it was too late. He learned that Theresa was engaged to another man and was to be married later that year. He sent her a brief note offering his best wishes, but decided that it would be inappropriate to call on her. Over the next few years, the other women he met did not compare in his mind with Theresa. Once again, as with the investigation into Ben's death, delay and inaction on his part had been costly. He wondered if he was destined to be a lifelong bachelor.

In December of 1849, when Monty returned to Washington for the full congressional session, the city was in a frenzy over what to do with the land won in the Mexican War. The Treaty of Guadalupe Hidalgo, which ended the war, stipulated that, for a payment of fifteen million dollars, Mexico would cede more than 500,000 square miles of territory to the United States, including California, and all of the land between it and Texas. Sectional divisions were higher than ever. Southerners wanted the new land to be slave territory. Northerners wanted it to be free.

Monty's former boss, Senator Clay, who had returned to the Senate at the same time that Monty began his term in the House of Representatives, outlined early in the session his plan to resolve the outstanding issues. Under it, California would be admitted to the Union as a free state, and the state of Texas would agree to significantly reduce its claimed borders and transfer the land given up to the federal government, in exchange for federal assumption of its debt. From this land, the territories of New Mexico and Utah would be created, with the existence of slavery in them to be determined in the future by a vote of their citizens. The sale and trading of enslaved persons within Washington City would be outlawed and, in a concession to southerners, a more forceful law concerning fugitive slaves was proposed, mandating that federal law enforcement and judicial officers assist in their capture and return and, to some extent, requiring the same of private citizens. Clay had initially combined all of the bills into an omnibus package, but that failed to pass the Senate. He then became ill with the beginnings of the tuberculosis that would eventually take his life, and had to leave the Senate for a while to recuperate. Senator Stephen Douglas of Illinois, a Democrat, picked up where Clay left off and led the effort. The bills were passed individually by the Senate. They then moved to the House, where they were also passed, as five separate bills. Monty voted for all of them, except for the fugitive slave provision, which he strongly opposed. President Millard Fillmore, who had assumed the presidency in July 1850 upon President Taylor's death from a stomach ailment, signed all of the bills of the Compromise of 1850 into law in September, and, after ten months, Congress finally adjourned. In early October, Monty was finally able to go home to Dayton.

It had been a long and grueling session. Although he had wanted stronger measures taken against slavery, Monty was generally pleased with the outcome. It was a good start, he thought. California was going to be a free state. Eliminating slave trade in Washington City was a step in the right direction. And the New Mexico and Utah territories could still be free of slavery, depending on votes there in the future. He had to hand it to his mentor and friend, Senator Clay. The Great Compromiser had done it again—as with the Missouri Compromise and the Nullification Crisis, he had brought the nation back from the brink of civil war. But more, Monty believed, needed to be done. To him, the compromise was a beginning, not an end, as to what needed to be done regarding slavery.

Monty was nominated by the Whigs during the summer of 1850 for a second term in Congress. When he finally got back home in early October, he spent a month campaigning around his district. It was his least favorite part of the job. He was not good at glad-handling voters, and his oratorical skills were even worse. He envied Senator Clay, who excelled at both, and wished that some of his former boss's talents had rubbed off on him during their years together. Despite his mediocre campaign skills, he won the election in November 1850 with almost sixty percent of the vote. He must be doing something right, he considered, and was pleased to have been re-elected by a larger margin than he had received two years earlier. After a few more weeks at home in Ohio, he would make the trek back to Washington in early December for the second session of the Thirty-First Congress, and then the beginning, in March of 1851, of the Thirty-Second Congress.

CHAPTER 43

March, 1851— As Monty's horse led him up the temporary construction road off of B Street, the rocky surface and ruts from wagon wheels made the going slow. He wondered if coming had been a wise decision. But how could he not? He owed it to Ben. Not like he was meeting this stranger in some dark alley in the middle of the night. It was daylight, and he was in the middle of the nation's capital. He thought he would be safe. The wind on the cloudy day whipped around him. Thankfully, the rain from the morning had stopped.

The unsigned note, stuffed in an envelope and slid underneath the door of his congressional office, had been brief. "For truth about death of Lt. Geddis, meet Sunday 2 pm at Wash. Monument site. Come alone," it had stated. The cloak-and-dagger aspect of it bothered him. If this person had information, why not give a name, or walk into the office and ask for a meeting? Ben had been dead seven years. What could this person know about Ben's death? He had to find out.

It was the second week of March, 1851. Monty was in Washington City for the special session of the new Congress, the beginning of his second term. The session would only last a couple of weeks. He would then head back home to Ohio for several months and return in the late fall for the formal session that would begin in December.

He looked at the unfinished structure in front of him. After more than two years of construction, it had risen, he guessed, to around six stories, about the height of the National Hotel. Stacks of huge rectangular white marble stones, lifts with ropes attached to steam engines, several wagons, and construction equipment, surrounded what was going to be, when completed, an awe-inspiring monument honoring the general who had led the Continental Army during the American Revolution and who had become the nation's first president. Monty had seen sketches of the design in newspapers at the time of the laying of the cornerstone on the Fourth of July in 1848. The Washington Monument was to be an obelisk, fifty-five feet square at the ground, and rising more than five hundred and fifty feet into the air, surrounded at its base by a Roman-style temple, with thirty columns in a circle, and, above the main entrance, a statue of George Washington, standing in a chariot, and driving six horses. They have a lot more work to do, Monty thought, as he dismounted and tied his horse to a hitching post. For now, it looked like a giant marble cube, perched on the crest of a small hill.

The site was deserted on this dreary Sunday afternoon. He walked around a corner and saw a man sitting on a bench near one of the steam engines, his boots covered in mud. No sign of a horse. He must have walked here, Monty surmised. The man wore a canvas traveling topcoat that had seen its better days, and his hands were thrust into the deep pockets. He gazed down and his dark slouch hat made it impossible to see his face.

"I wasn't sure if you would come," the man said, as he lifted his head and stared at Monty.

Monty could not believe his eyes. Several seconds lapsed before he could get the word past his lips.

"Sam?"

CHAPTER 44

March, 1851— Monty felt a rush of emotions. Surprise. Suspicion. He cocked his head, still in disbelief. "What's going on? Why all the secrecy?," he asked. He took a step toward Sam and started to extend his right hand.

"No," responded Sam, curtly. "You will not want a handshake from me. Sit down." He motioned to a block of marble on the ground next to Monty.

Monty complied. "Are you alright?"

"I can't stand it anymore." Sam took a deep breath, exhaled, and then bit his lower lip. "You think you make the right decision." His eyes began to moisten. "Then you realize how terribly wrong it was, what it led to, and you can't take it back."

"I'm lost. *What* are you talking about?"

"That day," Sam began.

Monty needed no explanation of that. The day of the plot, of the explosion. A day he had thought about, sometimes dwelled upon, every day since.

"I warned the *Princeton* of the plot."

Monty's eyes narrowed. He grabbed a clump of his hair with his right hand, then slowly released it. "Why?" He paused for a few seconds. "How?"

"When I woke up, I was having second thoughts. Had been, frankly, for a couple of days. Could I really let the president of the United States be killed? I hated the man, but he was the president. I am an officer in the Army. But could I implicate you and Ben in a plot to kill him, knowing what that would mean? It ate at me all morning. I came up with a plan that, I thought, could solve both problems. I got the horse all set and in place for Ben, if needed. I took the steamship out from the fort around noon, as we had planned, still not certain what I was going to do."

Monty looked on, dumbfounded.

"I got to the middle of the river and saw the *Princeton* in the distance through my spyglass, and coming straight toward me. I was about a mile upriver from Mount Vernon, knowing that the cannon would be fired for a final time when the ship got there, and when Ben would shoot the president. I pulled out the flags and poles for hand signaling that I had put in a bag in the storage locker. I had studied the Navy codebook that morning. I got out the flags I needed. The one for danger, and the ones to spell out T-Y-L-E-R, using the code. I had already covered over my ship's name and number, pulled down the flag, changed out of my uniform, and covered my face as much as I could."

"Continue," said Monty, in disbelief, as he slowly turned his head from side to side.

"I waited. When I could just make out a sailor in the crow's nest, and the uniforms of some of the officers on the deck, I grabbed the flags and signaled the message. Three times. I didn't know then if they saw it or not. I got out of the way before the ship got any closer."

"How do you know they got the message?"

"Because they kept Tyler where he was, below deck, and guarded him."

"No. He stayed below deck to listen to a song," said Monty. "That's why he was not behind the cannon when it exploded."

"That was the cover story they came up with. They didn't want the public to know of an assassination threat. There was a song being sung, but that was not why he stayed where he was. They were about to move him into the captain's quarters when the explosion happened."

"How do you know this?"

"Because . . . because Ben told me."

"You saw Ben after the explosion? When?"

"The night before the funeral of the victims. My unit was called to march in it. We traveled all day from Fort Washington and got into the city late. Quartered at the Navy Yard. I snuck out, around ten or so. I wanted to make sure that you and Ben were all right, that Ben was not injured, and that neither of you had been arrested. I stopped by your room first, but you weren't there. I then stopped in to see Ben. Tapped on the back window, as we always did after the landlady had locked the door for the night. Rather than go down the hallway and unlock the front door, he just helped me in through the window."

"The night he was killed?"

"Yes. He told me what had happened, about him being in position, of Tyler not being there, of the explosion, and of his head injury. He was in a foul mood. Angry that Tyler had escaped death, both from his hand and from the explosion. He told me that he had been visited by another officer, I think he said it was a commander, earlier that evening, who had come by to drop off his coat and pistol, and to check on how he was recovering from his head injury. Ben said this officer told him that the ship had gotten a signaled message, minutes before the explosion, of a threat to the president and that they kept him below deck and closely watched. It saved Tyler from being killed in the explosion."

"You said you didn't know that day if your message was received. If it had not, were you going to let Ben freeze and drown in the water?"

"No. I had decided that I was going to signal the ship and, if that failed and he carried out the act, I was going to honor my promise to you and Ben and get him to shore and on his way. I had the horse waiting near the fort."

"Well, I suppose that's something. What does all this have to do with Ben's death?"

"I am not a good liar. Ben figured out that the warning had come from me. I guess it wasn't hard to deduce. Other than you, who else could it have been? He became irate. Started to attack me. I pushed him and he stumbled and fell backward, hit his head on a corner of a table, and was unconscious. I couldn't revive him. He appeared to be dead as soon as he hit the floor. A pool of blood spread on the rug. I panicked. How could I explain it to the police without risking them finding out about the plot, and implicating you, Ben, and myself? I ransacked the room, to make it look like a burglary. Went out the back window, the way I had come in. I cannot count how many times since then that I tried to muster the courage to tell you, but couldn't. How could I tell you that I betrayed you and Ben, and then that I killed Ben? It was an accident, but I killed him." Tears streamed down Sam's cheeks.

"We met together months later, Sam. More than once. We told stories of Ben," said Monty, his voice rising with each word. "We read his letter to his parents and shed tears. And all that time, you said not a word to me about any of this. You son of a bitch!"

"I'm telling you now." Sam's eyes darted. He could not look Monty straight in the eyes. "My life has been a living hell these past seven years. Not only did I betray my friends, kill one, and lie to the other, but I was wrong. I compromised my morals. I detest slavery. It has grown since then, I believe, due to my actions. The things I have seen done to slaves in South Carolina are unspeakable. Beatings. Lynchings. I feel like it is my fault, that if Tyler had been killed, maybe their lives would be better by now. Or at least they would have some hope."

"Why come to me now?"

"Because it's over. I can't take it anymore. Be stronger than I was, Monty. Fight for what you and Ben and I talked about those years ago. In my pocket, I have a note confessing to Ben's death."

Monty watched as Sam began to pull something out of the pocket of his coat. It was not a note. "No!," he cried, as he rushed toward Sam. He was too late.

Sam put the barrel of the pistol under his chin and pulled the trigger. Monty reached him as his lifeless body began to slump to the side.

CHAPTER 45

*J**une, 1852—* When the train from Washington City to Baltimore arrived at Camden Station, Monty pulled out his pocket watch. On time, he said to himself, just over two hours. On the ride, he thought about Sam's suicide, as he often did. It had been just over a year. The sight still haunted him. The note he had found in Sam's pocket said nothing of the assassination plot, only that Sam and Ben had an altercation over a "personal dispute," that Ben's death had been an accident, and that he regretted having made it look like a burglary. How, he wondered, could he have been so wrong? He had been all but certain that Fenwick, likely with Stockton's acquiescence, had killed Ben. He had never suspected Sam. Detective Lawrence had examined the scene of the suicide, and the note, had a few questions for Monty about his friendship with Sam and Ben, and had marked Ben's case as solved.

He also recalled an eerie memory from the day of Sam's death. When he got back to his room, he saw, on the table by his bed, the Ben Franklin quotation book that he had given to Ben. He opened it to a random page and one of the first quotes he came across startled him. "Three can keep a secret, if two of them are dead." He was, he then realized, the sole survivor of the three who had been involved in the plan to kill Tyler. Maybe it was a sign, he had thought at the time, that he should get the failed plot, and its aftermath, out of his mind for good and move on. God knows he had tried since then to do so.

The railroad cars on this hot June day had been full. He had exchanged pleasantries with a few of his fellow Whig congressmen, and a couple of senators, before boarding the train. All were headed to Baltimore this Friday morning for the second day of the Whig Party's 1852 presidential nominating convention, to determine the party's candidate to run against the unexpected Democratic nominee, Franklin Pierce, who had been nominated just a couple of weeks earlier in the same convention hall.

Monty waited several minutes at the station for a hack to become available. He climbed in and the driver slowly made his way slowly down Pratt Street, dodging an array of carriages, wagons, pedestrians, and an occasional pig. The city was bustling with activity. Over the past twenty years, since 1832, when conventions became the method used by the nation's political parties to select their nominees for president, Baltimore, due to its central location, and its ease of access by turnpikes, steamships, and railroads, had been the site of most of these national political gatherings. As his driver turned left onto Calvert Street, Monty saw a small brass band, in red uniforms with gold trim, coming toward him, horns blaring, and headed for the Hall of the Maryland Institute, where the convention was being held.

A long line of carriages waited in front of Monty's destination, the sprawling six-story Barnum's City Hotel, the city's finest, and among the best in the country. He had the driver drop him off in the large square in front of the hotel, and grabbed his small bag, having only brought a couple of changes of clothes. Hopefully, he would only be staying two nights. He gazed at the monument in the middle of the square, which he had read about but had never seen. The Battle Monument, about fifty feet tall, had been erected in honor of the city's defenders against the British attack during the War of 1812. Monty walked over to the base of the monument and studied its Egyptian base, topped with a Roman column, which was circled with bands inscribed with the names of the soldiers who fell in the battle. A statue of a female figure stood above the column, her right hand holding a wreath aloft, and her face looking to the east, to the scene of the battle.

Turning back toward the hotel, Monty could see, in the distance, to the northwest, the top of the city's other famous monument, dedicated to George Washington, a glistening white marble column with a statue of the first president on top. Much more impressive than the stump of a monument to the great man that sat in Washington City. If time permitted, he hoped to inspect it up close as well. He now understood why President John Quincy Adams, on a trip to the city in the 1820s, had called Baltimore the Monumental City, a nickname that had stuck.

After he checked into his room at Barnum's, Monty made his way to the Fillmore campaign headquarters, located in one of the hotel's suites. He supported President Millard Fillmore, a New Yorker, for the nomination and had been asked by Fillmore's campaign team to come to Baltimore to try to sway some of the delegates from Ohio to support their man. Monty was surprised that he had been recruited for this task. He liked the president, but was not an ardent supporter. In his opinion, Fillmore needed to do more to restrict and oppose slavery. Despite this, he was willing to help out, since he thought the president was definitely preferable to the other two men seeking the nomination. It was a three-man contest for the 1852 Whig nomination. Fillmore and General Winfield Scott were the two frontrunners. The third candidate, Daniel Webster of Massachusetts, had much less support, almost none outside of his native New England, but he had hopes of being a compromise nominee.

Monty couldn't stand Scott, another military man, like Harrison and Taylor, trying to use his popularity with Whig voters from war to get to the presidency. Scott, from everything he knew about him, was vain and arrogant, and held no true political beliefs. Although very obese, he was meticulous with his appearance, always wearing ornate uniforms and feathered helmets. "Old Fuss and Feathers," his soldiers called him. All show and no substance, said his detractors. Scott, Monty believed, shifted his position on the issues depending on his audience, or with whomever he last spoke.

Webster, the other contender, Monty thought, was even worse. He had to admit that he was biased, given Webster's battles over the years with Senator Clay for the leadership of the Whig Party. The man could not be trusted and wanted too much to be president. Monty never forgave Webster for staying on as secretary of state in Tyler's cabinet back in 1841, after the rest of its members resigned in protest over the vetoes of the bank bills. Now, he was back in the same office, again serving as secretary of state, under Fillmore, and was running for his party's presidential nomination against the man in whose cabinet he served. Disloyalty never sat well with Monty. Besides, Webster had only a few delegates committed to him. He was not going to win the nomination. He was, Monty decided, either too vain to realize this, or intentionally wanted to make sure that whoever got the nomination would lead a divided party into the fall campaign.

"Welcome, Congressman Tolliver. Thank you so much for coming. We are in for a tight contest and appreciate your help," said John Barney, a former congressman from Maryland, and one of Fillmore's managers at the convention.

"Glad to be here," responded Monty, "Where do things stand?"

"Nothing much of substance was done yesterday. Typical of an opening day. We're looking good on getting the platform that we want adopted. We control more of the state delegations than Scott and Webster, so we have more of our people on the committees than they do."

"Is it still one delegate from each state on the committees?," asked Monty.

"Correct," replied Barney. "We expect the platform committee will propose a plank supporting the Compromise of 1850 as being the final word over slavery. That is our main policy issue. We don't think the Scott men will make a strong effort to defeat it when it gets to the floor. That would be a big victory for us."

"I was not aware that was the position on slavery that you were taking. What about the delegate count for the nomination?"

That is not as good. Looks like we are neck and neck with Scott. Your Ohio delegates are almost all for Scott. We hope that you can help peel a few of them away to support the president. Tonight, the voting on the presidential nomination is set to begin."

"I will do all that I can. What about Webster? Any movement with him?"

"Hell no. Damn stubborn fool won't budge," said Barney, in a disgusted tone. "It's a disgrace, I tell you. A sitting secretary of state challenging his own president for the nomination of his party. If the man had any decency, he would have resigned months ago. I told Millard that he should have fired the ingrate, but he wouldn't do it."

"Incredible," said Monty. "I was with Senator Clay a few days ago and he said basically the same thing."

"How is Henry? I didn't know that he was still receiving visitors. I've not been hearing good things."

"As you know, I used to work for him and we are still close. He is limiting whom he sees. He is sick and weak, but his mind is still sharp. We had a good conversation earlier this week."

"When you go into the convention hall, you will see that there is a large portrait of him hanging at one end. Clay and Washington are the only ones so honored. You may have seen in the newspapers that there was a nice tribute to him yesterday during the opening session."

"No, I was not aware of that," replied Monty.

"Yes, it was quite moving," said Barney. "The delegates from Philadelphia presented the Kentucky delegation with a large framed medallion of Senator Clay. Everyone on the floor and in the gallery was on their feet, applauding. And then, there was a moment of silence for the senator's health. Henry Clay is the one man over the years who has held this party together. I fear what will happen to us Whigs without him."

"Agreed," said Monty. "I will see him again next week and will give him the details of the tribute. He is very interested in the outcome of this convention and believes that President Fillmore is the right man for the party, and for the country."

Barney handed Monty a piece of paper. "Here is a list of the names of the Scott delegates from Ohio that we think could be persuaded to come over to our side. They are staying here at Barnum's. See what you can do."

"I will do my best. I am staying here also." Monty glanced at the list of about ten names, recognizing only about half of them.

Late that afternoon, Monty found at the hotel's bar a few of the Ohio delegates who were on his list. He gave his best Fillmore pitch. Despite the fact that he was a congressman from their home state and considered something of an up-and-coming star in the Whig Party, he could not budge them from their support for Scott. At best, he got a promise that, if Webster were to drop out, and if enough of his delegates went to Fillmore to put him within a few votes of the nomination, they would consider switching to the president in order to put him over the top.

That evening, Monty sat in the gallery at the convention hall as the voting on the presidential nomination began. To win, 149 delegate votes were needed. Barney was right. It was neck and neck. Fillmore had a slight lead on the first ballot, with 133 votes, compared to Scott's 131, and with Webster far behind at only 29 votes. When the tally was announced by the secretary of the convention, the man sitting next to Monty looked at him and said, "Looks like Webster is the most powerful man here tonight." Monty looked at him and, reluctantly, nodded. "Damn Webster. Only twenty-nine votes and he can determine the outcome," he muttered under his breath. After a few more ballots that night, there was little change in the strength of the three men and the convention adjourned.

The next morning, Monty found four more of the Ohio delegates on his list, who were having breakfast at the hotel. He asked to join them, and they agreed. Unfortunately, his pitch for the president again fell short. Fillmore was, they told him, an uninspiring congressman from New York who was lucky to have been put on the ticket with General Taylor as vice president at the last convention in 1848. Taylor's death had put Fillmore in the White House. He had not won it on his own and, in their view, could not in the coming election. What was needed, they told Monty, was another general, a military hero, as Taylor had been. Scott, they told him, was the man. He, along with Taylor, they noted, had been the two generals who led the American army to victory in the Mexican War. Only Scott, they confidently said to Monty, could beat the Democrats in November.

Monty thanked his fellow Ohioans for their time, excused himself, and went back to his hotel room. He was angry. How could people be so stupid? Or maybe, he pondered, he was the stupid one. He plopped down on the bed and stared at the ceiling. Why was he still a Whig, and what was he doing here? The only man of substance that this party had ever nominated for president had been his mentor, Henry Clay. The two others, Harrison and Taylor, had been military men, nominated mainly for their ability to attract votes. Both had died in office. Now the party looked poised to nominate Winfield Scott, another general. Moreover, he wondered, did he really believe in the Whig agenda anymore? He detested slavery, wanted its spread to be stopped, and for it to be eradicated from the country. He had even plotted to kill a president over slavery. By adopting a platform stating that the Compromise of 1850 was the final word on slavery, the Whigs were regressing. And this was a platform that Fillmore, the man he was supporting, had strongly endorsed. Fillmore, if he won the election, was not going to do anything about slavery. To Monty, the status quo was unacceptable.

As he was prone to do, Monty made a snap decision. Enough was enough. He packed his bag and checked out of the hotel, leaving a note at the front desk for John Barney advising that he had met with most of the Ohio delegates on the list given to him, was unable to sway any of them to move to Fillmore, and that he had decided to return to Washington City.

As he sat in the nearly empty Baltimore and Ohio Railroad car headed back to the nation's capital that afternoon, Monty thought about his future. He was done with the Whig Party, he decided. He would finish up some things over the next couple of weeks, would then resign from his seat in Congress, and head back to Dayton. It would be good to resume his work at the foundry, to be of help to his father, and to try to start a family. That had been the plan all along. Maybe he never should have accepted the offer to run for Congress. He let out a sigh of relief. It felt good.

CHAPTER 46

June, 1852— Once back in Washington City, Monty followed the news from the convention. Almost hourly, updates from Baltimore were posted on a message board in front of the telegraph office a couple of blocks from his boardinghouse. On Sunday morning, he walked over and read the last telegram from the previous evening. The convention held a marathon session on Saturday, with forty more ballots taken, and there had been little movement. The last ballot had Scott moving into a slight lead, with five more delegate votes than Fillmore, and with Webster still far behind. The gossip on the streets on Sunday was whether it would be Fillmore or Webster who would drop out and endorse the other since, together, they had more than enough votes to defeat Scott.

At work on Monday, Monty noticed that little was getting done in the clerk's office of the Senate. Everyone was wondering what was happening in Baltimore. Around noon, word arrived that a few more ballots had been taken that morning and that there was still no winner. Not getting much accomplished, Monty left in the mid-afternoon. He decided to stop by the telegraph office on the way home. As he walked up, a young man ran out of the door, a piece of paper in his hand. "It's Scott!" he shouted, as he made his way through the crowd that was milling around the message board and pinned the latest telegram on it. Monty waited for those in front of him to read it. As they walked away, he heard one man say, "Fillmore was the better man." Another muttered, "That idiot Webster." When he got closer, Monty saw that General Winfield Scott had been nominated on the fifty-third ballot, with ten votes more than needed. The final tally was 159 for Scott, 112 for Fillmore, and 21 for Webster. The outcome only confirmed for him the decision that he had made on the train ride back from Baltimore on Saturday. Another general nominated, and on a platform that opposed doing anything further about slavery. He could not remain a Whig.

* * *

The next day, Monty went to the National Hotel to see Clay, to discuss the convention and its outcome with him. The knock on the door was answered by James, who had a worried look on his face. "Come in, Mr. Tolliver. He's not having a good day." Monty walked to the doorway leading to the bedroom and saw the senator stretched out on his bed, covered with a blanket, his eyes half closed. He could hear labored breaths.

"Damn shame about the convention," Clay said, as he noticed Monty's presence, barely turning his head. "Come in and have a seat." He looked weaker, Monty thought, than he had at the last visit. His voice had less volume.

"What a disappointment," replied Monty, as he pulled a straight back wood chair next to the bed. "Nominating Scott, another military man with no political experience. Just like with Harrison and Taylor. Denying the nomination to the party's own sitting president."

"Webster did this. Unforgivable," said Clay. "His few delegates could have easily put Fillmore over the top. It's no secret that I've had my differences with Daniel over the years." He paused and let out a few coughs. "I knew he was vain, but his arrogance really took control of him this time. He's Fillmore's secretary of state, for Christ's sake."

"Now we can add disloyalty to his list of sins. I've never cared him since he decided to stay in Tyler's cabinet."

"Way before then for me," added Clay.

Monty decided to change the subject. "You were spoken of often at the convention. They had a large portrait of you hanging above the delegates. You and Washington. Pretty good company, I would say. I was not there on the opening day, but there was a medal in your honor presented to the Kentucky delegation. Many people asked me to pass on to you their prayers for your health."

"Yes, I read about the presentation in the newspapers. I am grateful for it. I've dictated to my son, Thomas, a letter of thanks and he is working on sending it out. I agree with you about the outcome of the convention. We Whigs may have nominated the only man who Pierce, that unknown, can beat. I don't have a good feeling about the election."

"Nor do I," replied Monty. "I can't even vote for General Scott, much less publicly support him. But my disgust with the party goes beyond his nomination. Sir, I have done a lot of soul searching over the past couple of days. I plan to tell the party folks back in Ohio that I am going to resign my seat in Congress. I am leaving the Whig Party."

"Never make rash decisions, Monty. It's always best to take some time and think things through."

"I've given it a lot of thought and my mind is made up. It's not only that the party keeps nominating unqualified generals for president, but I have moved far beyond where the party is on slavery. The platform adopted in Baltimore says that nothing further needs to be done about slavery. We cannot have slavery in any of our territories, and we need a plan to get rid of it where it already exists. Sooner, not later. I don't see the party ever supporting this."

"Sounds like you are now a full-fledged abolitionist."

"I guess you can say that I am."

"Maybe I should have been," replied Clay. "As I have lain here these past months, I have come to realize how much my generation failed the country on the slavery issue. How I failed it. The founding generation had to compromise to get the Constitution ratified and the country on a firm footing. I don't believe they intended for this evil to continue. Jefferson said of slavery that we had 'a wolf by the ear,' and it is ten times more dangerous now. In my time, we should have taken steps. I should have pushed more strenuously for gradual emancipation, or even something more drastic." He paused, needing to gather more strength before he could continue speaking.

Monty looked on, surprised by what he was hearing. He reached out a hand and gently placed it on his mentor's arm. "Go on, but only if you feel that you are able."

"We bandaged it in 1820," Clay continued, the volume of his voice becoming fainter. "But Texas ripped the bandage off. We got another bandage put on in 1850, but I fear that one won't last long. When it comes off, the wound will likely be so deep and infected that no healing will be possible. Abolition may now be the only cure, but the South will not stand for it, and it will tear the country apart. Maybe all of my work for compromise between the North and South was in vain. Just delaying the inevitable. I am glad that I will not be around to see it."

As he spoke to Monty, coughing between every sentence or two, Clay became more philosophical. "I wonder if it was worth it. My public service. What did I accomplish? I could have had a more comfortable and much less stressful life as a lawyer and farmer in Kentucky. In fifty years, a hundred years, will anyone remember Henry Clay?"

"You are talking nonsense, sir." replied Monty. "As long as there is a United States, your name will be remembered with admiration and respect. You did your best with the cards you were dealt. You accomplished more with that hand than anyone else did. The Union still exists, because of *you*. Had you gotten the opportunity to be president, perhaps you could have done more. But you can't blame yourself that lesser men occupied that office."

"I appreciate the flattery, Monty." Clay turned his head and looked at the small slit of sunlight coming in between the maroon curtains covering the only window in the darkened room. "I am not afraid to die. I had always imagined it would be at Ashland, surrounded by Lucretia, my children, and my grandchildren. And here I am in this damn hotel room."

"In a way, it is fitting that you are here in Washington City. You have given so much to our country." Clay let out a few deep coughs and Monty noticed his eyes close. He removed his hand from the senator's arm and stood up. "I will come again soon," said Monty. He saw a faint nod of the head in response.

CHAPTER 47

June, 1852— A few days later, on June 29, as Monty walked to a meeting near Capitol Hill, one of his last before his resignation from Congress took effect and he went back to Ohio, he heard the ringing of a church bell. Strange, he thought, for early afternoon on a weekday. He heard another bell ringing a couple of blocks away, and then another. As he walked, he noticed shopkeepers pulling down their shades and closing up. Quickly realizing the news being conveyed, his eyes began to well up with tears. The six-month-long death watch in the nation's capital was finally over. A well-dressed woman holding her young daughter's hand came toward him. "What has happened?," she asked. "Senator Clay has died," Monty responded, passing her just in time to notice her reach into her purse, pull out a small handkerchief, and bring it to her eyes. He would not be going to his meeting. He turned and headed up Pennsylvania Avenue toward the National Hotel, where he had been three times over the past couple of weeks to reveal dark secrets and to reminisce with the one man in the world whom he had most admired and respected.

* * *

Henry Clay was the first American statesman whose death was mourned nationwide in real time. The widespread use of the telegraph in the late 1840s and early 1850s had revolutionized communications and the speed with which news traveled. Only eight years earlier, in 1844, the famous words "What Hath God Wrought" had been transmitted by Samuel F. B. Morse through a copper wire strung on chestnut poles between Baltimore and Washington. Since then, telegraph poles and wires crisscrossed the country. News of the deaths of Franklin, Washington, Adams, Jefferson, and, more recently, even Clay's nemesis, Jackson, in 1845, had taken days, even weeks, to travel by horseback and riverboat across the length and breadth of the growing United States.

Within an hour of Clay's death on June 29, 1852, church bells throughout Washington began to toll. They were slow, somber rings that, upon hearing, most knew the message that was being delivered. The Great Compromiser was dead. The click-clack of the telegraph spread the news like a wildfire. Clay's son Thomas, who was at the bedside when the last breath was taken, quickly sent off a message to the family in Lexington. "Our father is no more," it read. Early that afternoon, President Fillmore issued an order closing the federal government. Congress adjourned. An era had ended.

* * *

As Monty approached the hotel, he saw that a large crowd had already gathered in front. He pushed his way through and into the lobby, spotting a clerk that he knew.

"Where's Thomas? Can you take me to him?," he asked.

"Yes, congressman, follow me," replied the clerk, and he led the way up a back staircase to Room 30, adjacent to the suite where the senator's body still lay.

There were about five or six men in the room. Monty recognized Thomas, Senator James Jones of Tennessee, whom he knew resided at the hotel, and Reverend Charles Butler, the chaplain of the Senate. What does, what can, one say at such times, Monty thought. He went up to Thomas and gave him an embrace.

"I am so sorry," he said, as tears began to roll down both of their cheeks.

"He thought of you like another son," replied Thomas, "and told me how much he appreciated your recent visits."

"I will treasure every one of those moments," Monty lied, recalling how reluctant he had been to tell Clay about the 1844 Tyler plot. Still, uncomfortable as it was, it had been a strange relief to get it off his chest and to have his story heard by a receptive, if not sympathetic, ear. We will have to agree to disagree, he remembered Clay saying to him. And during their visits, he had the opportunity to also discuss and relive the good times, and those memories he *would* treasure.

Senator Jones addressed the group. "As you know, I live just upstairs, and Thomas called for me this morning when he knew the end was near. We were both at his side. Tragic as this is, it is not a moment that has been unexpected, and we in the Senate have been working on plans for a funeral for some time.

Tomorrow, there will be a procession from here to the Capitol. There will be a service in the Senate chamber, and our colleague will then be taken to the Rotunda for public viewing. The residents of Washington City will want to pay their respects to this great and good man. We believe that the nation will also want to honor him. Therefore, our plan is for the body to be taken by train, first to Baltimore, on to Wilmington, Philadelphia, New York, and Buffalo, and by steamboat to Cleveland, and then on to Lexington. There will be public viewings in each city. We expect more stops to be added along the way. A group of six senators, both Whigs and Democrats, will serve as honorary pallbearers and will accompany Henry's body until he is with his beloved Lucretia for the last time."

* * *

A week after Clay's death, as his funeral procession was winding its way through Ohio, a lawyer in Springfield, Illinois, organized and led a tribute to The Great Compromiser. Shops in the Illinois capital were closed in honor of the occasion, their fronts draped in black. In his politics, Abraham Lincoln had always been a Clay man. Lincoln would say, years later, in his famous debates with Stephen Douglas, that Henry Clay was his "beau ideal of a statesman." After a service at the local Episcopal Church, Lincoln and the throng of mourners walked in procession to the nearby Illinois Statehouse. There, in Representatives Hall, Lincoln mounted the rostrum and began a eulogy of his political idol.

Lincoln began by noting that Clay was born in 1777, only a year after the nation's birth, and that "The infant nation, and the infant child began the race of life together." In a public career that spanned a half century, Clay, Lincoln noted, had been the "most loved" by his supporters of all American politicians, and the "most dreaded" by his opponents. When the nation had been in despair and its very existence in jeopardy, during the Missouri controversy, the Nullification Crisis, and the recent turmoil that had led to the Compromise of 1850, Clay had been "the leading and most conspicuous voice" in finding a solution and bringing the nation together. It was Clay, said Lincoln, throughout his career, who "seems constantly to have been regarded by all, as *the* man for a crisis . . . the task of devising a mode of adjustment, seems to have been cast upon Mr. Clay, by common consent— and his performance of the task, in each case, was little else than, a literal fulfilment of the public expectation." Clay's failed quests for the White House, observed Lincoln, did not tarnish his image. "There has never been a moment since 1824 til after 1848 when a very large portion of the American people did not cling to him with an enthusiastic hope and purpose of still elevating him to the Presidency. With other men, to be defeated, was to be forgotten; but to him, defeat was but a trifling incident, neither changing him, or the world's estimate of him."

On slavery, he noted Clay's belief, since his early career in Kentucky, favoring gradual emancipation, followed by colonization of freed Blacks to Africa. It was an approach with which Lincoln, the man who one day as president would issue the Emancipation Proclamation, agreed with at that time. "Cast into life where slavery was already widely spread and deeply seated, he did not perceive, as I think no wise man has perceived, how it could be at *once* eradicated, without producing a greater evil, even to the cause of human liberty itself."

Clay, Lincoln continued, stood for the Union because he believed that the cause of liberty and freedom around the globe depended on a united and strong America. "He loved his country partly because it was his country, but mostly because it was a free country . . . Whatever he did, he did for the whole country. In the construction of his measures he ever carefully surveyed every part of that field and duly weighed every conflicting interest. Feeling, as he did, and as the truth surely is, that the world's best hope depended on the continued Union of these States, he was ever jealous of, and watchful for, whatever might have the slightest tendency to separate them." Without the life of Henry Clay, concluded Lincoln, the country would be in a much worse place. "Such a man the times have demanded, and such, in the providence of God was given us."

* * *

On the same day as Lincoln's eulogy of Clay in Illinois, Monty finished packing up his belongings in his room at his boardinghouse in Washington and assisted the driver in carrying the trunks out to the waiting carriage. It was a beautiful, early July day. As he took his seat in the open carriage for the first leg of his long trip back to Ohio, he stretched his neck and looked up at the deep blue sky. The heat of the sun felt good on his face. He reflected on his time in the city. Fate had been good to him. He had come here a decade and a half ago to learn to be a lawyer. When that had not worked out, he had become a trusted aide to one of the most powerful and respected men in the country, had worked in the clerk's office in the Senate, and had been elected to and served in the House of Representatives.

Not bad for a kid from Dayton, he thought. He recalled what Sam had said to him a year earlier, on that terrible day, just before Sam had ended his own his life. Be stronger than me, he had said, work to make things better, to rid the country of slavery. Ben, also, surely would have wanted him to. *How* he might do this, he had not a clue, but he would. Of one thing he was certain—staying in Congress as a Whig was not the answer. As the carriage veered to the left off of Pennsylvania Avenue and headed for the train station, he turned his head to keep the dark green dome of the Capitol in his vision as long as possible. He resolved that he would see it again.

AUTHOR'S NOTES

The events discussed in this book concerning the political battles between President John Tyler and the Whig Party, the long illness and death of Senator Henry Clay, and the *Princeton's* fateful excursion on the Potomac River, all occurred and are well-documented. Fictional characters (Monty Tolliver, Ben Geddis, Sam Shipley, and some other minor figures), have been added. Tyler did remain below deck at the time of the explosion on the *Princeton* to listen to a song, likely saving his life. There was an estrangement between John Ericsson and Captain Robert Stockton over Stockton taking credit for the *Princeton's* design and innovations. The general view of historians is that the Peacemaker had defects in its design and in the repairs made to it, and that Stockton bore some culpability for the explosion, but avoided any consequences due to his friendship with the president and his political connections.

Below is more information about the historical figures and other things discussed in the book.

Henry Clay:

Although he was never elected president, Clay is still remembered as one of America's greatest statesmen. He is consistently ranked by modern observers as one the most influential legislators in the nation's history. Known as The Great Compromiser, his nickname was well-earned. The Missouri Compromise in 1820, the legislation diffusing the Nullification Crisis in the 1830s, and the Compromise of 1850, would never have been passed into law without him. It has been said that, without him, the Civil War would have been fought years earlier, and possibly with a different outcome. Clay wrestled with slavery his entire career. A slaveholder himself, he repeatedly denounced the institution as evil, but tried to steer a middle course, criticizing abolitionists as well as southern slavery extremists. His solution was for gradual emancipation, followed by transport of freed Blacks to Africa. Upon his death, Clay was the first person given the honor of lying in state in the Rotunda of the United States Capitol. It is estimated that well over a million Americans paid their respects to him during his two-week funeral procession, which went through seven states and many large cities in the North and what is now known as the Midwest, a testament of the respect the American people had for the man and for his public service.

President John Tyler:

The first vice president to assume the presidency upon death of a president, Tyler is generally placed near the bottom of rankings of United States presidents. His persistence and ultimate success in annexing Texas changed the makeup and map of the country, which many believe led directly to the Civil War. His position that he was, in fact, the president, and not an acting president, was followed by all later vice presidents who assumed the office after the death of a president, and was confirmed in the Twenty-Fifth Amendment to the Constitution, ratified in 1967. A few months after the *Princeton* disaster, the widowed Tyler married Julia Gardiner, then twenty-four years old, whom he had been courting before the explosion, and whose father was one of its victims. Tyler's ardent support of slavery led him to side with the Confederacy during the Civil War and, at the time of his death in 1862, during the midst of that conflict, he had been elected as a Virginia member of the Congress of the Confederate States of America. He is the only president to have renounced his status as a citizen of the United States.

John Tyler, III:

The third eldest child of President Tyler, John worked, along with his older brother Robert, as a secretary for his father in the White House. Beginning in early adulthood, he had problems with alcohol that lasted throughout his life and, due to this, was mostly estranged from his wife and three children. Although intelligent and handsome, he always seemed to be in the shadow of the more accomplished Robert. He was trained as a lawyer, but was never successful in that profession, and moved from job to job, including stints as a writer and journalist. During the Civil War, like his father, Tyler sided with the South, and he held an administrative job with the Confederate government in Richmond. After the war, he became a Republican and received an appointment from President Garfield for a low-level patronage job working for the attorney general. It is said that he lived out his later years talking, to anyone who would listen, of his power and influence during his father's presidency. He died at the age of seventy-six in Washington in 1896.

Robert Stockton:

Captain Stockton's reputation survived the explosion on the *Princeton*, despite his involvement in the design of, and the repairs made to, the Peacemaker. He continued to serve in the Navy during the Mexican War and was instrumental in the taking of California from the Mexicans during that conflict. The city of Stockton, California, is named for him. After the war, in 1851, he became a United States senator from his home state of New Jersey. He served for only two years in the Senate, resigning to pursue business interests. He died in his hometown of Princeton in 1866.

John Ericsson:

The Swedish engineer and inventor remained in the United States and became a citizen. Bitter over his experiences with Captain Stockton and the federal government over the lack of recognition of, or compensation for, his work on the *Princeton*, he avoided, for many years, further work for the government. He was given free rein to develop his inventions and designs at the New York foundry of his good friend, Cornelius DeLamater, with great success. Shortly after the outbreak of the Civil War, desperate for a ship to counter the *Merrimack*, a former United States naval vessel converted into an ironclad by the Confederate Navy, President Lincoln's secretary of the Navy, Gideon Welles, turned to Ericsson. Despite his reluctance to work with the government again, Ericsson submitted an innovative design for an armored ship with a rotating turret that housed large cannons, which became the USS *Monitor*. The battle of the ironclads, the *Monitor* and the *Merrimack*, in 1862, was one of the most famous naval engagements of the Civil War. The *Monitor* and other ironclad ships that he designed for the Union made Ericsson a hero in the North and he finally got the recognition and acclaim that his talents deserved. He died in 1889. A statue and monument to Ericsson is on the National Mall in Washington, just south of the Lincoln Memorial.

USS Princeton:

After the explosion in 1844, plans for more warships based on the *Princeton's* design were shelved, and the modernization of the United States Navy was delayed for years. This occurred despite the fact that the tragedy was caused by a cannon, and had nothing to do with the ship's innovative engineering. Eventually, screw-propeller driven ships, of which the *Princeton* was among the first, replaced paddlewheel steamboats in both military and commercial use. During the Mexican War, with a new captain, the ship patrolled the Gulf of Mexico, and was then sent to the Mediterranean Sea. When the *Princeton* returned to the United States in 1849, it was found to have rotted boards in its hull. Rather than replace them, the ship was torn apart and sold for scrap, only six years after its highly celebrated 1843 launching in Philadelphia as the nation's new state-of-the-art warship.

A study on the remnants of the cannon that exploded, the Peacemaker, released by the respected Franklin Institute in

September 1844, found several flaws in the weapon's design. The welding that forged the iron bars from which it was made was inadequate, leaving seams between the pieces, and the hammers used to beat the pieces together did not sufficiently remove slag particles and other impurities. Moreover, the method that Stockton used to try to arrest the cracks that developed during test firing, by welding metal strips onto the base of the weapon, was found to be deficient. Only rings that were heated and shrunken onto the base, which was the method that Ericsson had used on the other cannon, the Oregon, were successful in preventing additional cracking.

Today, only two parts of the *Princeton* survive. The Oregon is on display near the main gate of the United States Naval Academy in Annapolis. The ship's bell is in Princeton, New Jersey, located in a park surrounding the city's Battle Monument.

Whig Party:

In the 1852 presidential election, the Whig Party's nominee, General Winfield Scott, lost in a landslide to Franklin Pierce, the Democratic nominee. The Whigs carried only four states, compared to twenty-seven for the Democrats. The tally in the Electoral College was 254 for Pierce and only 42 for Scott. The Whigs were never competitive on a national basis again. The party was hopelessly divided over what to do about slavery. Its northern members helped found and joined the new Republican Party, and its southern members either went over to the Democrats, or joined a nativist third party, the American or Know-Nothing Party, that arose in the mid-1850s. At a sparsely attended Whig Convention in 1856, the party nominated former President

Millard Fillmore, who had also been nominated by the southern faction of the American Party. Fillmore carried only one state in the election, which was won by Democrat James Buchanan. By 1860, the Whig Party had ceased to exist.

Dolley Madison:

The wife of President James Madison was known for being a charming hostess during her husband's administration, which ended in 1817. Then, after two decades at their Montpelier estate in Virginia, she returned to Washington in the late 1830s, after her husband's death. She lived in a small townhouse on Lafayette Square and again became a fixture at the city's social events. Due to the spendthrift habits of her only child, a son from her first marriage, she had to sell the Virginia estate and lived meagerly in her later years, with financial assistance from her many friends. Emotionally distraught over her experience on the *Princeton*, it was said that she never spoke about the events of that day. She died at the age of eighty-one in 1849.

1315 Duke Street:

In the mid-1840s, this three-story townhouse in the heart of Alexandria, Virginia, was the site of Kephart & Company, a slave trading firm. The previous owner, Franklin & Armfield, had operated at the location since the 1820s and was one of the largest dealers in purchasing enslaved people from nearby Virginia and Maryland slaveholders and shipping them to New Orleans and Natchez for resale at large profits. The business later became known as Price, Birch & Company, which continued to operate at the site until Union troops captured Alexandria in 1861, during the Civil War. The building still stands and is today the home of the Freedom House Museum, which honors and tells the story of the thousands of enslaved people who passed through its doors in the mid-nineteenth century.

Mary Ann Hall:

Known today as the "Madam on the Mall," she owned and ran what the Smithsonian has called "the classiest and most famous brothel in all of Washington, D. C. . . . that catered to a rather illustrious clientele." Her brick house on Maryland Avenue was located on what is now the National Mall and only a short distance from the Capitol. The National Museum of the American Indian stands on the site. When the brothel opened its doors, in addition to Hall, six young women lived there. The business grew and prospered, with eighteen residents by the 1860s. During the Civil War, Hall was convicted of "keeping a bawdy house" and was fined, but was not shut down by the authorities. The brothel continued in operation until her death in 1886, by which time she had accumulated a sizeable estate. She is buried in Washington's Congressional Cemetery.

ACKNOWLEDGMENTS

I would like to express my appreciation to several people for their assistance in the preparation of this book. My thanks to Larry Giambelluca and Snowden Stanley for reading the first draft and offering helpful suggestions. I am grateful for the skilled work of the team at Historical Editorial, Jenny Quinlan for designing the book's cover and Aaron Redfern for developmental editing. I am indebted to my son, Nate, and to my friend, Doug Spiro, for their technical assistance. Finally, as always, I thank my cherished wife, Beth, for her loving support.

ABOUT THE AUTHOR

Stan Haynes, an attorney, spent his legal career as a litigator with a Baltimore law firm. A graduate of the College of William & Mary and of the University of Virginia School of Law, he has had a lifelong interest in American political history, particularly concerning the presidency. In addition to *And Tyler No More*, he is the author of two books on the history of presidential nominating conventions, *The First American Political Conventions* and *President-Making in the Gilded Age*. He resides in Maryland. Visit his website at *www.stanhaynes.com*.